To/
Barbara Singleton
My Sister in Christ
What a blessing to
know you.
Faustina Yalley
(7/20/10)

Ordinary Mr. Yalley,
Extraordinary
Gift from Above

Ordinary Mr. Yalley,
Extraordinary
Gift from Above

Faustina Korley

TATE PUBLISHING & *Enterprises*

Published by Tate Publishing & Enterprises, LLC
127 E. Trade Center Terrace | Mustang, Oklahoma 73064 USA
1.888.361.9473 | www.tatepublishing.com

Tate Publishing is committed to excellence in the publishing industry. The company reflects the philosophy established by the founders, based on Psalm 68:11,
"The Lord gave the word and great was the company of those who published it."

Book design copyright © 2008 by Tate Publishing, LLC. All rights reserved.
Cover design by Nathan Harmony
Interior design by Stefanie Rooney

Published in the United States of America

ISBN: 978-1-60696-506-1
1. Fiction, Christian, General
08.11.05

Dedication

This book is dedicated to my mother, Mrs. Florence Adikpe, who became a widow at the young age of thirty-four and was left alone to raise seven children. Thank you, Mother, for all you've done for us. We are all who we are today because of the foundation you were able to give us. To my husband, who has been my support all these years, your wisdom and support have brought me to where I am today. I love you, Joe. And to my children, for being my greatest cheerleaders when I started writing this book. Miss Harris, thank you for your support and for being a dear sister in Christ. To all my friends and anybody who had ever said a prayer for me to push me into my destiny, and to my family, to you all, I say thanks. And lastly I say a big thanks to Tate Publishing for believing in me and giving me the opportunity to call myself a writer. God bless you all.

The Divine Gift

Mr. Yalley looked out through the front window of his house and saw six-year-old Sam crossing the street. Sam lived with his mother, who was a single mother. Mr. Yalley thought to himself, *Where is this child going on this cold Saturday afternoon?* At that moment the doorbell rang.

"I got it, honey!" he shouted to Mercy, his wife.

He opened the door, and there stood Little Sam with a grin on his face.

"Mr. Yalley, my mom says can I stay with you for a little while? She has to go somewhere."

"Sure, Sam," Mr. Yalley responded, and then he looked out toward the street and saw Grace, Little Sam's mother, standing near her car.

"Thanks, Mr. Yalley, for your love and kindness," Grace said and waved her hand with a smile.

Mr. Yalley waved back and said, "You're

welcome. Anytime, Grace. We are always glad to help you out."

Mr. Yalley looked down, and Little Sam was still standing there, so he playfully ran his fingers through his hair and said, "Come on in, Sam. It is always good to see you."

Back in the house, it dawned on Mr. Yalley that he had just had a dream or vision. He knew he did not doze off in the chair while reading the newspaper, but he remembered going to the front window and looking through and seeing Little Sam in the same clothes, crossing the street, and he wondered where he was going, and then the doorbell rang. He opened the door and saw Little Sam standing there. *Oh my God! I just had a vision and saw what was about to happen.* This thought brought chills all over his body, and the hair at the back of his head stood up.

Mr. Yalley sat down and was lost in his thoughts about the awesomeness of what he had just experienced. He instantly knew that God was giving him a supernatural gift. He immediately prayed to God and said, "God, I know you are the giver of all gifts, and you said in your Word that every good and perfect gift comes from above, and if this is you, I receive this gift and all the responsibilities that will come with it. Help me always to humble myself before you so that you can work with me. In Jesus' name I pray, Amen."

After this prayer the peace of God came all over him, and he just sat there enjoying himself in God's presence and thanking God for all his goodness in his life.

Little Sam joined Mrs. Yalley in the kitchen, and he went on and on about how he wanted a puppy, and his mother said that he couldn't have one yet because he couldn't take care of it, but he knew he could, because he was six and could make his bed, take a bath, and read a book all by himself.

Mrs. Yalley listened quietly whilst cooking lunch. Suddenly

Little Sam stopped talking, looked up at Mrs. Yalley, and said, "You think I can take care of a dog?"

Mrs. Yalley answered and said, "There is more to having a dog, but I know you will do your best. God gives us things at different times in our lives, and you just have to pray to God and be patient. He will let you have a dog when the time is right."

"You mean the God that lives in the sky?" Little Sam asked. "Do you think he knows me? Will he listen to me?"

Mrs. Yalley turned and looked into his innocent eyes.

"Oh, I'm glad you have an idea about God. He knows you, dear. He even knows the number of hairs on your head."

"That's a lot to count," Little Sam said with a surprised look on his face.

"That's easy for God," Mrs. Yalley answered. "He knew you before you were born. He created every part of your being, but most of all he loves you so much and can't wait to hear your prayers."

"Okay, I'll pray to God about the puppy when I go to bed," said Little Sam.

"Good, he will like that," she told him.

Mr. Yalley listened to part of the conversation and said to himself, "We need to start praying for Sam and his mom to come to know the Lord." Simultaneously Mrs. Yalley was thinking about the same thing. They both found out later and praised the Lord for another manifestation of a couple being one flesh and united in spirit.

"Lunch is ready," Mrs. Yalley called out.

Mr. Yalley got up and said, "What's the surprise this afternoon?" Mrs. Yalley always wanted to surprise him with lunch, so he was not allowed to come to the kitchen when she was preparing lunch. Mr. Yalley enjoyed this game all these years and had never been disappointed once. Lunch was always something that he would enjoy, and he thanked God for giving him a wife like Mercy. He stepped into the dining area, and on the table was one of his many favorite dishes: broccoli, chicken, and rice casserole, and apple pie for dessert.

"Thank you, dear. You are the best. Sometimes I wonder whether restaurant operation and management are in our future." He planted a warm kiss on her forehead and sat down to enjoy his meal.

"Little Sam, where are you? Come join us," called Mrs. Yalley. Little Sam was watching cartoons in the family room. "Come have lunch with us," Mrs. Yalley called out again.

Sam walked toward them and said, "I already had lunch with my mom."

"What did you eat?" asked Mr. Yalley.

"Cheese pizza," he answered, "and I'm really full."

"Sorry about that. This really tastes good!" said Mr. Yalley, putting a spoonful of the casserole in his mouth. "Do you care for some apple pie then? I bet you still have a little room in your tummy for something sweet," Mr. Yalley said as he tickled Little Sam.

"Okay I'll eat the apple pie," he said, laughing.

Mrs. Yalley sliced him a piece and added a scoop of vanilla ice cream on top. Little Sam sat down and began to enjoy his pie, kicking his feet under the table and moving his head from side to side at the same time. Mr. Yalley looked up and saw the innocence and contentment on his face, and he remembered his only son, Paul Jr., who was then in college, when he was at that age. He held onto the thought for a moment and remembered how he loved his mother's homemade apple pie and how anytime they had some in the fridge, he wanted more. He would come and say, "Dad, do you want a piece of pie?" Mr. Yalley would say no, and Paul would leave for a while then come back and ask the same question again.

"Dad, you sure you don't want a piece of pie?"

Mr. Yalley would then realize that Paul wanted some more

pie and didn't know how to ask. Mr. Yalley remembered calling him back to the family room and asking him to sit on his lap. He kissed his son's forehead and said, "Paul, you know how much I love you, right?"

"Yes, Dad, but Jesus loves me more because he is love," said Paul.

"You are right, Son. You know, because of his love for us, he wants us to come to him with confidence and ask him for anything, and he will give it to us. He makes us wait or gives us what he knows is best for us. God is your heavenly father. You don't see him with your eyes, but because he is in your heart, you know he is there. I am your earthly father, and I love you very much. So if you want something, what do you do?" Mr. Yalley asked him.

"Dad, I will come to you with confidence and ask you or Mommy, and you will always give it to me, make me wait, or give me what is best for me."

"You got the message, Son. I love you so much. Now let's eat some apple pie." Father and son would then move to the kitchen for apple pie. These recollections brought a sweet smile on Mr. Yalley's face.

"Penny for your thoughts," Mercy said when she noticed the smile on his face.

He smiled at her and said, "I was thinking about Paul."

"Oh dear, you just spoke to him yesterday."

"Yea, but that is not it," said Mr. Yalley. "I just remembered a conversation we had when he was just Little Sam's age."

Mrs. Yalley smiled and said, "He was such a lovely boy."

Just then Little Sam looked up and said, "It's all gone. I ate it all, and that was yummy. Can my mom have a piece too?"

"Okay, we will send her a piece too," said Mrs. Yalley.

"What a lovely, thoughtful, and nice boy you are," Mr. Yalley said, looking in Sam's direction. He knew instantly that Sam would be a very lovely boy the first day he met him.

Mr. Yalley remembered standing on the porch in front of his house. He saw a moving truck pulled in front of the house across the street from his house, with a car following. A little boy and a woman came out of the car. The woman ran up the stairs to open the door, and the boy stood still, looking around as far as his eyes could see. When he noticed Mr. Yalley standing there, he smiled and waved his hands boldly and said, "Hello!" and began to walk toward him. When he got to where Mr. Yalley was standing, he said, "Sir, my name is Little Sam. I am six years old and I'm your new neighbor. Are there any kids around here?"

"Nice meeting you, Little Sam, welcome to the neighborhood," Mr. Yalley responded. "There are kids your age around. You will meet them with time." Just then a lady came out, calling out for Little Sam; she looked up and saw Mr. Yalley talking to him. She hurried toward them and said, "Sir, I am so sorry about that."

"For what?" Mr. Yalley responded. "He was just introducing himself to me. You have a very lovely and intelligent boy here."

She smiled.

"My name is Grace Luken," she said and stretched out her hand.

He shook it.

"Welcome to the neighborhood," he told her.

She thanked him with a smile and turned around to go, with her hands resting on her son's head. Little Sam turned around and said, "See you around, sir."

"Paul Yalley is the name. Sorry I did not tell you my name." Just then he thought it would be nice to invite them to dinner. He called after them and said, "Miss Luken, why don't you and Little Sam have dinner with us tonight?"

Her eyes lit up and she said, "That's very thoughtful of

you. Thanks a lot, but I already bought a takeout dinner on our way here. Some other time, Mr. Yalley."

He then told her that anytime she needed help with Little Sam, he and his wife would love to help. She thanked him again, and the look on her face showed how grateful she was for the offer. Although Mr. Yalley was a stranger, Grace had a good feeling about him immediately after she shook his hand. When she got to the stairway of the house, she turned briefly and had a quick look at Mr. Yalley. She noticed that Mr. Yalley was still standing there and looking at them. She waved at him with a smile. Mr. Yalley waved back, and she quickly ran up the stairs and vanished into the house. He stood there and wondered who she was, what her story was.

Mr. Yalley went back inside and told Mercy about the encounter.

"Let's invite them over for dinner," she said and smiled.

"I already did that, but she said they bought takeout dinner on their way here."

"Oh, okay, we will do it one day during the week to welcome them to the neighborhood," said Mercy.

"Sounds good to me," Mr. Yalley responded. That night as the Yalleys kneeled beside their bed to say their nightly prayers, Mr. Yalley prayed for their new neighbor and her young son, that God would protect them in their new environment. He also prayed that whatever way God wanted them to help her that he would give them the wisdom they needed to do that and fill their hearts with love toward them.

They were able to have lunch together one Saturday afternoon and got the chance to know more about Grace and her young son. She had just been divorced and decided to relocate and start afresh. The memories she had made with her husband in the first home they bought together were just too many for her to live there alone in the shadows of them. She felt it was best for her emotionally to give up the house and move out. They discussed it, and her move became part of her settlement. Her ex-husband was still very active in Little Sam's life. He talked to him every night and saw him every other weekend, she told the Yalleys.

Grace took up on Mr. and Mrs. Yalley's word to help her out with Little Sam, and so far the Yalleys had watched him for her on two other occasions. It had been a year since Grace and her young son moved into the neighborhood, and the Yalleys had become like a family to them.

They heard the doorbell rang. Little Sam ran to the door. "That's my mom," he shouted.

"Okay," said Mr. Yalley. "Let's open the door first." Mr. Yalley opened the door, and there stood Grace. "Hey, lady! You are back."

"Thanks a lot!" she said. Little Sam jumped into his mother's arms. "Hey, big guy, did you miss me?" she said.

"You want to come in?" Mr. Yalley asked.

"No thanks, you have seen enough of us for today," Grace responded.

Mrs. Yalley came to the door. "Don't forget the pie for your mom," she said.

Little Sam reached out for it, and Grace thanked them for their kindness. Mother and son walked away hand in hand.

God have mercy on them, Mr. Yalley prayed as he and his wife watched them go.

The Surgery

That night Mr. Yalley woke up in the middle
of night. He was about to get out of bed and go
help his wife in the bathroom when he realized
that Mercy was still in bed sound asleep. He
looked at the digital alarm clock, and the time
read 2:45 a.m. It then dawned on him that he
was dreaming. The more he thought about the
dream, the more troubled his heart became. In
the dream he saw Mercy holding on tightly to
her abdomen, and the look on her face showed
she was in terrible pain. The dream was so
vivid that he thought it was real. He immediately knew there was something wrong in
her abdomen. He began to pray immediately,
Lord, I bring Mercy before your throne of grace.
Whatever is going on in her abdomen, I plead the
blood of Jesus Christ over it. She is your righteous-
ness, so there is no infirmity in her body. You have
healed all her sicknesses and cure all disease. No
weapon formed against her shall prosper. I release
your fresh anointing from the top of her head to the
sole of her feet, and by your stripes she is healed.

In Jesus' name I pray. Amen. The peace of God came all over him, and he knew everything would be all right. Before he fell asleep again, he remembered Mercy's yearly checkup was the following day, and he decided that when they went he would suggest and insist that they take an X-ray of her abdomen. He looked at the time again, and it was 3:52 a.m. He couldn't believe he had been up for over an hour. He changed positions and drifted off to sleep.

Mrs. Yalley always woke up at 5:00 a.m. to spend time with God, take a shower, and go to the kitchen to cook breakfast by 6:45. Mr. Yalley, on the other hand, was a late sleeper. He woke up at 6:30 a.m., had his morning devotion, took a shower, and went to the dining room for breakfast every day at 7:45. This routine started after their retirement, but they never missed their evening prayers together.

"Good morning, honey," Mr. Yalley greeted his wife as he sat down.

"Do you want to start with orange juice or coffee?" Mercy asked her husband.

"Orange juice, please," he said as he sat down. Mercy looked at her husband and knew there was something heavy on his mind.

"Did you sleep well last night?" Mercy asked.

"Yes, I did. God gives sleep to those he loves," he answered. "When is your appointment?"

"Eleven thirty," she answered.

"Let's try and leave home by 10:00 a.m.," he told her. Mr. Yalley appreciated his wife so much and did not take her for granted. Mr. Yalley was a fast eater, so he always finished his food first, but today he was eating slowly, and Mercy noticed that but did not say anything. When he was done, he stood up and said, "That was a good breakfast. Thanks, honey. I am the luckiest man on earth to have a wife like you."

Mrs. Yalley smiled and said, "You are always so sweet, honey."

"I am ready for the appointment," Mrs. Yalley said as she emerged from the bedroom.

"I can't believe it's ten o'clock already," Mr. Yalley responded. "Let's have a little talk before we leave the house."

Mrs. Yalley came to sit down, anxious to know what was on his mind.

"Honey," he started, "something is happening to me, and I am convinced God is entrusting me with a gift. Yesterday, before Little Sam came to the door, I saw him crossing the street as I was looking through the front window. When the doorbell rang and I opened it and saw him standing there, I realized that I had just had a vision, because I didn't get up from my sit till I stood up to open the door."

"Hmm..." Mrs. Yalley said and sighed. "That's interesting."

"And then last night I had this vivid dream about you. You were standing in the bathroom, holding your abdomen, and the look on your face showed you were in pain and couldn't move, so I got up to help, only to realize that you were still in bed sound asleep. I lay in bed and prayed for you. Somehow I feel there is something going on in your abdomen that God wants me to be aware of, so I want us to suggest or insist that your doctor order an X-ray to be done or whatever needs to be done."

Mrs. Yalley sat there, lost in her thoughts but with peace on her face.

"Honey, I have never doubted anything that you've told me, so we will do as you say," Mercy finally responded. They then prayed that God's favor would go before them so that the doctor would agree to their request.

On their way to the hospital, they were both quiet and lost in their thoughts. Mr. Yalley was actually busy remembering how he first met Mercy, a place he loved to visit in his memory.

Mr. Paul Yalley Sr. got a job as a production manager in the mines, so they moved to a small mining community. Mr. Yalley remembered that as a sixteen-year-old who was beginning to have a voice to express himself about likes and dislikes, he didn't like the move at all. He asked his dad to stay behind with their next-door neighbor, who was just like family to them, but he said no, and Paul Jr. knew nothing could persuade him, so he never asked again. The day finally came, and they moved to Little Bethlehem, a very warm and friendly community. At sixteen Paul Jr. had no girlfriend but was beginning to notice girls. They settled down in their neighborhood and schools. Their next-door neighbor's son, Nick, became Paul's friend.

A smile beamed on Mr. Yalley's face when he thought about Nick. *I wonder where he is* now, he thought.

Nick and his family went to a near by church called Let the Redeemed Say So Church of Christ. Nick's dad came to invite them to their upcoming church picnic, but the Yalleys were not churchgoers, so they were not interested in any church activities. Paul Jr. had attended a couple of church functions when invited by a friend, so he decided he would accept the invitation on behalf of his family and go by himself, which was okay with his parents.

Let the Redeemed Say So Church of Christ had their yearly picnic on Easter Sunday, and it was always a fun day for everyone who attended. They always had lots of food, cakes, cookies, pies, drinks, and activities for all ages. The day finally came, and Nick came over, and together they walked to the church. When they got to the church grounds, the fun had already begun. Nick quickly joined a group of teenagers and began to introduce Paul Jr. to them. A few knew Paul Jr. already from the neighborhood or from school. Later on a group of girls joined them. They all sat under a big tree, talking, eating, laughing, and having fun. Paul Jr. was really enjoying himself and becoming very comfortable with all the faces he was meeting. One thing he felt and noticed was that there was so much love in the atmosphere, and that really made him feel at home. He looked up, and his eyes were looking into the eyes of the girl sitting across from him. His heart missed a beat, and somehow he knew he had to talk to this girl. He asked Nick later on about her, and his response was, "Hey, meerr, stay away. Don't even think about it. Her father is Pastor Matthew, the pastor of the church, and he is very strict with all his children." Paul just listened and didn't say a word, but in his heart he knew that was his girl.

The picnic was a success, the turnout was great, and everybody had fun. On their way home, Paul Jr. made up his mind that he would attend Pastor Matthew's church next Sunday so that he could lay eyes on her again. It seemed that was the only way he could see her because they went to different schools. When he got home, he told his family about all that went on and how he felt at home and how he had decided to go to the church with Nick the next Sunday. After all that talking, the only response he got was from his mother.

"That's not a bad idea," she said. She is the only one who encouraged him to follow his heart's desire, and he really loved her because of that.

When Paul Jr. went to bed that night, he couldn't stop thinking about the girl, whose name he'd found out was Mercy, and before he drifted into a deep sleep, he spoke quietly to himself, "I am going to marry her someday." This brought a smile on his face. Little did he know he was speaking his future into being.

Sunday came fast, and he was anxious to go to church. The service started at 10:00 a.m., but he was ready by 8:30. Paul Jr. walked around the house anxiously till 9:30.

"Dad, Mom, I'm off to church. See you all later," he shouted as he walked out the door.

At Let the Redeemed Say So Church of Christ, Sunday services were always a time to celebrate who they were in Christ, so when Paul Jr. was a few yards from the church, he could hear this sweet melody, and it was the sound that finally drew him closer and closer to the steps of the church. A young man met him at the door and gave him a warm welcome with a handshake.

"You are welcome to the house of the Lord, for this is the day that the Lord has made for you. Rejoice and be glad," said the usher. Paul Jr. didn't know what to say, so he just smiled. The young man led the way and showed him where to sit. The people around turned and gave him a friendly smile; a few shook his hand and welcomed him.

When the singing stopped, somebody prayed for the service and for other prayer requests, then announcements were made. He then thanked all those who came to the picnic and made it a success and also how those who didn't come missed a fun day from heaven. There were laughs here and there when he said that. Offering was taken, and as they passed the offering plate around, Paul Jr. had a little money on him, so he did what he saw people doing. They took the money to the front, and somebody blessed the offering whilst the choir sang a thanksgiving song.

After all that, the pastor came forward to preach the message for the day. It was about a man named Lazarus who died and was buried and was brought back to life by Jesus after three days. It was a very interesting message to Paul, so he listened attentively. Pastor Matthew told the congregation how we are all dead to sin and without Christ our sins make us stink like dead bodies before God, but if we give our lives to God, we come alive and become born again, and with this, when we die, we are assured eternal life in heaven. Receiving Jesus Christ as our personal savior and inviting him into our heart is our passport to heaven, and without that we will surely end up in hell when we die.

Paul Jr. knew immediately that he needed Jesus Christ in his heart, and whatever it took to do that, he was ready. He started wondering what he had to do. Then the pastor said anybody who wants to give his or her life to Jesus Christ should come to the altar. When Pastor Matthew said it the second time, Paul Jr. stood up and joined several people at the altar. The pastor prayed over them and told them to pray this pray after him:

"Dear God, I thank you for today and for this moment. I come before your throne of grace this day, admitting that I am a sinner and that I need a savior. I repent of all my sins, and I ask you to forgive me. I invite you into my heart and make you Lord of my life. I surrender my life to you. Help me to know you more and more. In Jesus' name I pray. Amen."

It was a simple prayer, but whilst Paul Jr. was praying, he felt a warm feeling come all over him, and when it was over, he felt so light-headed it was as if a load had been lifted off his shoulders. The difference really amazed him because he did not know he was carrying any load. He was glad he felt free, light-headed, at peace, and full of joy all at the same time.

The pastor told them to turn around and face the congregation, and everybody stood up and gave them a standing ovation as they welcomed them into the family of God. After the benediction people came forward to shake their hands or give them a hug. Paul looked up as somebody was hugging him and saw Mercy walking toward them. His heart began to beat fast as he wished she would approach him. His wish came true.

"Congratulations!" she said in a sweet voice as she stretched her hand to shake his. He was so excited that he shook her hand so hard that it showed on her face.

"Sorry, I think I shook your hand too hard," Paul Jr. said nervously.

"Oh! That's okay. I am fine," Mercy responded. "We have a youth Bible study on Wednesday at six thirty, and our youth Sunday school starts at 9:00 a.m. It will be nice if you could come," Mercy told him.

"Thanks for letting me know. I will surely come," said Paul, smiling at her.

That was the beginning of a friendship between Mercy and Paul Jr. They always did things in groups, but all their friends knew they liked each other. Finally they left for college, Paul Jr. studying administration and Mercy going into nursing. They couldn't wait to read sweet letters from each other or talk on the phone for hours. In their second year of college, Paul decided to propose to her that spring break when they visited home. Mercy decided to visit her sister for three days before coming home, and that worked out perfectly for Paul Jr. because he really wanted to surprise her.

Paul Jr. had grown so much in the Lord and wanted to do everything right. He told his dad what he wanted to do and asked him to accompany him to ask permission from Mercy's parents to marry her. It had been four years since Paul had given his life to Christ, and since then his dad, mom, and three siblings had come to know the Lord as well. God had been faithful to his Word when he said he would save us and our households. His parents related to each other better, and because of that their house now felt like a home. He had a good relationship with his dad, and Mr. Yalley felt honored to accompany his son to his future in-laws' house.

When they got there, as usual, the Matthews gave them a warm welcome; they knew Paul Jr. and Mercy were sweethearts. Pastor Matthew was glad to see Paul Jr. come to know the Lord before Satan dragged him into any sin that he would live to regret, and to watch him to become the fine young man he was now in the Lord was such a blessing. Everyone in his family was now a member of his church. They already knew Paul Jr. and Mercy would eventually marry, but when? It was only a matter of time. Somehow they were not surprised when they saw father and son at their doorstep. Before they started any discussion, Pastor Matthew prayed and thanked God for the fellowship and asked that his will be accomplished in all that they discussed.

Mr. Paul Yalley Sr. started by thanking them for the warm welcome, and he went on to say that, as they all knew, Paul Jr. and Mercy had been friends for four years, and they loved Mercy as a daughter, and he believed the Matthews also loved Paul Jr. as a son. He went on to say that he was really honored to accompany his son to tell them what was on his heart.

"Over to you, Son," Mr. Yalley told his son as he tapped his back.

Paul Jr. looked at his dad and said, "Thanks, Dad."

Paul Jr. turned and faced the Matthews, and rubbing his two palms together, Paul Jr. spoke and said, "I love Mercy very much, and I can't imagine my life without her. With my parents' blessing, I am here today to ask your permission to formally engage her."

If only they could see beneath his clothes; he was shivering and sweating; this was not easy for him to do, but the most important thing was that he had told them his heart's desire.

Pastor Matthew responded and said, "Son, we have heard you, and you have our permission to marry her. We don't think we could wish for a better husband for her like you, Paul. You have our blessing."

Paul Jr. breathed a sigh of relief, stood up, shook Mr. and Mrs. Matthews' hands, and thanked them for accepting him as their son-in-law. After that Paul Sr. stood up and did the same.

They all decided that the Yalleys would join the Matthews on Saturday evening for a little get-together dinner. They would call it a spring break party. When Mercy came back, they would suggest it to her and ask her to invite Paul and tell him to invite his family as well. Paul's mom would bake them Mercy's favorite dessert, cheesecake with strawberry topping. She would hide the ring in the cake, and when it was time for the dessert, she would serve it and give Mercy the slice with the ring.

When she discovered it and said, "What is this?" Paul would then stand up and propose to her whatever way he wanted to.

On that note, Pastor Matthew prayed and thanked God for his goodness and answering their prayers by blessing their second daughter with a godly man as a husband. He then prayed a special blessing on the Yalleys. After that they all chit-chatted for a while, and the Yalleys said their goodbyes and left. On their way home, Paul Jr. was so excited but didn't want to show it. His father read his mind, so he said to him, "Son, I know how it feels and am so happy for you."

Paul wasn't surprised he read his mind, because he knew parents are good at that. He just smiled and said, "Thanks, Dad."

Paul Jr.'s mother had a surprise for him and was waiting anxiously for them to get back. When they finally walked through the door, before they could tell her anything, she knew everything had gone well. Paul told them all that happened, as well as the dinner plans. They all congratulated him with teasing here and there as laughter filled the Yalleys' house. Paul Jr. asked his mother to accompany him to the jewel shop the following day to buy the ring. Mrs. Yalley didn't say a word, because she was waiting for that moment. She stood up and went into her bedroom and came back with a little jewel box, handed it to Paul, and said, "That has been taken care of."

"By whom?" he asked as he opened the box, only to see a beautiful antique-looking diamond ring. He jumped with excitement and said, "Oh, Mom! I remember this ring. Grandma Delores gave it to me when I was six; she told me to give it to that special girl I decide to marry one day." Paul Jr. couldn't believe he had forgotten all about this. Grandma Delores had died a couple of weeks after that, and Paul Jr. remembered crying so much during the memorial service as a child; that had probably made him forget all about the ring. Paul Jr. was so happy his grandma had seen this day and made plans for it. He gave his mom a big hug and said, "Mom, we are really set, and I can't wait for the big day to come."

Mercy made it back safely, and as planned the party was suggested, and she was asked to invite Paul and his family to the get-together dinner party. She loved the idea and was so excited that Paul Jr. and his family would be spending time with them, so she quickly called him and invited him, as well as his family. Before they knew it, it was Saturday, and Paul's big moment was only hours away.

He lay in bed as long as he could just to control his anxiety. He began to pray, thanking God for his tender loving kindness, his mercy, grace, and faithfulness in his life. He thanked God for where he'd brought him and where he was leading him to. Paul's heart was full of gratitude, and to his surprise he started sobbing like a baby without knowing why, but it was all about the presence of God preparing his mind and heart for the day ahead of him.

"Paul! Are you going to get out of bed today?" his mother called out, and before he could answer her, he heard a knock on his door.

"Son, are you okay?" his father asked behind the door.

"I'm okay, Dad. I will be out in a little bit," he responded. Paul Jr. emerged from his room after a while, hungry for breakfast.

"There he comes," said his mother. "We were getting worried about you. Are you okay?" she asked him, looking straight in his eyes and noticed that his eyes were red, but she decided not to comment on it.

"I'm fine. I was just enjoying a quiet moment by myself," he said. "Good morning, Dad," he said as he joined his dad at the breakfast table.

"Good morning," Mr. Yalley responded. "Did you sleep well?"

"Yes, I did," Paul answered.

Mr. Yalley decided not to ask any more questions, because he knew his son had a lot on his mind, so father and son sat there in silence and ate their breakfasts. After breakfast Paul hung around his mother as she made the cheesecake. When it was done, they hid the ring in it and marked the spot with a strawberry that looked different from the rest.

"What a delicious looking cake. A cake with a mission," said his mom, and they both began to laugh.

Finally it was time for them to leave, so they all headed out, feeling very excited about the rest of the day, but on their way to the Matthews' house, everybody became quiet in the car, just lost in their own thoughts for a while.

"I can't believe the little boy I brought from the hospital is on his way to engage a girl," said Mrs. Yalley with a laugh, breaking the silence. They all started laughing.

"Well, time goes so fast, and I am glad he turned out to be this fine young man, and we are all so proud of him, aren't we?" Mr. Yalley asked. Joy and Mabel, Paul Jr.'s two sisters, who were sitting beside him at the back, responded positively.

"So, do you have a date in mind? I didn't want to ask before the engagement, but somehow I feel like asking," Mr. Yalley told his son.

"I have not really thought about it, but I have an idea, and

I want Mercy to agree before we announce the date," Paul answered.

"That's a good idea, Son," Paul Sr. told his son.

"Ooooh! I can't wait for that day. I need to start looking for my dress," said Mrs. Yalley, giggling.

"Oh Mother, we are not even engaged yet, and you're thinking about shopping for your dress?" said Paul.

"Nice excuse to go shopping," said Mr. Yalley to his wife. Just then they arrived at the Matthews' house, and Mr. Yalley pulled into the driveway.

Mercy and her sisters were standing outside, so they quickly walked toward them. Paul Jr. had not seen her since she came back, and he was glad she was the first person he saw.

"Mercy!" Paul shouted as he rushed out of the car, excited to see her.

"Hi, Paul! It is good to see you, and I'm glad you could make it," Mercy said with all smiles.

"Well, we are glad to be here," Paul responded.

"Hello, Mercy!" said Mr. Yalley.

"Oh, hello, Mr. and Mrs. Yalley! I am glad you all could come," Mercy said in her usual sweet voice.

"Thanks for inviting us," Mrs. Yalley told her.

"I have nothing to do with this. My parents had it all planned, but anyway, you're welcome," Mercy responded.

"Okay then, we will see you inside," Mr. Yalley said as the family proceeded to leave Paul behind to chat with Mercy and her sisters.

"Paul, we are going to the store to pick a few items for my mom. You want to go?" she asked.

"Sure," said Paul. With all smiles they hopped into Mercy's car and took off. Paul was just glad God had given him the opportunity to chat with her a little bit before he popped the big question.

"You know, the party planner forgot a few items. I guess

she had too much to do. She really went out of her way to cook today. I helped her a lot, and I hope your family will enjoy all the dishes," Mercy told him.

"I am hungry already," said Paul, rubbing his stomach.

"Well, get ready to eat till you can't walk," Mercy said, laughing.

"I am ready!" said Paul in a funny voice. This brought more laughter in the car. "This is great. Thank you, Lord," Paul said to himself.

"What did your mom bring? I saw your sister holding something?" Mercy asked Paul.

"I can't tell you right now. It is a surprise," Paul answered.

"I love surprises," Mercy responded.

You are about to have the biggest surprise of your life then, he thought and smiled to himself. Just then Mercy turned and noticed.

"Penny for your thoughts? What are you smiling about?" she asked him.

"Just glad to see you and also thinking about the good food I am about to enjoy," Paul answered.

"That is so sweet. I am glad to see you too, and with the food, I assure you, you will not be disappointed," said Mercy.

I don't even care about that food now, girl. I just want to let you know you are mine for life, thought Paul.

When they got back home, everything was set with everybody sitting at their places at the table. Mercy and her sisters quickly unpacked the things and took their place at the table as well. Pastor Matthew prayed and thanked God for keeping their children safe in school and bringing them home safely. He thanked God for bringing the two families together, and he prayed that many more gatherings like this would continue. He also thanked God for being their provider and the source of everything they would ever need from generation to generation. He then thanked God for the hands that prepared the food and the heart that chose the delicious dishes and that God would continue to bless their labor of love. Lastly he asked God to bless the food and nourish their bodies as they ate. And everybody responded, "Amen!"

The food was really good, and everybody seemed to be enjoying themselves. Paul Jr. was enjoying the food, but anxiety wouldn't allow him to relax. He felt the eating should have come after the proposal; with that he would have a reason to eat and celebrate.

But anyway, I like the way everything is going on so far, he thought. Mercy seemed not to have any clue at all; she was her giggling self, eating and having fun.

"Paul, do you like the chicken, broccoli, and rice casserole?" Mercy asked him from across the table. Before Paul could answer, Mercy's mother cut in and said, "She insisted we add that to the main course because that's your favorite dish."

Everybody suddenly had this look on their faces as they turned to look at the couple.

"Yea! That's true, that's my favorite," Paul answered. "Thanks for adding it to the dishes. I am really enjoying it."

Paul Jr. kept wondering why everybody was eating so slowly. If only they knew he was beginning to have sweaty feet in his shoes, they would stop talking and eat quickly so that the dessert could be served. *This dinner seems like forever,* he thought. Finally the dinner plates were cleared, and dessert plates were brought in.

"Time for dessert," Paul's mother said, "and I made somebody's favorite."

Mercy came back from the store and joined the family hurriedly at the table, so she didn't get the chance to be sneaky about the surprise Paul talked about. Paul's mom brought the cake out, and Mercy was surprised about how beautiful and big it looked.

"Wow!" she exclaimed. "Thanks, Mrs. Yalley. That's really

my favorite, and I can't wait to have the biggest slice and a second as well," said Mercy. With this, everybody began to laugh.

"That's okay, you can have as much as you want," Mrs. Yalley told her in a kind, sweet voice. Little did she know that in less than twenty minutes Mrs. Yalley would become her future mother-in-law.

Mrs. Yalley began to serve the cake, and Paul found himself thinking over and over again, *Moment of truth, moment of truth, moment of truth.* Mercy's mom prayed silently, *Lord, please don't let her swallow this ring, knowing the way she eats this cake.* Meanwhile Mrs. Yalley was serving the cake and passing them on, and she finally gave the fifth slice to Mercy, which was a little bigger than the rest. Mercy saw the size of her slice and said, "Good things happen to those who wait."

"That's so true," responded Mrs. Yalley.

Mercy began to eat her cake, and every eye was on her, but she was so busy enjoying her cake that she was not even aware of the eyes that were fixed on her. Paul Jr., on the other hand, had no appetite to eat his, but to avoid anybody saying anything about that, he started eating it in a playful way. Just then Mercy cut a piece and saw a metal-like something sticking out in the cake.

"There is something in my cake," she said and began to use her fork to investigate. "Oh my God! It's a ring," she said. Her immediate thought was Mrs. Yalley accidentally dropped her ring in the cake. "Mrs. Yalley, your ring is safe. I didn't swallow it. Let me rinse off the cake crumbs," Mercy told her as she stood up and quickly made her way to the kitchen. Everybody began to talk about the incident, pretending they were surprised.

Paul Jr. stood up and said in a whisper but to everybody's hearing, "This is the long-awaited moment." He walked toward the kitchen and stood at the entrance. When Mercy came out, she was holding the ring at the tip of her finger and was admiring it, and she nearly bumped into Paul.

"Let me see it," Paul spoke up.

She gave it to him and said, "This is the most beautiful ring I have ever seen."

Just then Paul took her hand and said, "Mercy, you know by now that I love you very much, and I have no doubt that you love me too, even though we have not really expressed that kind of depth of feeling toward each other, but there is always this sweet air of love blowing over us when we talk on the phone or when we see each other. With much fasting and prayer, I am certain that you are my one true love, and I have decided that I want to spend the rest of my life with you."

Mercy had one hand covering her wide-open mouth as tears began to run down her cheeks.

"With the support of my family and permission from your parents, I want to ask you, Mercy, will you marry me?"

Mercy looked at her parents and saw the approval on their faces, so she turned to Paul and said, "Paul, I love you and cannot imagine a future without you. Yes! Yes! Yes! I will marry you."

Paul was still in control of his emotions, and he meant business.

"Mercy," he said, "this ring was given to me by my grandmother when I was six years old. She told me to give it to the girl of my dreams one day. She died a couple of weeks after that, so here I am today, fourteen years later, giving the ring to the girl of my dreams." He then took Mercy's left hand and said, "So with this ring we are officially engaged." With that said, he slipped the ring on her finger. Mercy was crying tears of joy. Paul gave her a hug, and that was their first close-body contact.

Lord, this is real, Paul Jr. thought.

There were cheers all over the room, as well tears of joy,

especially Mr. Yalley, who couldn't control himself. The ring made him remember his mother all over again, but he was so happy she made sure she was part of this beautiful day.

There was hugging all over the place. The Matthews gave their daughter a hug and congratulated her. They then shook Paul's Jr. hand and welcomed him into the family.

"Mom, Dad, I can't believe you all pulled this off like this," Mercy told her parents. "And you two, I did not know you were good at keeping secrets," said Mercy as she poked her two sisters on the side.

"We got you," said her little sister, laughing.

Pastor Matthew then asked everybody to join hands and make a circle around the couple. "Let us pray," he said. "Father, we thank you for this special day in the lives of these wonderful children you have given us. We pray your blessing over them, and we ask you to keep them safe and pure until the day they say their vows to each other. Remind all of us to pray for them always. We thank you for the date you are going to give to them as their wedding day. We know that you are on this journey with them, and you will surely be with them till the end. In Jesus' name we pray, Amen!"

"Amen, Amen!" they all responded.

Mercy opened her eyes and knew what her dad was going to say next.

"I want the two of you to listen to me carefully; we have no doubt the two of you have the fear of the Lord, and by the help of the Holy Spirit you do those things that please him, but I want you to know that temptation will be knocking at your door with all kinds of ideas, imaginations, and suggestions. The Bible says we should flee from temptation, so don't do anything that will help you open the door for temptation to come in. Don't hold hands or hug too long; if you have to do that, do it in the spirit of holiness. Your conscience knows what that is. No kissing at all. Always pray for each other for the strength to do what is right before God," he told them.

Paul Jr. thanked the Matthews once more for their love and acceptance; he then gave his two sisters-in-law a hug.

"You are now the brother we never had," they told him.

"I can't believe you pulled this off like this. For the first time in my adult life, I was clueless," Mercy told Paul as she poked him on the side. "I am really flattered and honored. I can't wait to be called Mrs. Yalley," Mercy added with smiles and excitement. Paul just listened as he admired every bit of her face, and for the first time his eyes began to notice how beautiful she really was.

"When do you think we should have the wedding?" she asked him as she sat beside him on the porch."

"That's what I want us to talk about," said Paul. "You know, we are both still in college, so we are not in a hurry. Let's bring our heads together and come up with something. Any ideas?" he asked her immediately.

"Not right now, but I am open to what ever you have to say," she told him.

"Okay, this is what I am thinking. Since we both have two more years of college, let's wait and do it right after graduation," Paul suggested.

"That sounds long to me, but since school will still keep us apart, I think that is a good idea," Mercy responded.

"We will wait and do it after graduation, settled?" Paul asked her, looking straight in her eyes to see whether she was really in agreement.

"Yes, settled!" Mercy responded with a little shout.

"I think is time for us to leave, so let's go back in and tell them what we've decided," Paul told her. When Paul and Mercy entered the house, Paul's family was actually getting themselves ready to leave.

"We have something to tell you all," Mercy said as they

stepped into the living room. Everybody stopped what they were doing to hear what the couple had to say.

"We have decided to wait and have the wedding after we graduate, so you all have two years to prepare for that day," Paul told them.

"That seems to be so for away, but it makes sense," Pastor Matthew responded.

"That is settled; the date will come later," said Mercy.

Paul and his family finally said their goodbyes and left. Paul felt like standing on top of their moving car with his arms open and the wind blowing in his face and shouting at top of his voice, "I'm engaged, I'm engaged, and I'm engaged to the most beautiful girl in the whole world."

The following day at church, Pastor Matthew announced the engagement to the congregation and asked them to be praying for them because they had decided to stay engaged for two years before saying I do. Almost everybody stood up and began to clap for them. Paul Jr. wasn't surprised but was so proud of himself for making the right decision; he got the pastor's daughter. Getting engaged enabled Paul Jr. and Mercy to open up to each other in ways they had never experienced. It was a wonderful two years of courtship. They talked on the phone almost every day, planned one-day surprise visits to each other at school, and made sure they spent a lot of quality time with each other during holidays. This enabled Paul Jr. and Mercy to know each other more till there was nothing left to know except to look forward to their wedding day.

Time really flies, and before they knew it, they were facing each other and exchanging their wedding vows three weeks after graduation. Pastor Matthew walked his daughter down the aisle and then officiated the ceremony. The two mothers put a lot of planning into it, and everything came out beautifully. Paul's dad was his best man, and Mercy's elder sister was her matron of honor. Paul Jr. and Mercy were so happy, and everybody was happy for them. Their parents were proud of them, and you could see it on their faces.

Two weeks after their honeymoon, they both started their jobs, Paul Jr. as an administrator at St. Joseph Hospital and Mercy as a nurse in the ICU for premature babies. They loved their jobs, and they were enjoying every bit of their marriage life. Plans to start a family immediately did not work out; month after month nothing happened. Checkups clearly showed that there was no reason why Mercy couldn't get pregnant. She was told by her gynecologist that the premature babies were having an effect on her emotions and it was taking a toll on her body, but she refused to believe that because she loved the babies so much, and she prayed for every premature baby in her care till they went home.

They came out into the world so little and fragile but with a will to live. As Mercy changed each baby, feeding or just rocking the baby, she prayed for each child with all her heart. No child under her direct care had ever died, and she gave all the glory to God.

Months turned into years, and before they realized it, they'd been childless for nine years. They decided a long time ago that they would enjoy each other and life to its fullest and allow God to take care of that problem on his own time, and that's exactly what they did. At the beginning of their tenth wedding anniversary, the long-awaited miracle happened. Mercy got pregnant unexpectedly; for weeks they thought they were dreaming, but it was for real, so they made sure they enjoyed every stage of the pregnancy. Finally, on a beautiful Sunday afternoon, Paul III arrived into the world, ten toes and ten fingers. Every good and perfect gift really does come from above; he was just perfect. At the age of thirty-two, Paul

Jr. and Mercy were the proud parents of a beautiful baby boy, and life couldn't have been any better.

Mercy decided that she would stay home and take care of their only child till he was ready to start first grade, then she would go back and work part time. That was twenty years ago. Paul was now a twenty-year-old nice-looking young man in college. He loved the Lord and desired to become a youth pastor in his local church.

At the age of fifty-two, Paul and Mercy retired and took life easy. They made the best out of each day that God blessed them with. Mr. Yalley could not imagine life without Mercy, the woman of his youth, his first love, his best friend, his companion, his cheerleader, his lover, the mother of his only child; life without her was unimaginable.

Suddenly he realized that his thoughts had sent him on a journey into the past, and he forgot all about Mercy sitting beside him; she had also been quiet all along.

"Are you all right, dear?" he asked her.

"Yea! I have been sitting at the foot of the cross, fellowshipping with my God," she told him.

"That's good," Mr. Yalley responded. "You will be fine. The good Lord will take of you as he always has," he added.

"So, what have you been thinking about?" Mercy asked him.

With a smile he said, "How we met, friendship, engagement, graduation, wedding, work, being childless for nine years, pregnancy, the birth of Paul, retirement, and how I love you so much and cannot imagine my life without you."

"You were really busy with your thoughts then," Mercy responded.

"Yea! They are thoughts that I will cherish until the day I die," Mr. Yalley answered.

"Me too," said Mercy.

Mr. Yalley reached out and squeezed her hand, brought it

to his lips, kissed the back of her hand, and said, "I love you, dear, and thanks for loving me back."

Such tender moments always brought tears to Mercy's eyes; she felt so blessed to be loved so sincerely.

"God help me to get a good spot to park," Mr. Yalley prayed as they pulled into the hospital parking lot. Just then a car was pulling out of a good spot. "Thank you, Jesus," Mr. Yalley said as he parked his car.

"We made it right on time," Mercy said.

"We have ten minutes, so let's hurry up," Mr. Yalley told her. A few minutes after that she signed in and was called in for a urine sample and blood test. Thirty minutes after that she was called into the doctor's office; the nurse did all she had to do and told them the doctor would see them shortly.

"Good morning, Mr. and Mrs. Yalley! It is always good to see you two. How is retirement life treating you?" Doc Prayers asked them when he entered the room.

"So far so good, Doc," answered Mr. Yalley.

Doc Prayers began to examine Mercy whilst Mr. Yalley looked on. Suddenly Mr. Yalley could see through Doc Prayer's clothes, and he saw a vein in his right leg that was very swollen. It happened in a split second, and because Mr. Yalley understood now that God was giving him a gift, he had such confidence and control, so he did not show any sign of surprise; he cleared his throat and just sat there. After the examination Doc Prayers told them Mercy's stomach looked a little big and unusual, so he ordered an ultrasound to be done on her stomach and abdomen. God had already revealed it to them, so they just went along with what he said.

"You will know the results by the end of the day," Doc Prayers told them.

"What is up with your right leg?" Mr. Yalley asked him.

"Oh, it started hurting yesterday, and I haven't had the time to pay attention to it," Doc Prayers answered. Then his face changed and he said, "Wait a minute. How did you know that? I have not even told my wife yet," he said.

"He is beginning to see things these days, like visions and in dreams," Mercy told him. "He saw something wrong in my abdomen last night in a dream," she added.

"That is true, and right now I saw a vein in your right leg that seems to be very swollen. You know what to do, so do it fast before it gets serious," Mr. Yalley advised.

"You know, I believe you, because as a Christian doctor I try to see beyond what my eyes can see. I knew there was something wrong with my right leg, but even as a doctor I didn't pay attention, and God in his divine grace decided to draw my attention to it through you before I found myself in big trouble. Knowing how busy I am, I would have taken some painkillers till the strongest dosage didn't work anymore, and then I would seek help. It could be too late by then. Anyway, thanks a lot. I will act upon it immediately," he told them. As they got up to leave, Mr. Yalley shook Doc Prayers hand and wished him all the best. Mercy then went in for her ultrasound, and they were free to go.

"Let's go eat Chinese food for lunch," Mr. Yalley suggested to his wife as they stepped out of the lobby.

"That sound good to me," she responded. They drove to their favorite Chinese restaurant, Xing-Xeng. As usual the line was long for lunch, but within a few minutes they were seated. Soon lunch was over, and they were heading out.

"Hey, Mr. and Mrs. Yalley!" they heard a voice call after them. They turned only to see Little Sam and his mother, Grace, standing in line to be seated.

"Hello, little fellow!" Mr. Yalley said as they turned and walked toward mother and son. "What are you up to, little man? No school today?" Mr. Yalley asked Little Sam as he ran his fingers through his hair.

"The school called me that he had a stomachache, so I

went and got him. The moment he got in the car he wanted to eat Chinese food, so here we are," Grace told them.

"Well, I am glad today is my off day. I wouldn't have known what to do," Grace added.

"Are you sure about that? We told you never to hesitate to call us when you need help," Mercy reminded her.

"Thanks a lot for assuring us that you will always be there for us," Grace told them.

"I know the Chinese food will do magic in this little tummy, and you will be all right by tomorrow," Mr. Yalley told Little Sam as he tickled his stomach. Little Sam's giggling and laughing turned a few heads to look at them.

"You see, the tickling has made you all right already," Mr. Yalley told Little Sam.

"Grace, on your next day off day, let us know so that we can all do something fun together," Mercy told her.

"I will remember and take you up on that," Grace responded.

"All right! You two take care, and we will talk again. Bye for now," Mr. Yalley told mother and son. As they turned to leave, Grace's number was called, and hand in hand mother and son walked toward their table.

"They remind me so much of Paul when he was at Little Sam's age," Mercy said with a smile.

"Well, he is all grown up now," said Mr. Yalley.

"Yea! My baby is now a man, and I just have to wait for my grandbabies," Mercy said with a little laugh.

"Me too," said Mr. Yalley.

When Mr. and Mrs. Yalley got home, they were surprised the doctor's office had already called and wanted them to call back.

"I pray everything is all right," Mercy said as her heart missed a beat.

"Honey, everything is in God's hand," Paul said, assuring her. "Go on and call them."

Mercy reached for the phone on the kitchen wall and made the call.

"This is Cynthia at Doc Prayers's office. Can I help you?"

"Yea, this is Mercy Yalley; I was just returning your call."

"Oh, hold on. Let me transfer you to his nurse," the secretary told her.

"Hello, Mrs. Yalley," came the nurse's voice from the other end.

"Hi, is everything all right?" Mercy asked her.

"Everything is not all right but not so bad either," she answered.

"What do you mean by that?" Mercy asked in a very anxious voice.

"Well, the ultrasound shows that you have a fibroid, and it is the fast-growing type, but the good news is that we got it at the early stage. Doc Prayers wants you to come tomorrow morning at 8:00 a.m. so that we can get you ready for surgery at 10:00 a.m.," the nurse informed her.

"That's fine with me, but can you hold on a second?" Mercy asked.

"Sure," the nurse said.

All along Paul was standing there, wondering what was going on. Mercy turned to him and briefly told him what the nurse said.

"Let me talk to her for second," Paul told her and took the phone from her. "Hello, this is Mr. Yalley. Mercy just told me what is going on. Is there anything we should be worried about?" Paul asked her.

"No, Mr. Yalley. She will be in safe hands, and she will be fine. Tell her not to eat anything before coming," the nurse told him.

"I will do that. Thanks a lot, and we will see you tomorrow morning," Mr. Yalley told her.

"Honey, you will be fine. I have peace about all this, so I know God has already done his part," Paul told her after hanging up the phone. "Let's call Paul and tell him about what is going on, as well as your parents," said Mr. Yalley.

"I was just thinking about that; it's as if you took the words out of my mouth," said Mercy.

"You know, we are one flesh, so we think alike," Mr. Yalley reminded his wife with a smile.

"Yea, I know! We are the marriage twins," Mercy said with a funny look in her eyes.

"I saw that look but no comment," Mr. Yalley told his wife, and for a moment they both forgot what was at stake.

"Let me call my parents, and you call Paul," Mercy suggested.

Mercy called her parents and told them about the situation and what was going to be done. Her dad, Pastor Matthew, prayed with her immediately and assured her their prayers during the surgery. Mr. Yalley then called Paul Jr.

"Hello, this is Tete, can I help you?" came Paul's roommate's voice.

"Hi, Tete, this is Mr. Yalley. How are you doing?" he asked him.

"Fine, thank you," he responded. "Paul is having a group discussion with some friends, so he is not here right now," Tete told Mr. Yalley.

"Okay then, tell him to call us when he gets back."

"I will certainly do that," said Tete.

"Thanks, bye!" Mr. Yalley said as he hung up. Shortly after that Paul came in, and Tete gave him the message.

"Hello, Dad! I got your message. Is everything all right?" Paul asked his Dad.

"Oh, hello, Son! How are you?"

"Fine, Dad. I just got back, and Tete told me you called. Is everything okay?" Paul asked his dad again.

"We are fine, Son, but your mom needs to go in for surgery tomorrow morning to remove a fibroid. They found out this morning during her annual checkup."

"You mean you find out this morning, and surgery is tomorrow?" Paul asked his dad in a worried voice.

"Yes, Son. This is the fast-growing one, and Doctor Prayers advised we operate immediately, but don't worry. Everything will be fine because God is on our side," Mr. Yalley assured his son.

"Let me talk to Mom," Paul told his dad.

"Sure, hold on," Mr. Yalley answered and gave the phone to his wife.

"Hello, Paul! How are you?" Mercy asked her son.

"Fine, Mom. Are you all right?" Paul asked his mother.

"Yes, I am all right. I am not anxious. I am at peace, and I still have the joy of the Lord, which you know is our strength. We cannot afford to lose that in the midst of anything," Mercy told her son.

"You sound really good, and it is good to know that," Paul responded.

"Just be praying. I'll go in at eight, surgery is at ten, and I will stay there for forty-eight hours," Mercy told her son.

"I will certainly do that, and you just take care of yourself," Paul promised his mom.

"I love you, Son. Bye! Here is your dad."

"Hi, Son. I will call you immediately after she comes out of surgery tomorrow."

"Okay, Dad. You take care, and I will be praying," Paul told his dad.

"Okay! Bye, Son," Mr. Yalley responded. Mr. Yalley in his thought was surprised that Paul of all people didn't insist he had to there for his mom. M*aybe he is too busy to get away,* he thought.

Paul III, on the other hand, had made up his mind that he was going to drive the five-hour journey and surprise his parents. He checked his planner and realized that he had no classes the following day and with the next day his classes started at 3:00 p.m., so the timing was just perfect. He then took a few minutes and prayed for his mom, dad, the doctor, and all the people who would be involved in his mother's life. He then thanked God for giving him the free time to travel. He decided to leave around three o'clock in the morning and get there around eight o'clock. He would go straight to the hospital and find a way to really surprise his parents.

"I hope to get there before they arrive," he said. He knew his mother would be so glad to see him; he couldn't wait to see the look on their faces. "I can't wait to experience that," he said aloud with a smile. "Tete, I will be traveling home early hours of the morning to be with my parents. My mom is having surgery tomorrow morning. I want to hit the road around three o'clock, so you wake me up when you get up at your usual time. I want you to be my alarm clock, I will be counting on you," Paul told him.

"No problem. I will do that," Tete promised him.

Tete, whose full name was Tetebi, which simply meant he was the firstborn son, realized that nobody could pronounce his name right in college, except a few students from his native land. After a couple of weeks, he got tired of the different pronunciation of his name, so he changed it to Tete. "To make it easier for you all now," he jokingly told some of his friends when they asked him about the change.

Tete was a very disciplined young man. He would go to bed around eight o'clock and wake up at 2:30 to study until 6:30 a.m. Then he would take a shower and eat breakfast, only to be back in bed by 7:30. He slept until he had to get up for class at 10:30 and then got ready and left for class at 11:30 a.m. Every now and then something would interrupt this routine, but most of the time he followed it religiously, and Paul really admired him for that. Paul and Tete had been roommates for one-and-a-half years, and they had grown to love each other as brothers. Paul was so glad when he found out that Tete was a strong believer. They connected immediately and became best friends. Paul remembered how he and Tete crossed paths.

Paul's roommate left to do an exchange program overseas, so Paul needed somebody to take his place. Paul decided to put the vacancy announcement on the school notice board. After praying that God would give him somebody he would love unconditionally, he stepped out to do just that. When he got there, he saw a young boyish-looking guy standing there reading the information on the notice board. Paul looked at him and immediately out of the leading of the Holy Spirit, he found himself saying, "Hi! My name is Paul, and I am looking for a roommate."

Tete look up, looked at him for a second, and said, "My name is Tete, and I am looking for a place as well."

"Great, you've found the perfect roommate. You want to have a look at it now?" Paul asked him.

Although Paul was very straightforward, somehow Tete knew God was leading him, so he found himself saying, "Yea, that will be great." Tete followed Paul silently without knowing what to say.

"Where do you come from?" Paul said, breaking a few minutes of silence.

"The City of Wisdom," Tete told him.

"Oh, so you are one of those wise people. I've heard a lot about your city," said Paul.

"Don't believe everything you hear. Yes, it is a unique city, but I don't think everybody who comes from there is full of wisdom," Tete responded.

"Well, I am aware of that, but to tell you the truth, your city has a good name out there," said Paul. After a while they both realized they'd been standing and talking as if they'd known each other for a long time. Paul then knew God had answered his prayers. They both hurried up to the dorm room. Paul showed him around, and Tete liked what he saw, but he had already decided he would roommate with Paul regardless of what he saw, because he had a good feeling about Paul. He spoke up and said, "I will take it."

"All right, you've found yourself a roommate, a friend, and a brother," said Paul as he stretched out his hand to give him a friendly handshake. They sat down and discussed the rent and other little bills they had to pay. When they were done, with all smiles Paul put his hand on Tete's shoulder and said, "Welcome to room number 6215."

"Thanks," Tete answered. "I will move in on Sunday evening, okay?"

"If you need any help, just call and let me know," Paul offered.

"Thanks for the offer. I'm going to go now, but I will see you later," Tete told Paul as he stepped out of the room.

"Bye! See you later," Paul shouted after him. Paul sat on his bed amazed about how God answers some prayers so fast. *Anyway, that is God. He always knows best.* With this thought Paul stood up and began to pray. "Father, thank you so much for giving me Tete as my roommate. I like him already. Help me to be what you want me to be in his life. I pray your blessings upon today and forever, Amen."

Tete moved in that Sunday as planned. They got along very well, and with time they got to know each other's backgrounds. Tete's dad was a Pastor, and he got saved at a very early age; he was the only boy among four sisters. They became the brothers they did not have to each other, sincerely looking out for each other, being there for each other, and praying together, as well as praying for each other. It had been a wonderful one and half years since they crossed paths.

They both knew God really brought them together.

"Paul! Paul!" Tete called as he woke Paul up.

"What!" he asked from a deep sleep.

"Time to get up and hit the road," Tete told him.

"Okay, thanks, man. I'm awake," Paul told Tete, still lying down. Tete stood there till Paul finally got up and sat on the bed.

"Good, you are awake now. Don't go back to sleep. I will be watching," Tete said as he turned to walk away.

"Thanks, I appreciate it," Paul told him. Paul took a few minutes to pray, and ended it with Psalm 23, as he did every morning. He took a quick shower, got dressed, got his backpack, and bid Tete goodbye.

"I will be praying for you all," Tete assured him.

"Thanks," Paul said as he stepped out of the room. Paul looked up to the sky and breathed in the early morning fresh breeze. *It is going to be a beautiful day,* he thought as he opened his car door. The journey was smooth, and after two hours he made a quick stop and bought a cup of coffee and a donut. He stretched his legs for a few minutes and hopped back into the car. Paul was excited and breathed a sigh of relief when he finally pulled into the parking lot of the hospital at 7:15 a.m. *Thank you, Lord. I* made *it earlier than I thought,* Paul thought. Somehow he knew his parents hadn't made it yet, but he decided to drive around both parking lots and make sure. There was no sign of their car, so he quickly went into the lobby and positioned himself in a corner where he could see both parking lots clearly.

He sat there, anxiously looking at all the cars coming in. Paul looked at his wrist watch, and it was 7:35 a.m. He wondered whether they were on their way. Just then he looked up, and there was his parents' car pulling into the parking lot.

He watched as his dad got out of the car, came around, and opened the trunk and then the car door for his mom, as he always did. He watched them and couldn't help it but smile. He decided that instead of surprising them in the lobby where a lot of people would be watching, he would rather walk to the parking lot and surprise them. As he stepped out of the lobby, he saw his mom come out of the car and walk toward his dad, who was taking her suitcase out of the car, both their backs were facing Paul so they did not see him approach them.

When Paul wanted to be playful he called his parents Mr. and Mrs. Yalley. "Hello, Mr. and Mrs. Yalley!" he called out as he approached them. They both turned immediately to make sure they were not hearing things, and Paul continued by asking, "Do you two know this young man?"

Paul's dad dropped the suitcase and shouted, "Son!" His mom rushed toward him with her loving arms wide open and stretched toward him. Paul walked into his mother's arms with a big smile on his face.

"Oh, Paul, I am so glad to see you. What a surprise," she said.

"That's exactly what I wanted it to be," Paul told them as he hugged his dad as well

"Son, you really did pull this one off," Mr. Yalley told his son. "Let's get going. Our check-in time is 8:00 a.m., and we have fifteen minutes to do that," Mr. Yalley told them. Paul picked up the suitcase and headed toward the hospital as Mercy rested her right hand on Paul's shoulder, whilst Mr. Yalley locked hands with Mercy's left hand.

"This feels right," Mr. Yalley said as they stepped into the hospital lobby. Mercy was checked into her room, full of joy mixed with peace, knowing that the two people she loved most were right there with her. A sweet red-haired nurse entered the room. Mercy read her name tag immediately, so she said, "Hello, Sarah."

"Good morning, Mrs. Yalley," the nurse responded. "I am always glad when patients read my name tag and call me by name before I introduce myself."

"That's my mom. She believes that is why the name tags are worn," Paul told Sarah.

"Anyway, I am your nurse today, and I want to assure you that you are in safe hands and everything will be fine," the nurse assured her.

"Thanks, that's good to hear," Mrs. Yalley responded.

The nurse took Mercy's blood pleasure and temperature. "Everything looks good," said the nurse. "Now I have these forms for you to sign, but I am going to go through each one with you, and if you have any questions, you ask before signing them," the nurse told her. After she finished going through the forms, she asked the Yalleys, especially Mercy, "Any questions?"

"No, everything is well understood," responded Mercy. After that she signed the papers as part of the hospital procedure.

"Thank you, ma'am," said the nurse. "Doctor Prayers will be with you shortly," she added as she got ready to leave.

"Thanks, Sarah," said Mr. Yalley.

"You're welcome," she responded as she walked out the door.

The Yalley family was lost in their thoughts when Doc Prayers walked into the room. "Good morning!" he greeted the Yalleys. He then noticed Paul. "Hey, young man, when did you get into town?" he asked him.

"This morning," Paul told him.

"He really surprised us, but we are glad he is here with us," said Mr. Yalley.

"Are you still keeping the girls away?" Doc Prayers asked Paul.

"Yep, Doc. It's all books until God says it's time," Paul answered.

"That's a good idea, son. Good things come to those who wait," Doc Prayers told him.

Just at that moment Mr. Yalley saw the name Joyce flash in front him. He sat up straight as he realized God had just shown him the name of his future daughter-in-law. In response to what was said, he found himself saying, "Yep! Good things happen to those who wait. When Joyce comes along that waiting will end."

"Who is Joyce?" Mercy immediately asked.

"I don't know," Mr. Yalley answered.

"Dad, is it your desire that I marry somebody call Joyce?" Paul asked his dad.

"No, Son, that is not my desire, but I think God has chosen that name for your future wife."

Doc Prayers spoke up and said, "Let's talk about this wife thing later. Now it is business time. He then gave Mercy a lecture on the procedure and what to expert; he finished by saying she was in safe hands and everything would be all right.

"Thanks a lot," Mercy responded.

"It is always good to know you are in good hands," Mr. Yalley added. Just then Sarah walked through the door with a wheelchair.

"Time is up, Mrs. Yalley," she said.

Hugs and kisses from the two men in her life really put her at ease.

"We will be praying for you," Mr. Yalley assured his wife once again as the nurse wheeled her away. Mr. Yalley put his arms around his son's shoulder as they walked to the waiting room. They sat in silence for almost thirty minutes, lost in their thoughts, but each knew what the other was doing, praying for the woman they both loved dearly.

"You want something to eat?" Mr. Yalley broke the silence.

"No, Dad, I drank a cup of coffee and donut on my way

here," Paul told his dad. "What about you?" There was no immediate respond, so Paul looked up at his dad, and he noticed that there was a look on his face that was very unusual. He kept looking at him for a while and realized that there was something going on in his mind. He sat still for a while, and from the corner of Paul's eyes he noticed that his father sat up straight and breathed a sigh of relief.

"Are you okay, Dad?" Paul quickly asked his dad.

"Oh, Son, I just saw what was going on in the operating room," he told him.

"That is divinely awesome. What did you see?" Paul asked his dad anxiously.

"Your mother is lying on the table surrounded by three attending nurses and two doctors. There was this wall of bright light around them like a wedge of protection, you know, and the entire instrument being used had a candle glow-like light resting on each one of them. When the nurse picked up an instrument to give to the doctor, the light followed the instrument and rested on the doctor's hand as he worked on your mom. It was so beautiful, and Mercy looked so peaceful and beautiful. Son, your mother is in safe hands," Mr. Yalley told his son, shaking his head all along in amazement about how awesome it was for God to allow him to see what was going on in the operating room, just to assure him that He is in control.

Father and son sat there lost in the awesomeness of God, and Paul couldn't find words to comment on what his dad had just told him, but he spoke up and said, "What about you, Dad, you want to eat something?"

Mr. Yalley cleared his throat and said, "Your mom was asked to come on an empty stomach, so I decided to do the same till everything is over."

"Dad, can I ask you what the name Joyce was all about,"

said Paul. Mr. Yalley sat up straight and tapped his son on the knee.

"I knew you were going to ask me about that sooner or later," he said. "Son, God is doing something new in my life that I can't explain, but I know he is blessing me with a supernatural gift of having visions, or dreams. I am beginning to see things before they happen. It started when I saw Little Sam crossing the street one cold Saturday afternoon, and I was wondering where he was going. Just then our doorbell rang, and when I opened the door, there he stood just as I saw him. I saw your mom's problem before she was diagnosed. I saw through Doc Prayers's right leg, he was in pain because he had a swollen vein. He was really surprised when I asked him what was wrong with his right leg, because he had not told anybody about it, not even his wife. Now the name Joyce. When Doc Prayers was talking to you, the name flashed in front of me, and I have no doubt that's going to be the name of your future wife," Mr. Yalley told his son.

"That's very interesting to hear, Dad. I know with God everything is possible. He is the giver of all gifts, and I am so glad that he chose to use you like this at this time in your life," Paul told his dad.

"Me too. I am so humbled, and I pray that he will guide and protect me from anything that will rob this gift from me, and I will do my best to honor him with it," Mr. Yalley added.

Paul listened silently as he nodded his head to all that his dad was telling him. They both sat in silence for a while. Then Paul looked at his wristwatch and said, "It's been an hour already. I am sure they are getting ready to come out because the doctor said it would take one and a half hours."

"I will be so relieved when this is over," Mr. Yalley responded. Just then he looked up and saw Doc Prayers walking down the hallway toward them. "Son, I think it is over.

There comes the Doctor," Mr. Yalley said. They both stood up immediately as the doctor approached them.

"Sit down, sit down, guys," he told them.

"We are fine," Mr. Yalley responded.

"Everything went on well, and I want you two to know that you have a godly wife and mother. The hand of God is really upon her; that is all I can say. They are getting her situated in her room right now. She is still out of it, and when she comes through, the nurse will come and call you," Doc Prayers told them.

"Thank you very much," said Mr. Yalley as he shook the doctor's hand. Mr. Yalley and his son sat done for a moment, and then a nurse came out and told them Mercy was awake. Father and son looked at each other and said, "That was quick." The Yalleys followed the nurse to Mercy's room, and before they entered Mr. Yalley noticed the room number was 315, and he immediately felt that God chose that room number for Mercy, to know that everything would be all right, for Mercy's birthday was March 15. He smiled as they entered the room. Mercy was awake, waiting for them.

"Hi, honey!" Mr. Yalley greeted his wife as he walked toward her bed with Paul following; they both gave her kisses and hugs. Mercy was alert by now and was ready to talk and tell them what she remembered before they put her to sleep. Father and son were glad to see she was her usual self.

"I think I feel better than I thought," she told them.

"Well, when you have Doctor Prayers on your side, you will certainly be all right," Paul jokingly said.

"I agree with you, Son," Mr. Yalley added. Mr. Yalley sat at the edge of the bed holding Mercy's hand, and Paul sat on a chair near the bed looking at his mom and noticing how pretty she looked in everything, even in a hospital gown. He found himself smiling. Just then Mercy turned and looked at him.

"What is that smile for, Paul?" she asked him.

"Oh! I am just admiring the prettiest mother in the whole wide world; everything looks good on her, even in a hospital robe," Paul told her.

Mr. Yalley started laughing.

"That's funny, but thanks for the compliment," Mercy told them.

"Let's pray and thank God for what he has done," said Mr. Yalley. When he finished praying, they heard another voice say the Amen with them. They opened their eyes only to see it was the doctor coming in to check on Mercy. The Yalleys were glad to see him again.

"When are you heading back?" he asked Paul, and just then Paul's cell phone rang. He looked at it, and it was his roommate.

"Hi, Tete, I was about to call you. My mom just came out of surgery," Paul told him.

"Is everything all right?" Tete asked.

"Yea, everything is fine," Paul answered.

"I am glad to hear that. Anyway, one of your study group guys called Peter came by to let you know that tomorrow's classes at 3:00 p.m. has been cancelled."

"Did he say why?" Paul asked him.

"Yea, he said the professor was jogging and twisted his ankle," Tete told him.

"Well thanks, Tete. That gives me one more day to spend with my parents."

"Great!" Tete responded. "See you when you get back. Bye for now, and say hello to your parents for me," Tete told Paul.

"Okay, bye and take care," said Paul. "That was my roommate. I don't need to go back tomorrow. My professor twisted his ankle, so classes have been cancelled, and that is the only class I have for tomorrow," Paul told his parents.

"That is good news. We are glad to have you for another day," Mercy told her son. Mercy looked tired and sleepy, so

Mr. Yalley suggested they should go home for a while and find something to eat. With hug and kisses they said their good-byes and left.

After a good meal, all that father and son wanted to do was to relax for a while, but relaxation soon turned into a two-hour nap in the living room. Paul III woke up first and realized he felt good in his mind and body.

"I really needed this nap," he told himself. He looked over, and there was his dad still sleeping in his lazy boy chair, he went over and shook him gently. "Dad, Dad, wake up."

Mr. Yalley opened his eyes and saw Paul looking down at him.

"How long have I been sleeping?" he asked.

"About two hours," Paul answered.

"Let's get ready and go back to the hospital," Mr. Yalley told his son as he got up from the chair and started stretching his arms. "That was a good nap. I slept like a baby. Well, let's hurry up and get out of here before your mother thinks we have forgotten about her," said Mr. Yalley. Father and son freshened up and changed their clothes and headed back to the hospital.

"Hey, guys, what took you so long?" Mercy asked them as they entered the hospital room.

"Oh, you thought we had abandoned you?" Mr. Yalley jokingly asked his wife.

"Not for a split moment. I guess I was missing you two and became anxious," Mercy told them.

"Well, after eating your delicious meal, we decided to relax a little bit, and we fell asleep. It was a good meal and a good nap, and here we are happy to see you," Paul told his mom.

"How are you feeling?" Paul asked his mom as he bent down to give her a hug.

"I feel great. I am not in pain or anything."

"We thank God and give him all the glory," Mr. Yalley cut in. He went over and sat on the bed and held Mercy's hand as he gazed into her eyes with love and tenderness.

"Everything is going to be fine," he assured his wife. Mercy squeezed his hand in response.

Mercy was discharged after spending two nights in the hospital, and she was glad to be home but sad she had to say goodbye to Paul, who would be heading back to school in a couple of hours. Mercy felt she needed to take a nap, but she decided she would stay awake and enjoy her son before leaving; they sat in the living room chit-chatting for a while. It was a calm atmosphere, and the Yalleys were enjoying one another.

"What was the name Joyce about?" Mercy asked her husband.

"Oh, Mom, you remembered. Dad said I'm going to marry a girl called Joyce. He told me about the visions and dreams he's been having."

"I saw the name Joyce in a quick vision and I'm sure that is the name of our future daughter-in-law," Mr. Yalley told his wife.

"Well, I can't wait to meet her then, the mother of my grandchildren," she teasingly said. "Mooom! Wait till I am married before you talk about grandchildren," said Paul.

"Well, that is faith, for my confession is evidence of the things I cannot see now," Mercy told her son.

"Okay, Mom, keep on hoping, and it will come to pass," Paul responded. Paul stood up and said, "I need to start getting ready to leave."

"You're right, Son. As much as we hate to see you go, I think that is a good idea, for we don't want you to drive late in the night."

"Do you want me to dish some food for you to take along?" Mercy asked.

"No, Mother! First of all, you are to stay off your feet, and secondly, I don't want to carry any food with me this time," Paul told his mom.

"Okay, whatever you say, mister," Mercy responded.

Paul took out all the clothes he came home with and replaced them with fresh clothes from his closet. He changed his shirt and put on a new shirt his dad had picked out for him recently. He admired himself in the mirror for a moment and said to himself, "My dad really has good taste." Paul sat on his bed, picked up his pillow, and squeezed it three times. As a little boy Paul felt that his bedroom was his little castle, and his bed and pillow were his best friends because they were always there for him, so when he was spending the night somewhere, he had to say goodbye to them. This became a ritual for Paul anytime they had to go somewhere and wouldn't be back for the night; the last thing he would do before stepping out of the house was to run to his room and squeeze his pillow three times, his special way of saying goodbye to his room, bed, and pillow.

"Paul! Are you saying goodbye to your bed and pillow?" Mr. Yalley jokingly asked his son as he passed by his bedroom door. Paul heard him loud and clear but did not respond. He got up, put his pillow back, straightened up the bed, picked up his backpack, gave the room a final look. *I guess I will be doing these goodbyes till I am married,* he thought and stepped out of the room.

"I was wondering when you were going to come out of your room," said Mercy as Paul approached her. Just then Mr. Yalley came out of his room and wanted to say something when Paul cut in and said, "Thanks, Dad! I love the shirt."

"You're welcome, Son. I was just about to say the shirt looks good on you."

"I love it, thanks. Well, as the saying goes, everything has an end, and I'm ready to hit the road."

"Son, we hate to see you go, thanks for surprising us and I know that helped your mother a lot," said Mr. Yalley as Mercy nodded her head with all smiles.

"Well, I am just grateful that God enabled me to be here," Paul responded.

"Well, that's the God we serve, allowing his goodness to follow you once again. Anyway, sit down for a moment, and let's pray before you leave," Mr. Yalley suggested. The three of them held hands as he prayed traveling grace over Paul. When it was over, Paul hugged his parents and promised he would call when he arrived. Mercy got up and walked her son to the door, although Paul insisted she shouldn't. Mr. Yalley then walked him to the car.

"Be careful, Son, and watch out for yourself," he told him.

"Okay, Dad, I will," Paul responded as he drove off with a grateful heart for having such wonderful parents.

Paul drove for three hours and made a quick stop to buy something to snack on. He picked a few items and a drink, and when he went to the cash register to pay, he noticed that the cashier's name tag read Joyce. She looked up as he approached and said, "Hi, will that be all for you?"

Paul just stood there, and then with a big smile, he jokingly said to the cashier, "Are you my future wife?"

The cashier looked up and pretending she did not hear him well, said, "What did you say?" with a surprised look on her face.

"I was just joking. My dad says I will be marrying somebody call Joyce."

The cashier started laughing and said, "Handsome, I don't think you want an old bird like me. You are looking at a grandmother of six."

"Wow! " Said Paul.

"Young man, my advice to you is that you believe what your dad said, because parents know best," she added, still laughing.

"I will take your advice, Joyce," Paul told her as he walked out of the store.

Paul drove off thinking about how any Joyce he met from then on would trigger something in his memory. Paul had never desired to have a girlfriend, although most of his friends had girlfriends. A couple of girls had shown interest in him, but Paul had always been careful never to do anything to lead them on, and eventually they just avoided him. His Christian friends who had girlfriends called it a holy relationship, because they claimed nothing was going on that was not pleasing to God, but Paul decided that when it came to that kind of love, he was not going to play with his emotions until he was ready. The thought of knowing the name of his future wife began to fascinate him, so he decided to pray for the Joyce in question.

"Father, I thank you for whoever she is. I bring her before your throne of grace, thanking you for your enabling power that has made her to understand that her body is the temple of God and she will pursue purity until the day she marries. Father, I ask you to help her to be strong and alert so that she can flee from temptation, and also that she will walk in wisdom so that she will not put herself in questionable situations. I thank you for her parents who are raising her to be a godly woman, but if she is not in a home like that, I pray your hand of protection upon her, Amen." When Paul finished praying, he felt such love and tenderness toward this invisible Joyce. *I love my mom, but this feeling is different,* he thought. *Thank you, Lord, for whatever you are doing. I leave everything in your hands, Amen,* he added. Little did he know that the Joyce in question had a story that would blow him away.

"I am finally here! Thank you, Lord," Paul said aloud as

he pulled into the parking lot of his dorm. He knew Tete would be fast asleep, so he decided he would try and make less noise, but when he used his key to open the door, he realized that Tete forgot to leave the chain lock alone. "He forgot. He chained me out," Paul said under his breath. "Okay, here we go," he said as he rang the doorbell. Paul waited a few minutes and rang it again. Tete woke up from a deep sleep and realized immediately that it was Paul and that he had locked him out. He jumped out of bed, walked quickly to the door, and looked in the peephole just to make sure, and sure enough it was Paul. He took the chain out, and opened the door.

"Sorry about that," he apologized as Paul stepped into the room.

"That's okay," Paul responded with a wave of his hand.

"Well, welcome back, and how is your mom doing?" Tete asked him in a sleepy voice.

"Thank God everything went on well, and she is doing fine. That reminds me, I need to call them, for they will be waiting to hear from me before they go to bed."

"Okay then, settle in. I am going back to bed, and I will see you in the morning," Tete told Paul.

"All right! See you in the morning," Paul responded. Paul called home immediately; his mom fell asleep whilst waiting. He told his dad he made it safely and that he would talk to them in the morning.

"Okay, Son, have a good night!" Mr. Yalley responded in a kind of sleepy voice.

Paul decided to go straight to bed so that he would be well rested in the morning. He changed into his pajamas, drank a glass of water, and went to bed. As he lay still in bed, he couldn't help thinking about the Joyce in question, who she was, what her life story was, her likes and dislikes, and how she would look. *I know beauty lies in the eyes of the beholder, but I want her to be beautiful in everybody's eyes, I want her to love the Lord with every fiber in her being, gentle, kindhearted, full of compassion, soft spoken, and loves children because I desire to have a lot of them, but of course I know it takes two to agree on that. I know I may not get all these desires, but, Lord, loving you with all her heart is enough for me.* With this thoughts Paul drifted off to sleep.

A month had passed. Three weeks after Mercy had her surgery she had no more pain, and she was back to her usual self and enjoying every bit of her life, but Mr. Yalley wouldn't allow her to do anything around the house because Doc Prayers advised her to take it easy for six weeks. Mr. Yalley took charge of the household chores and was really enjoying cooking for the first time in their married life. He seized every opportunity to put a smile on Mercy's face and make her feel like a queen. The Yalleys, for all these years, had kept the advice Pastor Matthew gave them when they were getting married. He told them that laughter is like medicine to the bones and that marriage without laughter, humor, and playfulness will eventually get boring and die. "Take things easy, laugh with each other a lot, and find ways to be playful with each other." This advice had enabled them to enjoy each other, and they could sincerely say they were each other's best friend. Mercy felt so strong in her body that she started thinking of not honoring her six weeks appointment but she knew Doc Prayers was going to call her personally if she failed to show up.

The night before the appointment Mr. Yalley intentionally reminded her twice, knowing the way she felt about it. Mercy got a little irritated but didn't show it. *Why does he keep reminding me?* she thought.

They went to the appointment the following day, and Doc Prayers was very pleased about how fast her incision had healed but still warned her not to lift heavy things for a while.

"Why would I even do that when I have these macho arms waiting on me?" Mercy jokingly responded.

"I'm glad to hear that. Call me if you suspect any change in your body. You are not completely out of the woods yet, although I know your total healing is in God's hands," Doc Prayers told Mercy with a little tap on her shoulder.

"Thank you very much," said Mercy.

"Well, not just our Doc but our brother in Christ, thanks for taking care of us once again," Mr. Yalley said as he gave Doc Prayers a firm handshake.

"You're welcome, and you two enjoy your day whilst some of us get back to work since we cannot afford to get off early," Doc Prayers jokingly told them.

"No comment, just go and get busy," Mr. Yalley responded, and the two men enjoyed a laugh while Mercy looked on with all smiles. Doc Prayers hurried off, and the Yalleys headed back home.

"What do you feel like doing today?" Mr. Yalley asked his wife the following day, but she seemed not to have an answered.

"I am serious, what do you feel like doing?" Mr. Yalley asked Mercy again.

"Okay, I have an idea, let's go visit my parents for the weekend and be back by Sunday afternoon," Mercy suggested.

"That is a good idea, for we have not seem them in almost three months," responded Mr. Yalley. "What time is it?" he asked.

"Twelve o'clock," Mercy answered.

"Let's pack a few things and hit the road so that at the latest we will be there by 4:00 p.m.," said Mr. Yalley.

Pastor and Mrs. Matthew were old and frail and lived mostly by themselves; they hardly traveled outside Little Bethlehem these days, so it was always a special time for them when their children, grandchildren, family members, and friends visited, especially from out of town.

"Let's call Paul and tell him about our movements," said Mr. Yalley as Mercy got up to go and start packing.

"That's a good idea," she responded.

"Hey, Son! How are you?" Mr. Yalley asked Paul when he picked up the phone.

"Fine, Dad," he responded. "What about you two?"

"We are fine, Son," Mr. Yalley responded. "How is Joyce doing?" Mr. Yalley asked Paul.

"Who?" Paul asked his dad.

"Joyce," Mr. Yalley answered.

Paul immediately remembered what he was talking about and starting laughing.

"You got me on that one," he told his dad, still laughing. Mr. Yalley then joined his son in the laughing.

"Until it comes to pass, we have to keep her alive in our thoughts," Mr. Yalley told his son.

"Okay, Dad! I heard you loud and clear," Paul responded with another laugh.

"Anyway, I called to tell you that your mom and I are going to visit your grandparents." "Well, that's nice. Is Grandpa P all right?"

"They are both doing fine. We just decided to spend the weekend with them," Mr. Yalley told his son. When Paul was five years old he stopped calling Pastor Matthew just grandpa and started calling him Grandpa Pastor. That lasted for a while, and then he started calling him Grandpa P. Surprisingly everybody liked it, and all the grandchildren started calling him Grandpa P.

"Tell Grandpa P and Grandma I say hello and that I will call and talk to all of you tomorrow," Paul told his dad.

"Paul, when was the last time you spoke to your grandparents?" Mr. Yalley asked his son. "Well, let me think, um, about two weeks ago, I will say," he answered.

"Knowing how busy you are, that is not bad, but do try and be in touch with them often. You know they love you dearly, and as they always say, you were their long-awaited grandchild, and secondly, none of us knows how long they have with us," Mr. Yalley advised his son.

"Okay, Dad, I promise I will do better," Paul told his dad. "Where is Mom?"

"She is packing a few things we will need for the weekend; you want to talk to her?"

"No, Dad, just tell her I love her, and you all have a safe trip."

"Okay then, love you and bye," Mr. Yalley responded.

Mr. Yalley put the phone down and stood there motionless just staring into space. Mercy passed by and noticed the look on his face; she looked at him for a moment and asked him, "Are you okay?"

There was no response from him, so she stretched out her hand to touch him when he spoke up.

"I just had a vision," he said.

"Really! What did you see?" Mercy asked anxiously. "You really scared me standing there motionless like that. What did you see?" Mercy asked him again.

"I saw Little Sam's dad telling Grace that the divorce was a mistake and that he wants them to be a family again," he told her.

"That's interesting," Mercy responded. "Well, this is a serious issue, so let's pray about it for them," she immediately suggested.

They quickly held hands, and Mr. Yalley began to pray, "Lord, I thank you for our marriage. You have blessed us with love, understanding, respect, and unity. We have enjoyed each other for all these years by your grace. We are blessed to expe-

rience what true love is. If you can do it for us, you can do it
for anybody else, so Lord, we come before you today, standing
in the gap for Sam and Grace. We know you have already set
something in motion on their behalf, and we pray that your
grace and mercy will soften Grace's heart and open her eyes
to embrace the second chance you are giving them. We pray
that no weapon formed against this reconciliation shall prosper. We also ask you to grant us traveling grace in our going
and coming. In Jesus' name we pray, Amen."

"Amen!" said Mercy.

"Okay, honey! Now it is in God's hands, so let's wait and
see the end of this story," Mr. Yalley said when he finished
praying.

"Are we ready to go?" he asked Mercy.

"Yes, we are," she answered.

As the Yalleys walked toward their car in front of the
house, they saw Mr. Luken getting out of his car and Little
Sam rushing toward him.

"Honey, this is becoming very interesting," Mercy told her
husband.

"Well, that's our God at work," Mr. Yalley responded.

Just then Grace came to the front door, and when he saw
the Yalleys, she quickly came down the stairs and walked
toward them. Little Sam was all over his dad, and Grace just
walked past them without saying a word.

"Where are you two headed to?" she asked as she got closer
to them.

"Going to visit my parents," Mercy answered.

"Oh, that's nice," said Grace with a smile.

"How are you doing?" Mr. Yalley asked her, looking straight
in her eyes.

"I am fine," Grace responded. "As you could see, Little
Sam is leaving for the weekend, and I am going to be all by
myself. I don't look forward to this separation at all, because I

am restless when he is gone. He needs both of us, so I just deal with it," Grace told them.

Mr. Yalley put his hand on her shoulder and said, "Grace, if Big Sam tells you anything before he leaves, please listen, okay?"

Grace was a little surprised about the advice, but she found herself saying, "Okay."

"You all have a safe trip and a wonderful weekend," she told the Yalleys and walked away, thinking, *What is all this about? Big Sam has something to tell me? What will that be, and how did he know about that?* She crossed the street to her house.

"See you when we get back," Mercy shouted after her as they drove off.

Grace turned and waved at them. "Bye!" she shouted back with a smile.

As she climbed the stairs to her front door, for a moment she remembered how the name Big Sam came into being. Little Sam was named after his dad, and everybody called him Jr., and when he was about four years old, he asked his dad why everybody called him Jr. His dad explained to him that he was named after him, so he was Sam Sr. He looked at him and said, "No, you are Big Sam, and I am Little Sam." From that day on, nobody could call him Jr. anymore, for he would start crying and insist his name was Little Sam and his dad's name was Big Sam, so Little Sam and Big Sam became the new names. A friend asked him one day, "Little Sam, when you become a big boy, we cannot call you Little Sam anymore."

Little Sam looked at his face and said, "I know that. My name will be Big Sam just like my dad," he answered calmly and continued to do whatever he was doing, so father and son became known as Big Sam and Little Sam.

Little Sam always wanted his dad to visit his room for a while before they left. Grace didn't not like that, but she loved to hear them carry on a conversation. She walked into the house, and to her surprise her ex-husband was standing in the middle of the room with a look on his face.

"Where is Little Sam?" she asked him.

"Oh, I told him to go to his room for a while because I wanted to discuss something with you," he told her.

"Me! About what?" Grace asked him with an attitude.

"Well, can we sit down?" Big Sam requested.

"Sure," Grace answered with a look that said, *I don't care whether you sit or stand.* They sat down, and Grace fixed her gaze on his face so that she would not miss any facial expression as he told her whatever was on his mind. Big Sam cleared his throat and began to rub his two palms together.

"Well, I have been doing a lot of thinking, and I have realized that the divorce was a mistake. It should never have happened. I want you to think seriously about this. Please, can you find a place in your heart to forgive me and my selfish actions and see whether you can give me a second chance? I want us to start over again, because I still love you and Little Sam dearly. We are family, and I want us to maintain that till we leave this world," he told her. Big Sam found himself on one knee and continued with a shaky voice, "Grace, I am really sorry for all that I have put you through, and I promise I will do whatever it takes to make this work this time around, if you will give me the chance. I feel I am dying slowly inside, I miss you so much. Please listen to my heart," he pleaded.

Grace was so shocked she could not even blink her eye. She felt her whole body was frozen. Big Sam stood up and sat down, almost on the verge of crying. It seemed like forever when Grace finally spoke up. Surprisingly her heart was very softened toward him, and somehow the love she had suppressed began rise up from the depth of her soul to her heart. Then she remembered what Mr. Yalley had told her a little while ago. She sat up straight suddenly, and that made Big

Sam stood up, thinking she was getting ready to leave without saying anything.

"No! No! Sam, sit down," she told him. Big Sam sat down and began to rub his palms together slowly; Grace then realized how nervous he was at that point. She smiled and said, "I miss seeing you do that."

"Do what?" he asked.

"The palm thing," she responded.

He looked down at his hands and said, "Yea! Yea! I am nervous. Who wouldn't be?" he told her.

Grace was surprised at how she wanted Sam back, but she decided to take it easy and put up a little bluff. She found herself responding almost in a whisper.

"Sam, I have heard all that you said. Give me time to think about it, and I will let you know what is on my mind," she told him.

"That sound good to me," he responded.

"Why don't we take Little Sam to his favorite restaurant for lunch before you two take off," she suggested, giving him a clue that her heart had softened.

"That sounds great, and Little Sam will love that," said Big Sam.

"Little Sam! You can come out now with your stuff. It is time to go," Grace called after him.

"But Dad has to come to my room first," Little Sam responded.

Big Sam looked at Grace's face and said, "Okay, Son, I am coming, and I have a surprise for you," he said as he walked toward his room. Little Sam was used to surprises these days, because his dad always had a surprise for him during their weekends together. In his little mind whatever surprise he had for him was not a big deal.

"Little Sam, are you ready?" he asked him as he entered his room.

"Yes, I am ready. You always come to my room before we leave, so I am waiting for you," he told him.

"Yea, I nearly forgot about that, because I was discussing something important with your mom. Guess what the surprise is? The three of us are going out to eat at your favorite restaurant before we leave," he told his son.

With this information, Little Sam stood up and in an excited voice asked his dad, "Is mom really coming with us?" He did not wait for the answer from his dad. He took off running through the hallway, shouting, "Mom, Mom, are you really coming with us?" he asked as he nearly bumped into his mom.

"Yes, Sam, I am going with you guys," Grace assured him. Little Sam began to jump up and down in front of his mom.

"I can't remember the last time we went out to eat together. I mean, you, dad, and I, this is going to be fun." Little Sam went on and on talking with such excitement. Big Sam just stood there speechless, watching him, whilst Grace was trying had not to cry when she realized how silently her son had been suffering over their family break up.

"I am ready, let's go," Little Sam shouted to the two of them.

"Are you sure?" his dad asked him.

"Yes, I am sure! I have everything in my backpack," he answered.

"Okay then, let's get going," Grace told them. When they stepped out of the house, Grace became very uncomfortable because she realized she may have to sit in her ex-husband's car for the first time after the divorce. She quickly said, "Let me drive my car, so that you don't have to come back and drop me off."

"Oh no, Mommy, we are going to eat together, so let's ride together," Little Sam responded.

"I don't mind dropping you off. After all, it is worth all

the trouble," Big Sam told his ex-wife with a smile. Grace didn't want to refuse the offer because of Little Sam, so she said, "Okay guys, I will ride with you two, but you know how I enjoy being chauffeured, so I will sit in the back," she told them. Big Sam realized immediately what she was trying to avoid, so to make it easy for her, he jokingly responded and said, "Okay, Queen of England, we are at your service." They all laughed happily for a moment as they entered the car.

Little Sam knew what he wanted, so he was the first to place his order. As they all sat down to eat, Big Sam and Grace in their thoughts couldn't stop the memories of outings like these. With a sigh he assured himself that it was only time that would bring times like these back into their lives. Just then one of Grace's co-workers walked in with her family.

"Hi, Janet!" she quickly said when she saw them just to break the silence at the table.

"Oh hi, Grace. I did not know we both have the same off days," said Janet as she walked toward her at their table.

"Well, you know my little boy, and this is his dad," Grace made the introduction. Big Sam stretched out his hand to give Janet a handshake and said, "Sam Luken, nice meeting you."

"Nice meeting you too. I work with Grace, and she is such a wonderful co-worker," Janet told Big Sam. He just nodded his head with a little sweet smile in response to what Janet said. In his heart he knew it was true, and he truly missed that.

"Well Grace, see you on Monday. Let me get over there before my kids order everything on the menu. Enjoy your meal," Janet said as she walked away.

"She has five kids?" Big Sam asked, sounding a little surprised.

"I had no idea they were all hers. She looks too young to have five kids. I will ask her about that on Monday," Grace responded.

"I don't want to eat any more," Little Sam told his parents.

"What do you mean you don't want to eat anymore? You have to finish your food," Grace responded without looking at Little Sam's plate.

"Tricked yah!" Little Sam said with a laugh.

Grace turned and noticed his plate was empty. "I will get you, alligator," she said as she stretched out her hand to tickle him.

Little Sam laughed as he jumped off his chair to avoid his mother's tickling.

"I guess we are all ready, so let's get going," Grace said. Grace kept wondering how long she should keep Sam in suspense as they drove her back home. *These are matters of the heart, and they need careful thinking,* she thought. She thought about the advice Mr. Yalley had given her, so she decided she had to talk to them before she made up her mind. She felt this was very important because it seemed Mr. Yalley knew something that she didn't know. *Before I make any decision, I have to seek their counsel,* she advised herself.

"Well, I am going to miss you, little guy," Grace told her son as he came out of the car. Grace was surprised to see her ex-husband come out of the car and walk her to the front door.

"Gracy, I really do appreciate you suggesting this lunch," he told her. Grace couldn't resist looking into his eyes before saying anything, for he was the only one who called her Gracy, and the way he said it always made her light headed, and she was amazed when those suppressed feelings toward him began to rush into her brain when he called her Gracy.

She did her best to control her emotions before saying, "You are welcome. I am glad we were able to do that. Anyway, drive safely." She waved at her son and quickly vanished into her house. Little Sam was watching, wondering what was going on between his parents. His little mind couldn't connect anything, so he moved onto something else.

"Is Mom sad I am leaving again?" he asked his dad when he entered the car.

"No, Son, she is not sad," he told him.

Little Sam kept quiet for a while and then said, "I wish we could all live together again." Big Sam turned and looked at his son and felt sorry for him.

"Be careful what you wish for," he said. "It can come true."

"Yea, I know," came a calm response from Little Sam.

This is a good wish, and I don't mind if it comes true, Big Sam thought. *I really do want her back. I want to change this situation and make things right. Oh God, I don't really know you personally, but I have heard a lot about you. Please help me.* He turned to look at his son, who was fast asleep. The cool air coming into the car always made him fall asleep.

The Visit

Mr. and Mrs. Matthew were so glad to have their daughter and son-in-law visiting. They ate dinner and sat down in their peaceful living room and talked into the night. Mercy sat near her mom, snuggling into her side as if she were a little girl, and her mom was enjoying every bit of it. Mr. Yalley later on shared what God had been doing in his life lately concerning the visions and dreams he had been having. The Matthews listened without being surprised; they knew what God could do through his children. When he finished, Pastor Matthew thanked God for choosing his son-in-law as a vessel to use. He prayed that God would give him wisdom so that he would know how to handle each revelation. Mr. Yalley was so glad to have such a godly couple as in-laws. It was a nice evening, and they all went to bed with peace and joy in their hearts.

They made it to church on Sunday, and Mercy was glad to be back. The Yalleys got the chance to sit with the Matthews throughout the service because Pastor Matthew preached once a month these days. Pastor Jacob, his assistant, preached a good message about standing in the gap for somebody, and that life is not all about us. Christ was made the ultimate sacrifice for us, and God expects us to do the same in our own little way, to be the one Satan has to deal with before touching somebody God has put in our lives. Not only for our families; it could be a stranger, a co-worker, a friend, or anybody you can think of who needs prayer for Satan and his demons to take their hands off them. The message really ministered to the Yalleys, and they left church realizing they needed to be interceding more for people, for they knew that there was always somebody to pray for other than themselves, and Grace and Big Sam were their new assignment.

The Matthews planned to eat lunch with the Jacobs immediately after church, but they had a little delay because most of the church members were glad to see Mercy and her husband and wanted to fellowship with them.

"I really do miss this fellowship," Mercy said as they finally drove off.

"Well, we can try and come once a month," Mr. Yalley suggested.

"That would be great," Mercy and her mom found themselves responding at the same time.

"Here goes the twins," Pastor Matthew said jokingly.

They were almost at Pastor Jacob's house when Mr. Yalley asked, "Who is Jeremiah?"

"He is one of our church members," Pastor Matthew answered from the backseat.

"Why are you asking?" he asked Mr. Yalley.

"Well, I don't know what is going on, but I just saw a woman crying and a nurse comforting her as they walked in a white hallway, and then the name Jeremiah flashed in front of me," he told them.

"Oh my God! Let's turn around and go to the hospital," said Mrs. Matthew in a worried voice.

"Signal the Jacobs to stop," Pastor Matthew told Mr. Yalley.

"Pastor Jacob, we need to turn around and go to the hospital," Pastor Matthew told him.

"Why? I was there last night, and he seems to be doing fine. We intend to visit him this evening," he told them.

"Well, we just need to go there right now," Pastor Matthew told him.

"Okay, let's go," he responded, wondering what was going on.

They all turned around and drove straight to the hospital. On their way Mr. Yalley broke the silence and asked Pastor Matthew what was wrong with Jeremiah.

"Mr. Jeremiah is a deacon in the church. He got sick about a week ago and was admitted there days ago. He seems to be doing fine from the report I heard yesterday. We visited him on the day he was admitted, and he was in great spirits. When they were praying for the sick this morning, his name was mentioned," Pastor Matthew said.

"Oh yea, you're right, I heard that," Mr. Yalley responded.

When they got to the hospital, the Jacobs knew what floor Mr. Jeremiah was on, so they led the way. At the reception area they saw a nurse helping Mrs. Jeremiah to make a phone call, and when she saw them, she ran straight into the arms of Mrs. Matthew, sobbing as she kept saying, "He is gone, he is gone, he is gone."

The nurse couldn't get all the numbers out of her before she ran off.

Mr. Yalley noticed the look on the nurse's face, so he went over and said to her, "Thanks a lot for helping her out. We will take it from here."

She looked up and said, "You're welcome, sir. I was a

woman without faith, and this man on his sick bed talked to me about the goodness of God and how he loves me so much to send his only son, Jesus Christ, to die for me. He prayed for me that God would open my eyes to embrace his love. This was yesterday morning, and I woke up this morning with a strong desire to go to church, but I couldn't because I had to be at work. I promised myself that next Sunday whether rain or shine I would make it to church," she told him. "We see death all the time, but when someone touches your life like this and dies the following day, it becomes personal," she added in a shaky voice.

"Well, I am glad you had an encounter with him. His mission in life was to tell everybody he came in contact with about the love of God, and I am glad he did it to the very end of his life on earth. Just honor his memory by doing what you promised yourself," Pastor Matthew told the nurse. She turned and gave Mrs. Jeremiah a hug.

"I am so sorry for your loss once again. Can you give me your number, for I will be honored to come and pay my last respects."

Mrs. Jeremiah tried to give her the number but couldn't remember all the numbers; they all noticed she was struggling, so Pastor Jacob quickly came to her rescue.

"That is my number. Call me in three days, and I will tell you about the funeral arrangements," he told the nurse.

"Thanks a lot! By the way, my name is Ruby. I just realized I dropped my nametag somewhere," Ruby responded.

"Well, my name is Pastor Jacob, and this is my wife, Naomi. The older couple is Pastor and Mrs. Matthew and their daughter Mercy with her husband, Mr. Yalley."

Ruby shook their hands as the introduction was being made. After that, she bid them goodbye and left, feeling so sad about the situation but glad she had an encounter with him.

Pastor Jacob turned to Mrs. Judy Jeremiah and asked, "Where is he now?"

"Still in the room," she answered in a shaky voice. "They will take him out in a few minutes, and then the funeral home will pick him up," she added with tears dropping down her face. Judy led the way silently, leaning somehow on Mrs. Jacob's shoulder as they made their way back to the room. When they entered the room, the white sheet had been pulled over his head, and there was this sweet fragrance in the room. They all looked at each other without confusion because they knew it was the Holy Spirit manifesting itself that way. They were all filled with peace and joy, and Judy started singing "It Is Well with My Soul." They all joined in, and although it was five of them, it sounded like a whole choir was singing. It was so beautiful that tears of joy started running down their faces, and for a moment they thought they'd stepped into heaven.

When it was over, they started hugging each other. They took the sheet off his face, and he looked like he was just taking a peaceful nap. Judy put her hand on his forehead and said, "Honey, safe trip, we will miss you very much. Thanks for being the most wonderful husband I could ever dream of. You are forever the love of my life. Please say a big hello to God for me, until we see each other again, farewell my love." Judy then hugged him for a moment and planted warm kisses all over his face before she released his body.

It was a moment that the Jacobs, the Matthews, and the Yalleys would never forget. Pastor Matthew started praying as he walked around the room, praising God.

"We serve a good God. He knows all things. He plans all things. Thank you, God, for your presence, comforting, and assuring us that all is well, and for filling us with your peace and joy. We love you, Lord, we love you, we love you, Lord, we are blessed to know you, Lord."

"Halleluiah! Halleluiah! Halleluiah! Praise God!" the rest kept responding.

The seven of them were really having church when they heard a knock on the door, and they all knew they were coming to pick up the body. Two men entered and made faces that seemed to say, *What is going on here?* One of them spoke up and said, "What is that smell? Did you all spray some kind of lady's perfume in here or what?"

"No, Son, that's the Holy Spirit manifesting his presence that way," Pastor Matthew said, and he quickly made the sign of the cross. The other guy began to back off till his back touched the wall, and then he slowly sat down on the floor and began to weep. They all turned to look at him, and his friend asked him, "Jerry, are you okay! Man, what's wrong?"

Pastor Matthew walked to where he was sitting and said, "Son, it is time to surrender."

"Yes, sir," he responded with tears running down his face, for he understood what Pastor Matthew meant, whilst his friend looked on with confusion.

"My mother has been praying for me for years to give my life to God. She always tells me, 'Jerry, God is about to arrest you one of these days.' I don't know what is going on, but I feel so sorry for everything I have done against God," he told them, sobbing. "Sir, can you please help me to make it right?"

Pastor Matthew asked Pastor Jacob to take over from there. He knelt beside him and took his hand as the rest made a circle around them. Pastor Jacob asked him, "You believe there is a God, right?"

"Yes, sir," Jerry answered.

"Jerry, there is a God in heaven who loves you very much, as a matter of fact he knew you in your mother's womb before you were born, and your destiny is in his hands. The only way you can know what he has in store for you is to have a personal relationship with him. We are all born sinners, and we cannot approach God with our sinful nature because he is a holy God. He wants all of us to become his children, so he makes a way out for us by giving his only son as a ransom for our sins."

"You mean Jesus Christ," Jerry interrupted.

"Yes, he sent his only son, Jesus Christ, to die for our sins, but I can assure you, if it were you alone, he would have still done that, and that tells you how much he loves you. For God to call you his very own you have to receive Jesus Christ as your personal savior by inviting him into your heart and making him Lord of your life. Are you ready to do that?" Pastor Jacob asked him. Only heaven knew how ready he was at that point.

"Yes, sir," he answered with every fiber in his being.

"Okay, Jerry, pray this prayer after me."

He nodded his head and closed his eyes. His friend moved closer and stood behind the circle, showing his support for what was going on. Only heaven knew where he stood with the Lord. Whatever it was with him, he had heard the gospel of Jesus Christ that leads man unto salvation.

"Dear God, I come before you this day as a sinner who needs a savior, and with a repentant heart, I ask you to forgive me my sins. I surrender my life to you, I invite you into my heart, and I want you to be the Lord of my life. I thank you that today I am called by your name. In Jesus' name I pray, Amen.

When Pastor Jacob was done praying with Jerry, Pastor Matthew stepped closer to Jerry, put his right hand on his head, and prayed over him.

"Father, we thank you for making Jerry your very own today. We pray your eternal blessing upon him, which will enable him to be glad with joy in your presence. We pray a wedge of protection around him so that nothing will distract him from what you have started in him. Father, create a hunger in his soul so that he will thirst for righteousness and seek you with every fiber in his being. We thank you that you who started the good work in him will see to its completion, in Jesus' name we pray, Amen."

"Amen!" Jerry shouted, wiping his face with his shirt as he stood up shivering from head to toe.

"Welcome into the family of God," they told him as each of them gave him a hug. Jerry felt the love of God all around him, and his face beamed with a smile that made him look very handsome.

"My mom will be so happy when she hears this," he told them. "Whose husband passed?" "He is mine, but not anymore. He belongs to God now," Judy said as she started tearing up. This was not just a job to Jerry today; everything became personal, so he stepped forward and took Judy's hand.

"Ma'am, I am so sorry for your loss. I pray God will be with you and your family," he told her.

"Thank you. Jerry," Judy responded.

They all made a circle around the bed and said their good-byes. Judy started crying again, and so Mercy quickly put her arms around her shoulders just to comfort her. They stepped back and made room for Jerry and his friend to do their job. The two men pulled the sheet over the body and wheeled him away, but before they stepped out of the room, Pastor Jacob gave Jerry his and Pastor Matthew's phone numbers, as well as the church address.

"Thanks a lot. I know my mom will love to take me to her church first, but I promise, you will see me one Sunday in your church," Jerry told them.

Judy assumed they decided to visit her husband after church, so she wasn't surprised when she saw them. She was so thankful to God for sending them her way just at the time she needed them most. Little did she know how God revealed the death to Mr. Yalley.

"Judy, let's take you home, or do you have your own car here?" Mrs. Jacob asked her.

"Yes, I do," she answered.

"Okay, let me ride with you, or if you wouldn't mind, I will drive you," said Mrs. Jacobs.

"Thanks, I think I will leave the driving to you," Judy told her. Judy sat in the car lost in her thoughts, wondering how she was going to break the news to her children. The Jeremiahs had three children. Jessica the oldest was eighteen and getting ready for college; Jethro was sixteen and looked just like his dad; and Johnny, the youngest, was twelve. Jessica took them to church, and the instruction was that after church they should go straight home, eat lunch, and wait for Judy to come home and get them so that they could spend some time with their dad. Johnny was really looking forward to the visit and kept looking out to see whether his mother was coming.

"Naomi, how am I going to tell my children about this?" Judy asked when she realized they were nearing her house.

"We are all going to help you do that. You know, let's pray right now," Mrs. Jacobs suggested. "Father, we thank you that you are the source of everything we will ever need on this earth, being emotional, physical, or mental well being. Children are a blessing from you, and I thank you for the lives of these children. We stand in the gap for them right now, and we ask you to send your ministering angels to surround them and grant them the peace and strength they need to go through this big change in their lives. You said your joy is their strength. Please fill them with a fresh heavenly joy and don't let the enemy rob them of that. I also pray that Jethro will not be burdened to be the man of the house but rather grow in your grace and wisdom so that he can be a wonderful brother to his siblings. Assure Judy that you are the Father to the fatherless and a husband to the widow, and that all will be well. In the name of Jesus, I pray. Amen."

"Thank you, Naomi, for everything," Judy said when she finished praying. Naomi reached out and turned on the radio, and "Great Is Thy Faithfulness" was being played. The two women sang along with all their hearts till they got to Judy's house. Pastor Matthew rode with Pastor Jacob to keep him company.

"God knows best, but I didn't expect Elder Jeremiah to leave us so soon," said Pastor Jacob.

"That is why all of us must be ever ready, before the Lord," Pastor Matthew responded.

The two men drove in silence for a while, and when they were nearing the house, Pastor Matthew began to pray for Judy to be strong emotionally as he broke the news to the children and also for the children's emotional well being from now on. Meanwhile, Mercy, her mother, and Mr. Yalley were doing the same thing. With all these prayers going forth on behalf of the family, the presence of God filled the house with a sweet fragrance.

Jethro went and sat on his father's favorite chair in the living room; he immediately smelled this sweet fragrance and started sniffing the air.

"Do you all smell that?" he asked aloud as he made all these faces.

"Smell what?" Johnny asked. Just then Jessica entered the living room.

"What's that smell?" she also asked. The smell became stronger; the three of them started sniffing the air.

"This smells really good, like a very expensive lady's perfume," said Jessica.

"I know what it is; it is the presence of God. Sometimes the Holy Spirit manifests itself that way," Johnny told them.

"Oh yea, you're right, little brother, let me breath as much as I can into my lungs," Jessica said as she started walking around the room and breathing in and out. Just then a car pulled up in their driveway, and Johnny looked through the blinds.

"That's mom," he said. "But Mrs. Jacob is driving her," he added.

"Really," said Jessica as she continued sniffing the air. Jethro immediately knew what had happened, but she kept quiet and just sat there feeling very funny in her stomach.

Johnny, still looking through the blinds, announced again, "Two more cars just pulled up." Jessica and Jethro quickly joined him at the window.

"I hope dad is okay. I feel funny in my stomach," said Jessica.

I feel the same, thought Jethro.

The doorbell rang, and Jessica ran to open it.

"Hi, family," their mother greeted as they entered the house. They all ran to give her a hug.

"We have been waiting for you so that we can to go and visit Daddy," Johnny told his mother.

"Well, that will come later," she responded as she pulled him closer to her side. The seven of them smelled the fragrance immediately as they entered the house; they looked at each other as they realized it was the same sweet smell in the hospital room, and with this they knew God had visited the children to prepare their emotions for the news.

"Jessica, come and give us something to drink," Judy told her daughter. Everybody was really hungry, so the cool water tasted like honey and was very refreshing. Jessica started feeling something was wrong, but he didn't want to start asking questions right away. Jethro knew his dad was no longer with them, and the thought of it made him very sick in his stomach, so he just sat there lost in his thoughts. Johnny, on the other hand, had no clue and couldn't wait for the visitors to leave so that they could go visit his Dad; he had drawn a beautiful picture for him the night before and was eager to give it to him.

"Jessica and Johnny, will you two join Jethro in your dad's chair," Pastor Matthew told them. They obeyed the instruction and quickly moved over. Judy was trying hard not to start crying, but her face gave it away. The children noticed that, and for the first time fear began to grip them.

"Children, we are here to help your mother to tell you something, and our presence here is to assure you that we love you all very much," Pastor Matthew told them.

Judy spoke up, trying hard not to cry whilst breaking the news to them.

"Jessica, Jethro, and Johnny, Daddy went to be with the Lord this morning," she told them.

Jethro already knew, but hearing it from his mom confirmed his worst fear. The three of them stood up with their mouths wide open and couldn't say a word. Jessica started crying, and Judy stood up and wrapped her arms around them and started crying. Soon the boys joined in. It was sad to watch, and Mercy and her mom started crying as well, and soon they all joined Mrs. Jeremiah. The men couldn't resist their emotions, so they started tearing up as well.

Pastor Matthew signaled the rest to get up, so they did and made a circle around them. They took turns praying for the mourning family. Pastor Matthew prayed for peace and strength, Pastor Jacobs prayed for faith and hope, Mrs. Jacobs prayed a wedge of protection around them so that the enemy would not use the situation to cause any confusion in their young minds, Mr. Yalley prayed for the funeral arrangements, and Mercy prayed and thanked God for all the people who would be reaching out to them in any way. When they finished praying, Pastor Matthew told them about how their dad led his life to the glory of God to the very end of his life on earth.

"He prayed for a nurse yesterday, and she has decided to start going to church. The men who came to carry his body, one of them got convicted in the room and started sobbing, and at the end we led him to Christ. I just want you kids to know this, so that you won't forget that your dad finished his race well. As you all know, he loved the Lord with all his heart and had a burning passion for every man to come and know the Lord, and this is the best spiritual legacy any father could leave for his children. I want you all to follow his example and live for Christ," Pastor Matthew told them. The three of them nodded their heads.

"Judy, we will ask to leave now. We know you have a lot of important calls to make," Pastor Matthew told her.

"Thank you all so much," she responded as she began to hug them one after the other. "I am so thankful to God that you all came to the hospital just when I needed somebody to lean on. God always looks out for us in times of trouble. He is truly our ever-present help in times of trouble."

"He sure is, and that is our God," said Mercy, and the rest nodded their heads in agreement.

Some friends went to the hospital and heard the news, so they came straight to the house. When Pastor Matthew and the rest were heading out, they were coming in.

Lord, don't let them stay too long. Judy needs a little private time with her children before tomorrow, Mrs. Jacob prayed.

The lunch they planned had now turned into dinner because it was past 6:00 p.m. when they arrived at the Jacob's. Mercy helped Mrs. Jacob warm the dishes and got the dining table ready. When you have death on your mind, especially the death of a dear brother in Christ, although you know where he is going and you will surely see him someday, it's still hard to deal with, and that can easily kill your appetite.

They were all dealing with this individually, but when it was time to eat, they found themselves enjoying the meal so much that for a moment elder Jeremiah was not on their minds.

"This is really good. I am not leaving without the recipe of the rice dish," said Mercy to Mrs. Jacob.

"Thanks! I am glad you are all enjoying the meal. Although we are mourning, we still need to eat to get our energy," Mrs. Jacobs responded. When they were done, the men moved to the living room to discuss few things, whilst Mrs. Matthew watched her daughter and Naomi clean up and put the dishes away. It has been a long day, and Mercy noticed her mother was dozing off, so she realized it was time for them to call it a day when she was done helping out. They said their goodbyes and left.

"What a day, but it is all in God's will," Pastor Matthew said as they drove off.

When they got home, the phone started ringing. Pastor Matthew was very tired, but as he always said, "You never know who is at the other end and what they need," so regardless of how he was feeling, he never ignored phone calls. He picked up the phone, and it was Paul III.

"Grandpa! Where have you all been? I have been calling the house since one o'clock," came his favorite grandson's voice.

"It's been along day, Son, but how are you doing?" he asked him.

"Fine, Grandpa P.," he answered. "Are you all okay?"

"We are all fine by the grace of God," Pastor Matthew responded. "One of our elders in church, Elder Jeremiah, just went to be with the Lord, so we spent some time with his family and then had dinner with the Jacobs."

"Oh! That is so sad to hear. You all must be very tired then," said Paul.

"Yes, we are tired, but we are okay," Pastor Matthew responded. "When are you coming down to see us?"

"I will surprise you and Grandma one of these days," Paul told him.

"Well, we will be looking forward to seeing you. Take care of yourself."

"Okay, Grandpa P," Paul responded.

"Here is your dad," said Pastor Matthew as he gave the phone to Mr. Yalley.

"Thanks," Mr. Yalley said as he took the phone from his father-in-law.

"Hello, Son, how are you?"

"Fine, Dad, I was really getting worried about you all. I thought something had happened to one of them, and you were at the hospital," Paul told his dad.

"Sorry about that. We were at the hospital all right, but it had nothing to do with us." "I am glad to hear that but so sorry to hear about the death of Elder Jeremiah," said Paul.

"Yea, that was sad, but we are rejoicing because we know where he is, and we will see him someday," Mr. Yalley responded.

"What happened to him anyway?" Paul asked.

"Well, from what I heard, he got sick about a week ago, was admitted three days ago, and he had a massive stroke and died this morning. He left behind a wife and three children, a girl and two boys. Jessica is eighteen, Jethro is sixteen, and Johnny is twelve."

"So the oldest is about to start college," Paul cut in.

"Yes, Son, you're right. They are very good kids and love the Lord so much, and I know they are going to be all right," Mr. Yalley told his son.

"I pray this will make them stronger than ever in the Lord," Paul added. "Where is Mom?"

"In the bedroom with your grandma. Hold on and let me give her the phone," Mr. Yalley told his son.

"Hi, honey! How are you?" Mercy asked her son, sounding very excited.

"Fine, Mom, I Just heard the news about Elder Jeremiah's home going," said Paul.

"Well, it has been a sad day for us, but not to God. He has shown himself so strong since it happened, and we know that he has already put a shield of protection around them. You know when things like this happen, Satan has a way of discouraging us and robbing us of our faith; that's why we should all be praying for them so that the joy of the Lord will continue to be their strength," Mercy told her son.

"You're right, Mom. Dad told me their names. I will write their names down, and I will be praying for them," Paul promised his mom.

"Son, they will appreciate that," Mercy responded.

"How is Grandma doing?" Paul asked.

"She is fine, just a little tired. She is getting ready for bed," Mercy told her son.

"Well, tell her I say hello. I guess you and Dad will head back tomorrow?" Paul asked his mom.

"Yes, we will try and leave in the morning. We intended to spend two nights, and here we are spending our third night, but it always feels good to be back home with your parents regardless of how old you are. Where your life began should always be a place where you look forward to coming back to and feeling at home whenever you visit. There are a lot of people out there who don't feel this way, so we should count ourselves blessed to have the family we have," Mercy told her son.

Paul listened attentively, and when his mother was done, he cleared his throat and said, "We are truly blessed to have the family we have. I pray every generation will keep it up."

"Your grandparents prayed for us and their grandchildren before we even started getting married, and we pray for you, your children, and grandchildren all the time. That's the only way the family legacy can be carried on from generation to generation, so as you pray don't forget to be praying for your children, grandchildren, as well as great-grandchildren," Mercy advised her son.

"Thanks Mom, for your advice. It is very important, and I will remember to do that," Paul told his mother.

"How is Tete?" Mercy asked Paul.

"He is fine, he went on a short trip with some friends," Paul told his mom. "Okay, Mrs. Yalley, you all have a good night's sleep and drive safely tomorrow," Paul added.

"All right, Mr. Yalley, we will. Talk to you later," Mercy responded as mother and son started laughing at their own sense of humor.

The Wait

Grace had been looking out of her window to see whether the Yalleys were back, but there had been no sign of their car. She became a little restless because she really wanted to talk to them before Big Sam came back, knowing that he would be expecting some kind of response from her.

"God, I need your help," surprisingly she found herself praying. Just then she heard a sound of a car, so she quickly looked out, thinking it was the Yalleys, but it was her ex-husband. "The moment of truth, what will I do?" she asked herself as she stood up reluctantly to go to the door. She took two steps, and she heard a soft gentle voice say, "Be still." She turned around quickly, thinking there was somebody behind her, but she was alone. Just then the doorbell rang, so she couldn't get the chance to dwell on what just happened.

Grace opened the door, and Little Sam jumped into her stretched arms. She started kissing him all over his face.

"I missed my prince for a whole month," she told him.

"Oh, Mommy, I was just away for the weekend," he responded.

"Yea, I know. I miss you so much that it feels like a month," she told him as she began to tickle him. Little Sam started rolling on the carpet and laughing hard. Grace was having so much fun with her son that for a moment she forgot all about Big Sam until he spoke up. He had been standing at the doorway watching mother and son play and have fun, and he wished he could join them, but he couldn't, so he watched with a big smile on his face.

"Hi, Grace," he said.

"Oh! Hi!" she responded, still laughing. "How did it go?" she asked him.

"Everything went on well. We had fun," he told her.

"Well, I am glad to hear that," she responded. Little Sam took off to his room to unpack all the new things he brought back.

Big Sam cleared his throat and said, "Grace, I want you to take your time and think about what I told you. These are matters of the heart, and I don't want you to feel pressured at all," Big Sam calmly told her.

Grace felt such relief that she didn't have to say anything in response to him now. She remembered the prayer that she prayed a little while ago, that God would help her and also the soft voice she heard that said, "Be still." She immediately realized that a God that she doesn't really know had bailed her out, so with a thankful heart she responded and said, "I am seriously thinking about it, and I will let you know what my heart says soon."

"Thanks, I am glad to hear that," said Big Sam. "Little Sam, I am leaving," Big Sam shouted out to his son. Little Sam came running to the living room dressed from head to toe in his latest matching outfit, a cap, a shirt, shorts, socks, and a pair of sneakers.

"Wow!" Mercy exclaimed, "And where are you headed to?"

"Nowhere, Mommy, I just want you to see my new outfit Daddy bought for me," he told her.

"Well, well, let me check you out. You look really nice and cute, like my prince," said Mercy to her son. "Now go and change and don't leave them on the floor."

Little Sam took off running back to his room, happy that his mom really liked his outfit.

Grace turned and looked at Big Sam without saying a word. Big Sam understood the look, so he spoke and said, "I know what you are going to say; I couldn't help it, I just had to get them for him." Grace could have been angry with him, but it was a different kind of feeling this time.

"The boy had too many clothes, that's all I'm trying to say. He is becoming very picky about what to wear these days, and I am afraid we will have a fashion monster on our sleeves by the time he turns ten," Grace told Big Sam calmly. Big Sam was surprised to see that she was not frustrated or angry, and there was no facial expression indicating anything else whilst she was talking to him.

"I certainly agree with you, Grace, and I promise to work with you on this," Big Sam responded, looking into her eyes with a heartfelt smile. Grace was very satisfied with his response, so the conversation ended on that note.

"Goodbye, Little Sam," said Big Sam. Little Sam came running into his arms.

"Bye, Daddy! Will you call me when you get home?"

"I think you will be fast asleep by the time I get home, so I will call you in the morning, little guy," he responded as he tickled him.

Little Sam laughed a little bit and said, "I think I have had enough tickling for today."

"Says who? Here comes another one," said his dad as he quickly reached out and tickled him again.

"Oh no! Daddy, not again," said Little Sam as he tried to run off to avoid more tickling. His dad quickly picked him up and gave him a big hug and a kiss.

"Love you, Son," he said as he put him down.

"Love you too, Dad," Little Sam responded. Big Sam turned toward Grace, who all along had been standing there watching them.

"Well, bye for now," he said.

"Bye," Grace responded with a little wave of her hand as she pulled her son closer to her side.

"Thanks," he added as he walked out the door.

Mother and son followed him to the car and waved goodbye together. Grace was surprised to see her hand up in the air, waving Big Sam goodbye, but somehow it felt good, and the whole thing seemed like he was just going on a trip and would be back.

"I wish we could all live together again," said Little Sam as they walked back to the house. "Wishes can come true, you know, so just keep on wishing okay?" Grace told her son in a very comforting voice as she rested her right hand on his shoulder.

"Dad said the same thing. You think alike," said Little Sam.

"What did you tell him before he told you that?" Grace asked him.

"I told him I wish we could all live together," said Little Sam.

"Oh, I see, we are really thinking alike. We are right by saying wishes can come true, so keep wishing with your heart, okay?" said Grace to her son. *Poor child,* she thought.

Big Sam drove in silence, lost in own thoughts. He realized how much he loved Grace and for the first time after the divorce, how hard it was for him to leave them.

"Grace is a wonderful, fun-loving woman who brought such balance into my rigid life. Now everything seems boring; loneliness is killing me and is getting worse each day. I cannot continue to live like this anymore. This was all a stupid mistake. I want my family back, oh God, help me," Big Sam found himself talking aloud as he started sobbing behind the steering wheel.

As Grace lay in bed that night, she couldn't help thinking about what was happening to her. "There is something happening that is beyond me. I thought I had closed every possible door in my heart for reconciliation, but here I am within forty-eight hours as if every door has been wide open within my heart. This is not me. I have to talk to the Yalleys," Grace said to herself as she drifted off to sleep. Little did Big Sam and Grace know that a loving God had already started working on their case, making the Yalleys his earthly representatives, for it was by no accident that Grace moved next door to them.

It had been a long day for the Matthews and the Yalleys, so they all decided to retire to bed early. As usual they gathered in the living room to have a prayer before going to bed. The day's event was so vivid on Pastor Matthew's mind, so much that he couldn't find words to say. They all sat there for a while and he finally spoke up and asked Mr. Yalley to pray, which he humbly did.

Mercy fell asleep as immediately as her head touched the pillow. Mr. Yalley, on the other hand, lay in bed and played the day's event over and over in his mind. He was so humbled by the awesomeness of God and how God had chosen to use him. He began to worship God silently with tears running down his face. In the midst of all that, Grace crossed his mind. *I wonder what happened in the Lukens's house,* he thought.

"*The beginning of a miracle,*" came the voice of the Holy Spirit.

"Thanks. I can't wait to see it unfold from beginning to the end," said Mr. Yalley in a whisper. A smile broke on his face. He turned and kissed his dear wife on her forehead. He lay there looking at her sleeping face till he drifted off to sleep.

Mr. and Mrs. Yalley planned to leave early in the morning, but Mrs. Matthew insisted they eat breakfast together before they leave, so she made sure she was up early to cook the breakfast before Mercy and her husband got up. Mercy planned to do that before going to sleep, but she couldn't beat her mother to it. She came into the kitchen, trying not to make any noise to wake her mother up, and was surprised to see her mother was almost done with the breakfast.

"Mom! When did you wake up to do all this? It is only 6:30," Mercy said with a look of surprise on her face.

"The usual time I get out of bed," her mom answered calmly. Mercy stood there not knowing what to say but appreciating her mother in her heart. Although frail, she still woke up at the same time every morning.

"Don't just stand there, help me lay the table," Mrs. Matthew told her daughter.

"Yes, ma'am!" Mercy responded in a childlike voice. Her mother turned and looked at her smiling face and gave her one of her looks.

At the breakfast table Pastor Matthew blessed the food, thanked God for the visit and prayed that God would grant them traveling grace so that they would make it back home safely. After breakfast Mr. Yalley thanked his mother-in-law for being such a great cook and feeding them before sending them off.

Mrs. Matthew smiled and said, "I hope my daughter is feeding you good breakfast at home."

"Oh yes, ma'am, if I give her the chance, she will feed me through my nose as well," Mr. Yalley said jokingly. "Anyway, we are grateful to have wives who can cook," he added as he clapped his hands.

"Thanks for acknowledging that. All said and done it is time to get up," Mercy said as she stood up and began to clear the table. Mercy cleaned up and put everything away for her mother before leaving the kitchen. After that she called Judy and talked with her for a while. She promised they would be back for the funeral. Judy tearfully thanked her for everything. The Yalleys couldn't leave as early as they had planned, but they were glad to heading out by 9:30 a.m. Mr. and Mrs. Matthew waved goodbye to their daughter and son-in-law as they drove off.

The Assignment

The Yalleys had been driving for a while when Mr. Yalley spoke and said, "We need to stop and buy gas at the nearest gas station."

"Why?" Mercy asked. "Your tank is only half empty," she added.

"Yea, I know, honey, I just feel I should top it up," said Mr. Yalley. He was experiencing something that he couldn't explain to his wife. All of a sudden, he had this strong desire to go to a gas station. He knew he didn't really need to buy gas, but for what other reason, he couldn't tell. They approached a gas station, and he felt that was not it, so he passed it.

"You are passing a gas station," Mercy quickly told him.

"I don't want to buy it from there," Mr. Yalley calmly told her.

They soon approached a second one, and he felt that was it, so he quickly pulled into the gas station and parked away from the pump.

"Why, are you not buying the gas anymore?" Mercy asked him with a look of surprise on her face.

"I will, but first things first," Mr. Yalley answered and got out of the car. Mercy began to get worried about his behavior, but she decided to keep quiet and watch. Somehow it did not occur to her that his behavior had anything to do with a vision or a dream. When Mr. Yalley came out of the car, he saw a vision of a young woman having a terrible headache, and a blood vessel was about to burst in her brain, and he heard the Spirit of God say, "She is my child. Go in and lay hands on her. I am about to heal her."

Mr. Yalley quickly walked into the store, and there stood the cashier with her head in her hands. She couldn't even look up when he entered. Mr. Yalley immediately stretched out his right hand and laid it on her head.

"In the name of Jesus, I command you, spirit of headache, to leave right now and never come back. You have no business in her life, for she is a child of God. In Jesus' name I pray, Amen." Mr. Yalley took his hand off her head, and she sat down on the chair behind her as if something pushed her to sit down. She was sweating all over her face as if she had been standing in the hot sun.

"Who are you? Are you a pastor or something?" she asked as she looked up to see who was standing in front of her.

"No, I am not a pastor. I am Mr. Yalley, and I was just passing through with my wife, and God directed me to come and pray for you."

"Really? Thanks a lot for obeying his voice," she said. "My name is Ruth," she introduced herself. She sat there lost in her thoughts for a moment and spoke up again. "I have been having headaches for the past four days, and I have been medicating myself with painkillers. It worked, but for the past one-and-a-half hours it got worse, and I thought I was going to die. I called my boss to come and relieve me so that I could go to the hospital. I begged God not let me die for the sake of my five-year-old daughter, Mary. I am all she has as at now. God really loves me, I am so thankful He sent an angel like you to bring my healing. A few minutes ago, I thought I was going to die, and now the headache is gone. I feel great and so sound in my mind. Thank you, Lord, and thank you too," she said as she stood up and stretched out her hand to thank Mr. Yalley. Just then her boss walked in, and without looking at Ruth, she said, "You can go now. By the way, can you drive?"

Ruth with all smiles said, "I am okay, Tori."

"What! A few minutes ago you were dying, and now you are okay? Are you playing some kind of April fool on me or what?" she asked with a funny look on her face.

"Tori, no, this is not an April fool at all. I always tell you that God will take care of me, and he has just done that. This story will knock your shoes off your feet," Ruth told her.

"What story?" her boss asked.

Mercy needs to hear this, thought Mr. Yalley, so he excused himself and went out to call her.

Oh Lord, what is going on with my husband today, she silently said as she got out of the car. Mr. Yalley held her hand, and they both entered the store together just as Ruth was about to tell Tori what happened.

"I have been having headaches, as you know, for the past four days, for the past one and a half hours it became so much worse that I thought I was going to die. I became very scared, and I found myself thinking about my daughter, Mary. I asked God not to let me die because of her. I was sweating, my head was wet, and I couldn't lift my head up, so I held my head in my hands, waiting for you to come so that I can rush to the hospital. Just then I heard somebody come in, but I couldn't look up, then I felt a hand on my head and somebody praying for me. He removed his hand, and I just slumped into the chair behind me. By the time I opened my mouth to ask him who he was, the headache was gone, and I felt great. I have been a Christian all this time, yet never have I experienced anything like this," Ruth told her whilst Mr. and Mrs. Yalley looked on.

Oh, I see, so this is the assignment Paul was on. Thank you, Lord for using him again, Mercy thought.

Tori, by now, was just staring at Mr. Yalley, as if to say, *What is your story, sir?*

Mr. Yalley, sensing that, spoke up and said, "This is my wife, Mercy. We were just passing through, and I had this strong feeling to stop at a gas station. We passed the first one, and I knew that was not it. When we were approaching this one, I knew this was the one, so I pulled into the station, and when I got out of the car, I saw in the Spirit."

"What do you mean you saw in the Spirit?" Tori asked.

"Well, it is like seeing a vision," Mr. Yalley answered.

"Hmm, okay!" Tori said, anxious to hear more.

"I saw a young lady having a terrible headache, and a blood vessel was about to burst in her brain. The spirit of God then told me to go in and pray for her, and that's what I did," Mr. Yalley continued.

God, thank you for using Paul to intervene in this young woman's life, Mercy silently prayed as she stood still beside her husband but with a sweet smile on her face.

Ruth was a young stay-at-home mom who got saved six months ago, and her life was radically changed forever. Her husband, Billy, couldn't stand the change, so he moved back home, but his mother wouldn't allow him to abandon his family like that. She kept nagging him about it till he couldn't stand it anymore, so he moved out from there to stay with a friend.

Ruth was forced to look for a job, and by the grace of God, she found one that was close to where her mother-in-law lived, so she took care of Mary while she went to work. Ruth had no doubt in her heart that Billy could come back home; her faith and hope was so strong she seemed not to be bothered about his moving out at all, because she knew it was a matter of time. Until that happened, all that she needed to do was to pray for him every day, and even little Mary prayed for her daddy every night. Ruth's first day at work was very stressful because Tori, her boss, was a woman without patience, but the joy and peace of God enabled her to handle everything well. Ruth had a long day, learning a lot of things and getting familiar with her environment, but before she knew it, it was time for her to go. She handed over her sales for the day to her boss and was ready to go home, but before she stepped out, she boldly asked her boss, "Are you a Christian?"

Tori looked up and said, "I didn't know I was hiring a Jesus freak," and then started laughing.

"I just want to tell you that Jesus loves you very much. Have a nice evening, and I will see you tomorrow," Ruth told her calmly and walked away. Tori watched her as she walked away till she was out of sight. She chuckled and said, "What have I gotten myself into?"

Ruth had been working in the gas station for four months and seized every opportunity to minister to Tori. She invited her to church Bible study and other church activities, and she was yet to accept one invitation.

"Ruth, if this Jesus you talk about so much loves you, why did he allow your husband to walk out on you and Mary?" Tori asked Ruth out of the blue one day.

"Well, to tell you the truth and more about my story, although we were married in church, we did not know God. We were in the world drinking, partying every weekend. I slowed down when Mary came along. My next door neighbor invited me to a revival in her church; I was bored and wanted something to do, so I followed her. That was the best decision I ever made in my life, because I left that church a brand new woman.

The change was so drastic that Billy felt he had lost the

woman he married to some kind of Jesus movement, as he called it. I don't blame him for walking out on us. I would probably have done the same thing, but I want you to know that Billy will come back to us, you wait and see," Ruth told her.

Ruth had already made it a point to pray for Tori every day and live her life in a way that it ministered to her. Ruth stood there as all these things flashed through her mind. Little did she know that the way she conducted herself had prepared Tori's heart for this moment. Now in her heart she prayed that what just happened to her would minister to Tori in a big way.

"This is very interesting," said Tori finally. "What should I do to know this kind of God who does things like this?" she asked them.

Mr. Yalley cleared his throat and faced Tori; he then took his time and explained the gospel of Jesus Christ to her. "This is not seeking God's hand but his face, so that you can have his free gift of salvation," he told her. Mercy prayed silently that God would soften Tori's heart so that she wouldn't walk away with a hardened heart.

Lo and behold, at the end of it all, Tori prayed and received Jesus Christ as her personal savior with tears running down her face. Her face immediately had a beautiful glow that told you God had touched her and washed away her sins. They all hugged her and welcomed her into the family of God. Heaven knew how happy Ruth was to see this happen right before her eyes. An elder in her church once told her that time invested in prayer would never be wasted, and she now realized how true that statement was. She felt happy for Tori and honored to be part of this beautiful moment in her life. The Yalleys said their goodbyes and drove off, thanking God for the lives of those two women.

Tori couldn't believe what had just happened to her, but

she felt so much at peace and humbled. She remembered the number of times she had ridiculed Tori because of her faith, and here she was surrendering to the same God. Tori wanted to say something to Ruth but couldn't find the words, so as she walked back to her office in the back of the store, she touched Ruth gently on her shoulder. Once in her office, she sat down and stretched her legs across her office desk. Tori sat there looking through the open window in her office, but her mind was busy thinking about her life as far as she could remember her childhood. Tori had mixed feelings about all these flashbacks, but one thing she was sure of: she was going to be okay from now on.

Tori was an only child just like her mother. Growing up she was taught not to trust anybody outside her family because there was nobody out there who could love her like her family. The family had a lot of fun traveling and getting together with other family members once in a while on special occasions.

They were not churchgoers and kept to themselves, and because of that Tori couldn't make friends or relate to anybody at school. She was quiet and a loner, and although very smart, this attitude began to affect her academically; because she started feeling nobody liked her anywhere she went.

When she turned sixteen, her parents decided to throw her a big party, so she decided to show off a little and also see whether she could make some friends. She came out of herself and invited all her classmates, twenty-six of them. Her mother put a lot of time into the decorations and everything else, and a lot of her family members showed up, but sadly only two of her classmates came. She did her best to have fun with them, but in her heart she was very offended, without realizing that you have to invest in relationship to reap a harvest. She decided on that day that she would enjoy her life the way it was and everything would be about Tori from now on.

She went through college with the same attitude; she had several roommates who couldn't stand her. "She is a very beautiful and smart girl with a beautiful smile if she allows herself to smile, but she is very self-centered. The girl has a lot of issues going on in her heart. She makes me feel I am disturbing her even when I sneeze," her last roommate had told a friend.

As the years passed by, Tori became more and more closed up within herself. Tori graduated with a degree in management but couldn't hold any job for long because she had to deal with people. Her parents couldn't help her when she complained about her life. Her mother would say, "Tori, you have everything going on for you. What do you need friends for? They will only bring trouble in your life."

"Mom, you don't understand. It's fun at my age to have a few girlfriends that I can do things with," Tori told her mom.

"Yea, yea, like I said, they only bring you more trouble to deal with," her mother responded.

"I'm twenty-six years old, have never had a date, and I'm still virgin," Tori continued.

"Hey! It means somebody will be first and get lucky," her dad cut in with a funny laugh.

"You two don't understand, and you are of no help. I am beginning to think the way you raised me is creating all these problems in my life," said Tori, feeling very frustrated as she hung up on her parents.

Tori lost her third job and out of frustration decided to give herself a break and move back home for a while. She called her parents and told them about her plans; they encouraged her to follow her heart. She went out to buy gas a week before the move, and at the gas station, she saw a notice in the window, "Now Hiring Manager." Something in her jumped at the opportunity, so she asked for the application form and filled it out immediately, and she was hired the following day. She called her parents to tell them about her change of plans, and they sounded happy for her, but in their hearts they felt, as usual, that it wasn't going to last.

Tori felt good about her new job and decided she was going to prove to herself and her parents that this was going to last until she decided to leave. A couple of weeks into her new job, one of her workers quit, so she posted the hiring notice in the window for a cashier. Ruth showed up, and she hired her.

Tori noticed that there was something different about Ruth; her temperament was very even, and she always had a sweet smile on her face, so she took interest in her, but she soon realized that she was one of the many Jesus freaks she had crossed paths with. Tori found herself refusing one invitation after another from her to her church programs. When Ruth told her that her husband had walked out on her because she became a Christian, Tori could not believe how stupid she was to allow something like that to happen to her. *I have been looking for just a boyfriend for all these years, and somebody throws away her marriage because of a Jesus she can't even see? This girl is so stupid,* she thought with a chuckle. Despite all that, for the first in her life, she couldn't resist the warmth and peace she felt around Ruth, but she couldn't stand what she represented at the same time. Little did she know that Ruth was her divine appointment.

Ruth knew that Tori was a woman living in darkness the moment she met her. She had no peace or joy in her life and always looked miserable. She was a hard-working woman, but when you looked at her, she was just an empty shell trying to make it through life each day on her own. The day Ruth gave her life to the Lord, she remembered the minister telling them, "You are all the light of the world now, and you are indebted to all those who don't know the Lord and are perishing in darkness. It is your responsibility to pray for them and seize every opportunity to minister to those who will cross paths with you."

The seed of prayers she sowed on behalf of Tori had born fruit right before her eyes. Tori became quite lost in her own thoughts with the peace of God all around her. Ruth decided to leave her a lone to enjoy the freedom she was experiencing in her heart. She looked at her time, and she realized it was time for her to go, but the girl who was to relieve her had not made it yet. Ruth couldn't wait, so she went to Tori's office to tell her.

She was sitting down quietly behind her desk, lost in her thoughts. She looked up when she heard footsteps and when she saw it was Ruth, she beamed with a smile.

"I guess you are ready to go?" she asked.

"Yea, but Adriana has not made it yet, but I have to leave right now," Ruth told her. The old Tori could have said with an attitude, "Can't you just wait a few minutes till she gets here?" but the new Tori said calmly with understanding, "Okay, just go ahead. I will take over till she gets here."

"Thanks a lot. I will see you tomorrow then," Ruth responded. As she turned to walk away, Tori spoke and said, "The Yalley guy said I should look for a good church and start attending. I guess I don't have to look far. I will just renew one of my many rejected invitations and follow you."

"Yea! That's a good idea, but you know, those invitations never expire; they are always valid," Ruth responded with a smile.

"Okay! It is good to know that, thanks," Tori responded as both women began to laugh together for the first time.

I have been working with this woman for all this time and never have I seen her smile or laugh so joyfully the way she just did. Thank you, Lord, Ruth silently talked to herself as she walked away.

Tori was surprised at herself when she laughed and it came so freely from the depth of her soul. She felt sorry for herself for suffering all these years emotionally, but at the same time she felt such love around her, and she knew she was going to be all right.

Back Home

"I wonder what happened at the Lukens' house this weekend," Mercy said as they were nearing their neighborhood.

"Something interesting with God's stamp on it," Mr. Yalley responded.

"Home at last," Mercy said as they entered the house. She put her bags down and slumped herself in the nearest chair. "Thank you, Lord, for bringing us back safely," Mercy prayed aloud. "What an interesting weekend. It was packed with stories and testimonies all to the glory of God," she added.

"You care for something to drink, Madam?" Mr. Yalley jokingly asked her.

"Just water," Mercy responded in a funny French ascent.

"At your service!" said Mr. Yalley, hurrying into the kitchen like a houseboy waiting on his madam. Mercy noticed how he hurried off and started laughing. Mr. Yalley came back with the water and started laughing as well. The Yalleys had always put smiles on each other's face with their jokes, pranks, and sense of humor. Like Mr. Yalley always said, "A cheerful heart does good like medicine."

"Thank you, Lord!" Mr. Yalley said as he sat on his favorite chair. "Lord, you are a good God, Lord you are a good God, thank you for everything. I am humbled to be called your child. I worship you this hour and lift you above all thrones, for you are the I am," Mr. Yalley continued to worship his God when he was interrupted by the ringing of a phone in his spirit and thought the phone was actually ringing.

"Mercy, pick up the phone," he told his wife.

"Why should I pick the phone?" Mercy asked him with a funny look on her face.

"Because the phone is ringing, and you are nearer to it," he told her.

"Paul, are you okay? The phone is not ringing. Either I am getting deaf or your ears are hearing things before they happen," Mercy told him.

"I guess so," he answered. "I heard the phone ringing, and I was wondering why you were not picking it up. I wouldn't be surprised if Paul called any moment from now," said Mr. Yalley. Just then the phone started ringing; Mercy turned and looked at her husband with a surprised look on her face. Mr. Yalley smiled at her as if to say, *I told you so.*

Mr. Yalley quickly stood and picked it up.

"Hello!" he said.

"Hi, Dad!" came the response.

"Hello, Son! How are you?" he asked him. Mercy's face lit up with a smile, knowing that it was Paul on the line.

"I am doing fine, Dad," he answered.

"What about Joyce?" he asked with a laugh.

"Well, I guess she is fine. I have been busy, and I haven't been keeping up with her," he told his dad.

"That is not good, Son, what does she think about that?" Mr. Yalley asked his son.

"She is busy too, so she understands," Paul responded.

"Hmm, my advice to you is don't ever allow business to rob you of your relationship," Mr. Yalley told his son as he starting laughing.

"Dad, this is not funny anymore. Ever since you told me the Joyce thing, it looks as if all the Joyce's have vanished into space. I hardly come across anyone called Joyce," Paul told his dad, sounding a little frustrated.

"Son, be patient, she will show up when the time is right. I am joking around with it, but to assure you, I do pray about it for you. Like I said, when the time is right, she will show up," Mr. Yalley told his son.

"Yea, I know, Dad, thanks. I called about an hour ago and no one picked up," said Paul.

"We came back about thirty minutes ago. We had a delay planned by God," Mr. Yalley told his son.

"What happened?" he asked in an anxious voice.

"Son, hold on and let me put your mother on the phone, as you know she is the one who is good at recounting stories."

"Come on, Dad, I want to hear it from you. Just try and tell me," Paul told his dad. Mr. Yalley realized how important it was for Paul to hear it from him.

"Okay, I will try; your mother will help me if I miss some parts," he responded.

Mr. Yalley took his time and told Paul about how God directed him to a gas station and the events that followed.

"You see, I told you, you can do it. I did not hear Mom say anything in the background, so I know you were on your own. Wow! What a story, Dad, you are more than Prophet Nathan in the Bible," Paul told his dad.

"I don't know about that, but I know God uses us in different ways to fulfill his mission on earth. He is a good God, and I am humbled to see myself being used like this by him," Mr. Yalley told his son as he became very emotional.

"Dad, that is great. It means he has set you apart for that ministry. I hope he will let you see more about Joyce," Paul told his dad with a little giggle.

"You never know, so let's keep our fingers crossed on that one," Mr. Yalley responded. "Okay, Son, take care of yourself, and I love you," Mr. Yalley said as he gave the phone to Mercy.

"Paul, how are you?"

"Fine, Mother!" Paul said. "Your weekend was really packed with stories to his glory, death, healing, and salvation."

"You're right, Paul, and we are so grateful to be part of it all. Let me boss you about this funny one. Your dad and I went to the store to buy a few items. We were standing in the checkout line when a beautiful lady walked in, and most people turned their heads to look at her. She was dressed very professionally; her hair and everything about her was just beautiful. Your dad grasped with a look on his face, so I asked him what that was about, and he said he just saw beneath the lady's clothes. I put my hand on my mouth and said, "You mean, you saw her underwear?' He nodded his head but with a serious face.

"God really have a sense of humor, but this is not funny. This is not funny; she has a terrible rash all over her butt and thighs. She is too embarrassed to see a doctor or tell anybody. The Holy Spirit said she has been self-medicating herself, but nothing seems to be working. She has been crying out to God, and he has heard her prayers. All that she needs is to rub All Purpose Thomas Cream on it," your dad told me.

"How do we give her this information?' I asked your dad, and he said we should pray she comes and stands behind us to check out, and he would then remind me about Aunty Mattie's cream. We would carry on this indirect conversation for the lady to get the information that she needed.

"Lo and behold, she came and stood behind us. I had eye contact with her, and I said hello. She responded with a nod of her head and a smile. Paul, she is a beautiful lady suffering under her expensive clothes. Anyway, we set the ball rolling.

"Honey, don't forget we need to go to the pharmacy and but Aunty Mattie's rash cream,' your dad said in a whisper but made sure the lady could heard the conversation.

"What is the name of the cream again?' I asked your dad.

"All Purpose Thomas Cream,' he said.

"He then went on to tell me how the rash was all over her butt and thighs but is getting better since she started using the cream. At the corner of my eyes I saw the lady was getting very uncomfortable, she then moved quickly to the next aisle, as if that one were moving faster. The most important thing was to pass on the information, and we did, and because God had a hand in it, we know she will rush to the nearest pharmacy and look for it.

The lesson your dad and I learned was that we can look good on the outside and be so ugly inside. Even as believers we put on masks that make us feel good on the outside, but what is going on in our life and heart is a different story. The funny part is we always forget how naked we are before God," Mercy told her son with a little laugh. "God have mercy on us," she added.

"This is becoming more frequent and very interesting, Mom," said Paul.

"You're right, Son, we are honored and we thank God for it all," Mercy responded.

"Well, let me leave you two alone, and I will be in touch," said Paul.

"Okay, Son, take care and we love you," said Mercy.

"Love you all too, bye," Paul said and hung up. Paul lay across his bed for a while. "I love people, and I walk in grace toward everybody, but do I have any gift that will be so extraordinary?" Paul spoke out aloud in the quiet room. He lay there just looking at the ceiling; chill came all over him, and he heard a still voice say,

"Paul, all that matters is you are doing the things that please me, and I love you." He sat up quickly. He looked around the room slowly with a funny face, then he realized that God had just spoken to his heart. He immediately went on his knees and began to worship and thank God.

The Yalleys just finished eating dinner when the phone rang and Mr. Yalley quickly picked it up.

"Hello!" he said.

"Hello, this is Judy," came the voice on the other end.

"Oh, Judy, how are you all doing?" asked Mr. Yalley.

"We are fine by his grace and mercy," Judy answered. "I was calling to let you all know that viewing will be on Friday at 4:00 p.m. and burial will be at 2:00 p.m. on Saturday."

"Judy, we will be there, and may God's hand continue to be upon you all, for all the comfort you need. Here is Mercy."

"Thanks, Paul," said Judy,

"Hi, Judy, all is well, okay," Mercy told her. "How are the kids?"

"They are doing fine and holding up well," said Judy.

"Is there anything you want me to help you with?" Mercy asked her.

"Thanks for asking, the food and drinks will be taken care of by the church ladies and some friends, and every other thing is taken care of, so you all just come and be there for us," Judy told her.

"Judy, if you think of anything that you will like me to do just call me, okay?" Mercy told her.

"I will, and thanks a lot," she said.

Mercy hung up and for a moment she put herself in Judy's shoes, and immediately she felt so cold. She stood up and cast down her imaginations and brought every thought to the obedience of Christ. "Life and death you put before us. I choose life," she said aloud.

At the Foot of the Cross

Grace left work that day wondering whether the Yalleys were back, and as she neared her house, she saw their car and her heart leaped with joy. She looked at her son and said, "Little Sam, we are going straight to the Yalley's house to spend some time with them. She wanted them to eat out before coming home, but Little Sam said he was not hungry, and she wasn't either, so she decided they would just snack on something before going to bed, so with that taken care of, she could spend some time with the Yalleys.

She rang the Yalley's door bell. Mercy opened the door and was so glad to see them.

"Come on in," she said and gave Grace a hug. Mercy closed the door behind them. She then put her hand on Little Sam's head and led them into the living room.

"Sit down and feel at home," Mercy told them. "Paul! Grace and Little Sam are here," she called out to her husband, who was in the bedroom.

Mr. Yalley came out and gave mother and son a hug.

"How was school today?" Mr. Yalley asked Little Sam.

"Fine, sir," he answered. "I have a new teacher call Mr. Peter," he added.

"Really! Where is the old one?" Mr. Yalley asked him.

"He went on *matality* leave," he told them.

"Oh, I see, she is going to have a baby. Well, we wish her well," said Mr. Yalley. "By the way, is maternity, not matality, but don't worry. You doing great with your pronunciations," Mr. Yalley added. He turned to Grace and said, "So, how are you doing, young lady?"

"Oh fine, fine, Mr. Yalley, but I just wanted to discuss something with you two. I hope I am not interrupting with your evening," she told them.

"Oh no! It is fine with us, and we have listening ears for you anytime," Mr. Yalley told her, looking in Mercy's direction for a second.

"Let's go to the formal living room and leave Little Sam here to watch something on TV," Mercy suggested. Little Sam told them what he wanted to watch, so Mercy turned on the TV for him.

"You want something to drink?" Mercy asked him.

"No, ma'am."

"What about you, Grace?"

"Not right now, thanks," Grace told Mercy.

I hope they will understand what am about to tell them, Grace thought. The three of them moved to the living room and sat down.

"You always keep this place so beautiful," Grace told Mercy.

"Thanks, it is all because you only have grownups living here," Mercy responded, laughing.

"Let's pray before we start," said Mr. Yalley, so with their heads bowed, Mr. Yalley prayed. "Oh Lord, we thank you for this day and your many blessings upon our lives. Give us wisdom in any way that Grace will need our help. We invite you to be part of this conversation, in Jesus' name we pray, Amen!"

Grace cleared her throat and said, "Well, it is about my exhusband. Little over a year ago, as I told you, we started having problems here and there, and he felt he wasn't happy anymore, so he went ahead and divorced me. It was a very painful time in my life. He was a very rigid and self-centered man but very kind-hearted when you got to know him.

"I moved away immediately to start my new life. The funny thing is, I have not even taken the time to change my name, which is a painful reminder of the life I left behind. When he came to pick Little Sam up for the weekend, he said he was sorry about his actions and that the divorce was a mistake. He said he realized he couldn't live without us anymore and that he wanted his family back. I remembered what you told me when you were leaving, to listen to anything he told me. I don't know why you said that, but somehow it softened my heart toward him, and I realized I still love him. Yes, I still love him but not in that way. I am bent on moving on and eventually embracing a new life. It's been over a year, and I am beginning to feel I am ready for something new in my life, then here he comes begging me to take him back. I felt I needed to talk to you two before I decide on anything. This is my story," Grace said as she breathed a sigh of relief.

"Well, well, Grace, this is good news to us," said Mr. Yalley. Grace's facial expression changed immediately, for she was surprised to hear that, but she was ready to hear more. Mr. Yalley continued, "You see, it is hard for a man to admit when he is wrong. It takes a broken man to say I am wrong or I'm sorry and really mean it. To tell you the truth, that is a good man. He has allowed his conscience to convict him, and he has buried all his pride, humbled himself, and decided to make it right. Grace that is a good man, and they are hard to find, and you know what? He did not decide this on his own without God's help," Mr. Yalley told her in a fatherly voice. Mercy was all along looking on with a smile on her face.

"What did you tell him when he brought Little Sam back?" Mercy asked her.

"Like I said, I wanted to speak to you two first, but when you didn't return as you said I found myself not knowing what to do. I asked God to help me, then I heard a voice say 'be still,' and I turned around, but there was nobody there. It was really strange, but when he came back, he asked me to take my time and think about it well, because it is a matter of the heart and he didn't want to rush me. That was such a relief. I then realized that a God whom I didn't have anything to do with had mercy on me and helped me out," Grace told them.

Mr. Yalley decided not to tell her anything about the vision he saw about Big Sam because these were spiritual things. She knew they were a godly couple, and she trusted them, so it was better for her mind to leave things that way than to tell her something that would make her think they were freaks.

"Grace, Mercy and I married in our twenties. We were married for ten years before we had Paul. We believe we were a couple made from heaven, but we had our own earthly problems. We have been married for thirty years now, and trust me: although we love each other dearly and never get tired of each other, we have walked through some trials, but because God is the foundation of this marriage, we have been able to deal with every problem we have encountered. Loving somebody without the grace of God is very difficult and sometimes impossible. Mercy and I will advise you to open your heart and give Big Sam a second chance, but before you do that, you have to give your life to God so that he can be the captain of this journey of marriage once again," Mr. Yalley told her. Grace sat down, quietly hanging onto every word that came out of Mr. Yalley's mouth.

Mr. Yalley continued and preached the gospel of Jesus Christ to Grace, and when he was done, the power of God was all over her, and in a shaken voice she told them she was ready to become a child of God. She called her son and talked to him about the love of God and how he wanted them to be his children, but before they become that, they had to pray a prayer with Mr. Yalley.

"That means we will be going to church on Sundays?" Little Sam asked his mom with excitement.

"Yes, we will start going to church on Sundays," she told him. "Come, come here and hold my hand," she added. Little Sam obediently went over and held his mother's hand.

"We are ready," Grace looked up and told the Yalleys.

Mr. and Mrs. Yalley stood up, held hands, and put the other hand on Grace and Little Sam's shoulders. Heaven rejoiced as mother and son were led to the Lord by the Yalleys. The Yalleys were so happy for them, and Mercy decided they should eat a piece of ice cream cake to celebrate. Mercy served everybody, and they sat down to enjoy their share.

"I feel so light headed, as if my body is empty," Grace told them.

"That is good because when God comes to indwell you, everything that burdened you vanishes and you feel free. That is why he said he whom the Son set free is free indeed," Mercy told her. When they were done, Grace helped Mercy to clean up and put things away.

"We will ask to leave now. Thank you for everything. I really appreciate your love and kindness toward us. Little Sam and I will not look far. We will follow you to church on Sunday," Grace told them.

"Oh! Sorry, we will not be here on Sunday. We are leaving early Friday morning to attend a funeral. The reason why we couldn't come back as planned was an elder in my dad's church died, and he will be buried this coming weekend," Mercy told her. "Our church is a very friendly church, and you will feel very welcome even if you go by yourself," Mercy added, trying to encourage her.

"No! We will wait for next Sunday," Grace quickly told them.

"That is fine, and we can't wait to worship with you and Little Sam. I am so excited," Mercy said with a little dance movement. Grace just looked on and smiled.

That night in bed the Yalleys thanked God for the new thing he was about to do in the Lukens' household and how Little Sam would witness how his family was restored. Grace on the other hand lay in bed enjoying the new person she felt inside. She thought about how she was going to tell Big Sam she had accepted his offer for a second chance. She gave herself a couple of options but finally decided on one. She decided that when Big Sam came to pick up Little Sam next weekend, she would cook his favorite meal and invite him to stay on for lunch, and then she would tell him what she had decided. "I don't know how early he will get here. I will try to wake up early and cook before he gets here. I can't believe this. I never thought this could happen. Anyway, it is all for the better," she said aloud with a smile.

The New Man

Grace went to work the following day with a new attitude. All her co-workers noticed that, and a few jokingly asked her whether she had a new man in her life. She looked at them with all smiles and said proudly, "Yes! I met someone last night, and he is the best thing that ever happened to me." With this they began to gather around her to hear more.

"Just last night, and you are so much in love? Who is he? What does he do? What car does he drive? Hey, is he handsome?" came the questions, one after the other. Grace kept shaking her head and laughing at how curious they all looked.

"Okay! Okay! I will tell who he is. I met him last night. Some friends introduced him to me, and for the first time in months, I understood what true love is. I slept like a baby with all smiles, and when I woke up this morning, the smile was still there, coming straight from my heart. His name is," she paused and pretended it was hard for her to tell.

"Come on, Grace, we've all shared our stories in this office all the time. We are happy for you, just tell us," one of them said.

Grace started fidgeting with her pen and pretending she was shy like a little girl. Their anxious faces made her laugh for a while. Finally she said, "His name is Jesus!" with a shout not too loud. "Jesus is my beloved's name."

"You! Come on, Grace, stop playing tricks," one of them told her.

Abigail, who was a born-again Christian, knew immediately Grace was not joking because she had been praying for her. She spoke up and said, "Congratulations, Grace! You finally met the big man upstairs. You want to tell us more?"

Grace always ignored Abigail because she felt uncomfortable around her, but now she felt drawn to her with such love, and she immediately spoke.

"After work yesterday I went to visit my neighbors to discuss something with them, and they introduced my son and I to this wonderful guy I had heard about but never paid any attention to what was said about him. The Yalleys are wonderful Christians, and they led us to meet him and the best part is, he was waiting with open arms to receive us. Now he is in my heart, and he has put this sweet smile on my face. As I told you, his name is Jesus. He is my savior and Lord now," Grace told them with confidence.

Most of them were looking at her as if she were crazy, because nobody had ever seen her like that since she started working there. They began to leave one after the other, a few making pretentious comments like, "Way to go, Grace, I am happy for you, but don't become a Jesus freak on us."

Grace realized that Abigail and two other co-workers were still standing near her with all smiles. The guy among them spoke up and said, "Grace, we are happy for you, and we welcome you into the family of God."

"Thank you all, I appreciate your support," she responded.

"Anyway, for your information, a few of us meet every Thursday afternoon from 12:30 to 1:30, that is during our lunch break in room twelve, the small conference room, to pray, and to tell you the truth, we've been praying for you, and we are humbled to be part of the sweet smile on your face," he told her.

Grace looked at their faces and said, "You've been praying for me?"

They all nodded their heads; she stood up and thanked them as she gave each one a hug.

Grace looked at the guy and said, "I never knew you were also..."

"Jesus freaks," they finished the sentence for Grace to her surprise.

"Well, welcome to the Jesus Freak club," said Abigail, and they all started laughing.

"We all go to different churches, so you can visit all three churches and see which one you like, or let me put it this way, pray about it, and God will direct your steps to where he wants you to be," Abigail told her.

"Well, I told my neighbor I would follow them to their church, but they are going out of town this weekend, so I decided I would skip this Sunday and go next Sunday," Grace told them.

"Just take your time because there is more ahead of you," Mary, the other lady, told her.

"Thanks, I will join you all on Thursday to pray, although I do not know how to pray," she told them with a giggle.

"Don't worry, there is more to learn on this journey with your new boyfriend, Jesus," said Abigail. With this they all laughed as they found their way back to their desks. When Grace was left alone in her thought, she realized why her three co-workers were different around the office. "From now on I pray that the way I lead my life should testify about me," she told herself with a smile.

The Funeral

The Yalleys left early Friday morning, and that was a good idea because Mercy became such a helping hand for Judy and the children. At the funeral home it looked as if the whole church was there. Elder Jeremiah looked like he was only taking a sweet nap; the children couldn't help it when they saw him all dress up but in the casket. They started crying loudly, and nobody could comfort them. Their mother joined in, and for a while there were no dry eyes there. It was so sad to watch, but there was also such joy in the atmosphere.

Let the Redeemed Say So Church in Christ was pack full by 12:00 Saturday afternoon, and extra chairs were brought in for more sitting for the burial service. The atmosphere was full of celebration; the choir was at its best, singing Elder Jeremiah's favorite's song, which the family requested. Judy stood up at a point and danced to one of her husband's favorite songs because she was so moved by the song and couldn't help it. A few friends joined in the dance, supporting her as she danced to His glory.

Jerry and Ruby from the hospital were in the crowd. They wouldn't have missed this home-going celebration for Elder Jeremiah for any reason. They felt honored to be part of all that was going on and so thankful that they were among the many lives that he touched.

When praise and worship was over, Pastor Matthew came forward to preach a brief message.

"I know Elder Jeremiah wouldn't want me to say anything today except to tell you about the love of God, which is the gospel of Jesus Christ, as he always put it. That is what brought God on earth through his son, Jesus Christ. When we come to know him, he entrusts us with his message of salvation, and we are supposed to pass it on or preach it as he gives us the opportunity, and that is exactly what Elder Jeremiah did till he took his last breath on earth. I tell you all, he finished the race well, and we are so proud of him. I want you all to stand up and give him a well deserving halleluiah clap," Pastor Matthew told them.

Everybody stood up and gave almost five minutes standing ovation. Pastor Matthew continued when they were all seated again.

"I learned that Elder Jeremiah doesn't want any time to be used talking about his life story. Instead the family wants you to read about him in the program, so I will leave it at that and do what he would love to see me do. I bet he is watching to see whether I am doing the right thing," said Pastor Matthew, and everybody started laughing.

Pastor Matthew took his time and preached the gospel of Jesus Christ to all who had listening ears. When he was done, he told them, "Today you've been exposed to the truth that will set you free. Tomorrow may not be yours. This is your day, this is your hour, and this is your moment. Come and receive his free gift of salvation. Come to the altar. This is your day, your special moment to become a son or daughter of the King," he told them as he appealed to their hearts. People began to walk to the altar from all corners of the church, and among them was Ruby, the nurse from the hospital, and as she stood there, she was so thankful for the life of the man who had brought her to this turning point in her life.

Pastor Matthew prayed the sinner's prayer with them and led all of them to Christ. After that he prayed a special blessing over them. He then told them to go on their right and make sure they get a free Bible and a devotional guide before they leave the building.

"You are welcome to make Let the Redeemed Say So in Christ as your home church or come worship with us next Sunday and have a feel of what we are about. Thank you and God bless you all," he added.

As they were led away to get their free Bibles, the church members began to clap for them and all the visitors joined in. Surprisingly they were fifty-four in number as if each one represented a year in Elder Jeremiah's life on earth.

Ruby decided that she was not going to look far, for she had found her church. She planned to come back the following day for the memorial service and every Sunday that she was off. She realized immediately in her heart that she had the responsibility to pray for her family. She could not play around at all. She had to be serious so that she could grow in the Lord and be able to witness to them. She had never owned a Bible, although she knew people who were not Christians but had Bibles in their homes. As she stood there waiting for her turn, she wondered what they did with them, or was the Bible just another book around the house? Soon it was her turn, and she received her very first Bible she could call her own, and a nice devotional guide. Ruby was so grateful and happy for all these blessings. *What an interesting but humbling way to surrender to the Lord, during a memorial service of a perfect stranger. I'm glad I crossed paths with him and I'm so honored to be among the many lives that he touched,* Ruby thought as she made her way back to her seat.

Judy wanted Mercy to be with her during the burial, so she stayed close by her side through it all. Death is painful, but when you know where your loved one is going, you can't help it but rejoice and thank God for making them his very own till you see them again. Mercy in her silent thoughts couldn't help but ponder over these things.

The reception was at the church, and Mercy was very impressed about how the church ladies and Judy's friends catered for the reception. *When the love of God is in your heart it shows in everything you do,* she thought.

"Wow! I'm so impressed. I can't wait to taste some of this mouth-watering finger food," Mercy whispered in her husband's ears.

"You are in mourning, remember?" Mr. Yalley responded.

"Come on, Paul, don't let me feel guilty. We are celebrating a godly man's home going," said Mercy.

"I know, honey. I was just teasing you. Come on, let's join the line and have a bite," Mr. Yalley told his wife.

A drawing was hanged on the wall facing the main entrance to the reception so that everybody coming in would notice it. It was a drawing that you didn't have to think hard to know it represented the Jeremiah family, but how it came to be was a very interesting story to everybody who heard it.

Jethro woke up Friday morning and told his mother that he had a dream about his dad. The family quickly gathered around him to hear what it was about.

"I dreamt dad was going on a trip, so I followed him to the car. He reached into his briefcase and brought out a well-folded paper and gave it to me. What is it, Dad? I asked him, and he told me it was something special, something forever. Go ahead and open it, Son, he said. I opened it and stood there admiring a very beautiful drawing. I looked up to say, Dad, this is beautiful, but he was gone, so I ran to the house to show it to you all, then I woke up."

The picture was two hearts with legs and arms, and a happy face holding hands and making a circle. Within the circle were three little hearts with legs, arms, and sweet happy faces. On top was this writing, "Love Forever in Life and In Death." When Jethro was done, they all sat there in silence admiring the picture in their mind's eye. Judy finally broke the silence

"Oh, honey, he came to assure us that he will love us forever," Judy told her children as she began to hug them. Johnny was a very good artist and without anybody telling him anything, he sat down immediately and drew the picture, so it became part of the decoration, and everybody who heard the story behind it was so moved and blessed.

That evening the children were so tired; they all went to bed early. Judy sat in her living room with some relatives that came from out of town. They were all talking, but her mind was not there. As she sipped her warm herbal tea to relax her mind and body, she kept telling herself, "I am a widow, Lord, I am a widow. I have a new name now, Judy the widow. I am in your hands, Lord, for I can't do this without you. I need you more than I have ever needed you. I know you won't leave nor forsake us, for you are still our shepherd. Help us, Lord."

"Judy, you need to go to bed. It's been a long day, and you need some rest," came her sister- in-law's voice.

Judy looked up and said, "I will, Maggie," but she never did. She fell asleep, and they covered her with a blanket, because she was sleeping so peacefully, and they decided to leave her alone, for that was a much needed sleep for her.

Actually Judy tried to get up from the chair, but her body

wouldn't because she felt so relaxed and comfortable. She was not surprised at all because that was her husband's favorite chair, and relaxing in it felt like she was relaxing in his arms. As she drifted off to sleep, she found her self thanking God for a good marriage, a marriage full of affection and the love of a man who would forever be in her heart. When she woke up in the morning, she felt very refreshed considering the situation, but she knew that was God, so she gave God all the glory and praise.

The church was packed full once again Sunday morning. It seemed everybody who attended the burial service was there for the memorial service as well. When the service was over, the Jeremiahs stood in the front, and almost the whole church lined up to shake their hands, hug them, or say something encouraging to them. One of the church members who designed T-shirts designed four big T-shirts for them. They had Elder Jeremiah's picture on the front, and on the back he printed these words, "One Life Touched By Many...Elder Jeremiah." Judy was so grateful for his thoughtfulness.

"This will be so comfortable to wear to bed," Judy told him.

"You're right! I made them soft and big for that purpose," he responded.

"Thank you very much; we appreciate all your love and kindness," Judy told him, as well as all the well wishers standing by. On their way home, Judy was so grateful to her church family. *This is what the family of God is all about, being there for one another in time of need,* she thought. She felt so blessed to be surrounded with such love; she had no doubt in her heart that they would be okay.

Mercy and Paul had a quick lunch with Mercy's parents after church. They left immediately after that. As usual the Matthews hated to see their daughter and favorite son-in-law go, but they were grateful to have them for two weekends in a row.

"Should we stop at the gas station and say hello to Ruth and Tori?" Mr. Yalley asked Mercy.

"Yea, that will be a good idea, and I know they will love to see us," Mercy responded.

"I hope they are both there," Mr. Yalley said as he pulled into the gas station. Hand in hand they walked through the door.

"Hello!" said Mercy. Ruth looked up from behind the counter, thinking it was a customer who needed help. She was about to say, "Can I help you?" when she recognized the people standing in front of her. With a shout and a big smile she said, "Mr. and Mrs. Yalleeey! Good to see you again."

When Tori heard that, she rushed out of the office and came to give them a big hug.

"Good to see you two again," she said with a warm smile.

"We went to a dear friend's funeral, and we said we can't pass by without seeing you girls," Mr. Yalley told them.

"Thanks a lot for thinking about us," said Ruth.

"I went to church today with Ruth, and it was great," Tori told them.

"That is good to hear. Keep going. It will get better and better," Mercy told her as she reached out to give her a hug.

"Do you two have a special prayer request that you want us to be praying about for you?" Mr. Yalley asked them.

"Oh yea," said Ruth, responding first. "My husband Billy left home because I became a believer and couldn't stand the change in my life style. His mother wouldn't keep him in her house any longer, so now he is moving from one friend to another. He is miserable out there, but he is being stubborn, and my daughter misses him so much. Please pray that he will come back home before he finds himself in trouble, for I know the devil is setting a trap for him each day," Ruth told them.

"With me, I want to get married. It's about time somebody looked my way and showed some interest in me. I am twenty-six years old and have never gone on a date. Nobody believes me when I tell them because they think I am a beautiful girl and that shouldn't be one of my problems," Tori poured her heart out.

The Yalleys listened carefully, and when they were done, he looked straight in Ruth's face and spoke to her out of faith, "By the end of this coming week, Billy will find his way back home, so just be thanking God for that."

Mr. Yalley then turned to Tori, took her two hands into his, and spoke out of faith to her, "Within a month you are going to meet your future husband. Do not be hard on yourself for not having a date all your life. You are a pure woman today, and not having a date has prevented you from going places and doing things that you would be regretting today. You wait and see how God is going to bless you for being a pure vessel today." With that they all held hands and Mr. Yalley prayed over them. He gave them their phone number and told them to call anytime. Ruth and Tori fell in love with the Yalleys, and in their hearts they knew they could always trust them.

As the Yalleys drove off, Mr. Yalley found himself praying for that godly man who was going to show up and sweep Tori off her feet.

"Amen!" said Mercy with a shout. "I can't wait to hear all about how Tori met Mr. Right."

"I wonder how she felt all these years because of that," said Mr. Yalley. "Thank God she is free now, and who the son sets free is free indeed," he added.

"Thank you, Lord, we are home. Thank you once again for your traveling grace," Mercy prayed aloud as they turned into their neighborhood. The Yalleys were so tired they both took a long late afternoon nap, and they felt refreshed when they finally woke up.

Miracles

"Hello! Mr. Yalley, this is Ruth from the gas station," came the voice on Friday afternoon.

"Oh hello, Ruth! How are you?" Mr. Yalley asked, sounding very excited to hear from her.

"Fine, Mr. Yalley," she responded. "I just called to let you know that my husband came back home this morning when I was getting ready to go to work. He apologized for being a jerk and walking out on us. Thank you very much for your faith and prayers. It is not even a week yet. God really sped up this prayer request. I never gave up hope that he would come back. I thank God for using you to bring me that assurance," Ruth told him with a grateful heart.

"Ruth, we are so glad to hear that, and we are very happy for you and little Mary. Hold on a second," he told her. "Mercy, come in here."

"What is it?" Mercy asked as she hurried toward her husband.

"That is Ruth on the line; she said her husband came home this morning as she was getting ready for work."

"Thank you, Jesus!" Mercy shouted when she heard the good news. "Let me talk to her," she told her husband as she reached for the phone.

"Ruth, this is wonderful to hear, and we give all the glory to God," Mercy told her.

"Yes, Mrs. Yalley, he came back very sober, quiet, and respectful. He apologized and for the first time in our lives, and he was very honest and sorry. Right there I knew the battle was over," Ruth told her.

"God has already finished Billy's story in heaven, but sometimes he releases it step by step. He has come back home. The next step will be giving his life to God, then witnessing to his friends, so whatever you do, don't rush him at all, just watch God do his work," Mercy advised her.

"Thank you very much, and I will be in touch," Ruth said.

"You are welcome, and be blessed!" Mercy said as she hung up.

The Yalleys held hands immediately and thanked God for his goodness and then prayed for the salvation of Billy.

"One more step to climb!" Mercy said with a little shout when they finished praying.

"You're right, honey, God is faithful. He will finish this story at his own time," Mr. Yalley told his wife. Mr. and Mrs. Yalley once again settled in their cozy living room to enjoy a quiet afternoon together.

Grace had been counting the days down, and now Saturday was just hours away.

"I need to start getting myself ready before tomorrow,"

Grace told herself after work. She went to the store and picked up a few ingredients to cook her surprise lunch. When she got home, Big Sam left a message that he couldn't make it early as he planned, but they should expect him around 1:30 p.m. After Grace listened to the message, she leaped with joy. "Thank you, Lord, for helping me out. I can get everything ready before he gets here. This is going to be fun. I am excited already, but I have to play it cool," she told herself. Everything seemed to be working in Grace's favor because normally Big Sam came to pick Little Sam up on Fridays, and if he couldn't make it, he would show up Saturday morning, but now with the time changed, everything would work out perfectly.

Grace had a good night's sleep but woke up early Saturday morning with a little anxiety. She decided to clean the whole house to get her mind off the main agenda for the day. After that her body felt relaxed but full of energy. *This was more than intentional workout,* she thought. With this energy she was ready to tackle her next agenda, which was cooking her well-planned lunch, so she went straight to the kitchen to do just that. Little Sam came in later on, hungry like a lion, looking for something to eat.

"Wow!" he said. "Are we having a party?"

"No, I am just cooking for somebody," Grace responded.

"Okay!" he said and went on his business.

Grace decided not to tell him anything yet or he would be the first to tell Big Sam what was going on. After breakfast Little Sam went to his room and got dressed. He came to the living room to watch TV whilst he waited for his dad. After waiting over two hours with no sign of him, he started getting restless.

"When is my dad going to get here?" he shouted after his mom.

"Soon, just be patient," Grace told her son.

Grace finished her cooking, took a shower, and got dressed

in a casual but pretty outfit. She started getting anxious and nervous, her hands begin to sweat, and all of a sudden she felt like throwing up.

Oh Lord, please help me. I want to be myself when I do this. Help me, Lord, for I know I am doing the right thing, she prayed. She went to the kitchen and drank a glass of cold water. She went and sat down in the living room and after a while she felt better and realized she was herself again. Just then she heard a car door close. Little Sam jumped from the couch and ran to the door.

"Wait, wait, check the window first before you go to the door," Grace told him.

"Mooom! I know is my dad," he responded.

Grace was about to tell him, "Just do what I say," when the doorbell rang. Little Sam quickly open the door and ran into his dad's arms.

"I have been waiting for a long time," he told his dad.

"Sorry, Sam, I had to go somewhere but am here now," he responded as he put him down and turned to say hello to Grace. He immediately noticed how pretty she looked, but he felt it wasn't appropriate for him to say anything. Grace, knowing him so well already, saw the look of admiration in his eyes when she looked up to respond to his greetings. That look was enough for her than any comment he could have made.

"Hi!" she responded. "How was the trip?"

"Oh, fine," he responded. Big Sam was standing as usual, waiting to walk out with his son for another weekend.

"Sam, you can have a seat," Grace told him.

"Thanks," he said as he sat dawn. *That is exactly what I wanted to do,* he thought. Little Sam came out dragging his backpack behind him.

"Dad, I'm ready," he said.

Big Sam turned to respond when Grace spoke first, "Little

Sam, put your bag down and come here," she told him, and without any question he did just that.

"I want us to have lunch together today, so I prepared some food, if that is fine with you, Sam," she said.

"That is fine with me," he responded calmly, but he was so excited he wanted to shout. "What about you, little guy?" he turned and asked her son.

"Alright, Dad," he said.

"Okay then, give me a few minutes to get the table ready," Grace said calmly as she stood up. Big Sam felt like asking her whether she needed help but decided against it. *It will look like I'm feeling too free or comfortable,* he thought, so he just sat there and waited to be called to the table.

"Okay, the food is ready," Grace told the two men in her life. Father and son walked to the table and sat down. Grace prayed and thanked God for her family and then blessed the food in Jesus' name. When she took the lid off the dishes, Big Sam realized she cooked his favorite dishes.

"Something good is about to happen," he said under his breath.

"When did you get up to do all this?" he asked her.

"Very early," Little Sam answered, "and she said she was cooking for somebody."

"Will that smart mouth keep quiet?" she told her son.

"Zip up," Little Sam said as he made a zipping sign on his mouth.

"Well, I am glad I am having a good lunch, which I haven't had in a long time," Big Sam told them.

Grace just smiled and continued to eat her food. In the middle of the lunch, Grace spoke up and said, "I have something to say, Little Sam, you are not that little anymore, so I want you to listen carefully. You know your dad and I are not living together anymore because we are—"

"Divorced," Little Sam cut in.

"You're right. Although we are still your mom and dad, we live separate lives," said Grace.

"That is why I live with you and visit my dad every other weekend," Little Sam explained further.

"That is my smart boy," Grace told him. Big Sam stopped eating because his stomach wouldn't take anymore until he heard the end of the speech.

"Well, your dad wants us be a family again," Grace continued.

"So that we can live together as a family again?" Little Sam jumped in and asked his mother.

"Yes, so that we can live together as a family," Grace told him as Big Sam looked on with a straight face but with a good feeling in his stomach. Hearing this, Little Sam got up and started jumping on his chair.

"Sam, sit down and let me finish," Grace told him in a serious voice. Grace turned to Big Sam and said, "Sam, I have decided to give our marriage a second chance, but I realize I can't do it on my own. I need God to help me, so I gave my life to God last Monday, as well as Little Sam, in the Yalley's house. Little Sam and I are now born-again Christians. I told them we would follow them to church this Sunday, so if you wouldn't mind, you can spend the weekend here and we can all go tomorrow," Grace told him.

Mr. Sam Luken's desire had come true. He had feelings of joy rushing to his brain, and he felt like climbing on top of the roof and shouting to the whole world, "I am the luckiest man on earth," but he kept his cool and decided to do what was appropriate. He stood up with all smiles. He took Grace's hand, and looking straight in her eyes, he said, "Thank you very much for listening to your heart. I know I don't deserve this, but I promise I won't disappoint you. I will stay as you suggested, so that we can go to church together." He turned to Little Sam and said jokingly, "If you wouldn't mind."

Little Sam with all smiles ran into his dad's arms without saying anything. He then jumped on his mother's lap and gave her a squeezed hug around her neck.

"I love you, Mommy," he told her.

Grace kissed him back and said, "I love you, Son. We are going to be all right."

After this Little Sam became very happy and excited, playing, talking, and running around. Big Sam ate a little more of his food and helped Grace to clean up. They spent the rest of the day talking and looking at old pictures that brought many sweet memories. There was peace and joy in the house because the right thing had been done.

Grace knew Sam had no place in her bed till they were married again. Thank God Little Sam had a bunk bed that he only loved to sleep on top, so she went in there and made the down bed up and got it ready for Big Sam. They had a light dinner, watched a family movie together, and went to bed, but before Grace went to sleep, she called the Yalleys and told them what she did and that they would follow them to church tomorrow. The Yalleys were so excited to hear the good news. Big Sam stepped outside before he went to bed to get his little suitcase he called "should in case." He always had clean clothes and every other thing to spend a night somewhere without bothering his host. He slept peacefully, feeling like a brand new man.

Little Sam was the first to get up the following morning. He was full of energy and was eager to dress up for church. He refused to eat breakfast because he said he wasn't hungry. Grace hurried up and got dressed, and before they knew it they were heading out the door. They met the Yalleys outside. They greeted each other, and Mr. Yalley told Big Sam to follow him.

Little Sam was a chatter box in the car as they followed the Yalleys in Big Sam's car. Grace wanted to sit in the back with Little Sam, but she realized her right place now was beside her husband-to-be in the front. Big Sam was glad she did, because it made him feel he was on top of the world. *I got my woman beside me,* he thought with a smile as he drove off.

Emmanuel Church of God had a praise and worship team that could bring you out of your little box. Anyone would find themselves having a good time, even if they were not familiar with the church's style. Big Sam found himself enjoying the song and clapping his hands as well. When it was over, he knew he was ready for whatever message the Pastor was going to preach.

Reverend Maxwell Praise was a very good teacher, and he delivered a powerful message. The message was about the unconditional love of God, but at the same time he expects us to obey him and do the things that please him. He went on to say that God is a loving and a forgiving God, but there are consequences for our actions. He told the congregation they couldn't do anything on their own without Jesus.

"Your life will never be complete without Jesus. There will always be a void that he alone can fill," he told them. A lot was said, but the idea that life is not complete without Jesus really got Big Sam's attention, and he decided right there that he need Jesus in his life.

Reverend Praise made the altar call for those who wanted to make Jesus the lord of their life. The praise team started singing, and Big Sam couldn't wait any longer. He stood up and excused his way out from the pew and started taking the steps that would change his life forever. Grace stood up and followed him, as well as the Yalleys, and at the altar Grace stood beside him, and the Yalleys stood behind them. They all prayed the sinner's prayer after Reverend Praise, and when it was over, he congratulated them and welcomed them into the family of God. The whole church stood up and clapped for them with shouts of praise here and there. Big Sam kept telling himself, "I am a born again Christian, I am a born again Christian, I am now a child of God, we are Christians," as he stood there a brand new man inside out.

Mr. Yalley couldn't help but to reflect on the first day he met Grace and Little Sam and the prayer he prayed that God would give them wisdom to be of any help to them. Little did he know that prayer would bear such fruit, a whole family coming to know the Lord and a marriage being restored, a little boy happy because he had his parents back together. "What a God we serve. Thank you, Lord," he said to himself.

Sam Luken felt strongly he should publicly apologize to Grace, so he told Mr. Yalley to ask the Pastor whether he could say something. Reverend Praise's response was, "Sure!" and he gave the microphone to Sam. Sam then held Grace's hand and turned to face the church.

"A little over a year ago, I divorced my wife without any reason except I was selfish. I realized I made a big mistake, so I buried my pride and asked her forgiveness and also asked her to give me a second chance, and she did. I told her I'm sorry in private, but right now from the bottom of my heart I want to apologize to her in public and also propose to her." With this he turned and faced Grace.

"Grace, I stand before the God who I just surrendered my life to and all these people, to tell you how sorry I am for putting you through those heartbreaking times. I am truly sorry, and I ask your forgiveness. I know with the help of God I will make it right this time," he told her as everybody listened to every word that came out of his mouth.

"I accept your apology, I forgive you, and I love you very much," Grace responded in a shaky voice because she did not expect anything like that at all from Sam.

"Now I want to ask you something very important. Will

you marry me again?" Big Sam asked her, looking tenderly into her face.

"Yes, I will marry you," Grace told him.

Big Sam reached into his pocket and brought out a beautiful engagement ring that Grace wanted, but they had never been able to afford.

"Wow!" she said with a sparkle in her eyes as she stretched out her finger for him. He slipped it on and gave her a quick kiss on the forehead. When it was over, there was no dry eye in the church as the congregation stood up to clap for them. The grace and mercy of God is so sweet when you experience it.

When the clapping stopped, Big Sam thanked them for bearing with him and that he couldn't think of a better place and time to do this, and on that note he gave the microphone back to the pastor and thanked him again.

"We could have a wedding right now," he jokingly told the congregation, and everybody begin to giggle, laugh, or clap their hands for them. Big Sam had never felt as good about himself and life as he felt at that moment. He took Grace's hand as they walked back to their seats for the benediction.

Many people came around after church service to congratulate and bless them with words of encouragement. The Yalleys then suggested they should all go out and eat lunch.

"What do you ladies care for?" Mr. Yalley asked, looking at Mercy and Grace at the same time

"Let's go to Xing-Xeng," Little Sam shouted.

"Well, I was going to say that," Mercy said and then turned to Grace. "What do you think?"

"Fine with me," Grace responded.

"Okay! Everybody, let's go to Xing-Xeng," said Mr. Yalley. "Thanks, little guy, for helping the ladies out," Mr. Yalley told Little Sam.

"You're welcome," he responded, feeling very proud for

helping. They got into their individual cars and followed each other.

"Mercy, you know Xing-Xeng is going to be crowded as usual. Pray that God's favor will go before us so that we can be seated quickly. I don't see the reason why a hungry man has to wait in a long line just to eat," Mr. Yalley told his wife with a laugh. Mercy prayed. When they got there, they were second in line for dine-in.

"Thank you, Lord," Mercy said. Within five minutes they were seated. By the time their orders came in, which was within fifteen minutes, the line was so long. Mercy looked up to heaven and said, "Thank you, Lord, for answering even the insignificant prayers we pray to you."

Mr. Yalley prayed and blessed the food, and the eating began.

"Grace, do you think it will be a good idea if we marry at Emmanuel Church of God," Sam asked her.

"That will be great," said Mercy, as if she were Grace's spokeswoman.

"Although I loved the place, we are not members yet. Wouldn't that be a problem?" Grace turned to the Yalleys and asked.

"I don't think that will be a problem at all, knowing my church and pastor, but I will ask him and let you know what he says," Mr. Yalley told them.

"I will really like us to do it within a month and very private," said Grace.

"That is fine with me. I do not think I want to go through another mega wedding," Big Sam told them with a laugh, and they all joined in laughing.

"Oh Grace, when I met you and Little Sam a little over a year ago, little did I know Mercy and I would be sitting here enjoying this moment with you two. God is good," said Mr. Yalley.

"All the time. God had all this planned all along. He is just using us to unfold it," Mercy added.

"Now I know why the two houses I looked at didn't go through. God wanted me right next door to you two," Grace told them with all smiles. She lifted her left hand up, and Mercy noticed the ring.

"Sam, what a beautiful ring you got her. That is so beautiful," Mercy said as she reached out for Grace's hand to look at it well.

"Thank you. She wanted it so badly, but we couldn't afford it then. Now I know she deserves every bit of it," Big Sam told them with affection in his eyes as he looked at Grace. Grace began to wiggle her fingers, showing off her ring.

"Isn't that beautiful?" she said.

"Any bride would die for a ring like this," Mercy added.

"I remember when Mercy and I got engaged, I gave her a ring my grandmother left for me to give to the girl I would marry. I was her first grandson, and she made sure she was part of that special day in my life," Mr. Yalley told them.

"It was a beautiful diamond ring; my fingers are a little fat now, so I can't wear it anymore. I will give it to Paul one day when he meets the girl of his dreams.

"Oh, what a sweet story, so how did you two meet, if I'm not being rude by asking you such a question?" Grace asked the Yalleys.

"Come on, what is rude about that? We love to share our love story, but I think we will tell you all about it another time," said Mercy as she turned to look at Little Sam. Big Sam and Grace realized that Little Sam didn't need to be part of such a conversation.

"All right, we will save it for another time," Grace said.

Lunch was good as usual, and everybody had their fill, and it was time to go. Big Sam wanted to pay the bill, but Mr.

Yalley insisted he had to pay because this was his way of congratulating them.

"Thanks a lot, we appreciate that," Big Sam said as he reached out his hand to shake Mr. Yalley's hand. He then told them he would be leaving shortly after they get home.

"Oh, we hate to see you go," Mercy said, making a sad face.

"So when do we see you again?" Mr. Yalley asked.

"I would love to come this coming weekend, but I can't. After that you will see me every weekend, and after the wedding we will decide what to do next," Big Sam told them.

"We pray traveling grace on you, and we will be looking forward in seeing again," Mercy told him.

"Thank you all very much for everything. Good neighbors are hard to come by, thanks," Big Sam told them.

It had been a wonderful weekend for Little Sam, and he didn't want his dad to leave. The thought of it made him sad, so he became very quiet in the car all the way home.

"Are you all right back there, Little Sam?" his mother asked him. He did not answer for a while, then he said, "I am sleepy."

"Okay, let's get home so you can take a nap," she told him.

When they got to the house, he quickly went to his room. Grace and Sam looked at each other and wondered what was going on. Grace followed him immediately.

"Are you okay, Little Sam?" she asked him.

"I am fine," he said and turn his face to the wall.

"You know I don't believe that," Grace told him.

"Why can't Dad stay? I don't want him to go."

"Oh, so that is the problem. Honey, I am so sorry you're feeling that way, but your dad had to go and start getting things ready because we will soon start living together, and that should make you give me a smile right now," Grace told him as she began to tickle him. Big Sam was standing at the door, so he spoke up.

"When I come back, not this weekend but the next one, I promise we are going to have a lot of fun, so start thinking of all the things you would like us to do before I get here," he told him. Little Sam was still not himself, so Big Sam suggested, "Get down and help me pack my things, then you choose one of your favorite movies, and we will watch it together before I leave. How about that?"

With this he jumped down from the bed, took off his church clothes, changed into play clothes, and quickly helped his dad to pack.

"All done, Son. Two hands are better than one," Big Sam told his son as he picked him up and swung him around. He was happy once again, so he started laughing and having a good time. Big Sam put him down and told him to go and look for the movie while he discussed something with his mom.

"Yes, Dad," he said and took off to the living room.

"Grace, let's talk about a few things I want you to take care of," Sam told her.

"Do you want us to sit down?" she asked.

"No, we can just stand here and talk," he responded.

"I was thinking about this last night, as we both know your parents are still mad at me about the way I treated you. They loved me like a son, and I disappointed them. I want to make it right by going there this coming weekend and apologizing to them before anything else," he told her.

Grace was surprised to hear that but quickly realized that she was dealing with a new Sam.

"I want you to call them and tell them about my plans to visit. Help me out or else I will be in trouble. God knows my heart. I just want to make things right," he added.

"They are still my parents, and I think that is a good idea. I will do that. Don't worry, everything will eventually work out," Grace assured him. Grace realized how important this was to him, and that made her respect him more.

"Call me and let me know whatever happens by Friday," he told her.

"I will," she answered.

Just then Little Sam shouted, "I found the movie and am ready!"

They looked at each other and smiled. They sat down with him and watched *Baby's Day Out*. A movie that he had watched more than twenty times, but it always seemed he was watching it for the first time. Soon the movie was over.

"I am so glad I watched a movie with you before leaving, Son," Big Sam said as he put his arms around his shoulders.

"Me too, Dad," Little Sam said with a smile full of contentment.

"Okay, now you know it is time for me to go."

"Yelp," he answered.

"Go and get me my suitcase then," he said.

"Yes, Dad," he said as he took off to do that.

Although Sam and Grace were happy they were back together, they would have to learn how to relax with each other all over again. When it was time for Big Sam to go, he couldn't help it; he pulled Grace toward him and gave her a quick hug and whispered "I love you" in her ears. Grace liked his move and was glad he did that.

Little Sam gave his dad a long hug before letting him go, and mother and son walked him to the car and waved goodbye.

"We are going to miss him, but he is in our hearts, so we are still together," Grace told her son as they walked back into the house.

"Mommy, this is the best weekend ever," said Little Sam as he jumped up and down in front of his mother.

"I am glad you feel that way, and I promise you there will be many more weekends like these ahead of us," said Grace to Little Sam, who by now was not paying attention anymore.

Making It Right

Grace had been dreading to call her parents for almost three days. Although she assured Big Sam that everything would be all right, she knew how angry her dad got when he heard Sam's name. He felt Sam not only disgraced his daughter but also betrayed the love and respect they had for him. Grace finally realized she needed to pray before making the call. Just then her phone rang, and when she picked it up, it was Mercy.

"Grace, I don't know why, but I felt I should call you. Is everything okay?" she asked her.

"Yes, everything is fine, but I know why you called," Grace told her.

"You do?" Mercy asked in a surprised voice. "Okay, tell me what my assignment is," Mercy said with a laugh.

"You know, my dad is very angry with Sam for divorcing me and doesn't even want to hear his name. He even finds it difficult to call Little Sam by name, so he comes up with all kinds of names like *my big boy, my prince, my little man,* or *guy*, etc., and that is always a reminder of his anger toward Sam. Sam was like the son he never had, and he really loved him, so when he divorced me, he felt betrayed, but to me that was not the end of the world. I let go and tried to move on.

"Unfortunately, he can't let go. It's been over a year, but his anger is as if this thing happened just yesterday, and now Sam wants to go over there and apologize to them and tell them he wants to marry me again. He has asked me to call and tell him about his coming over the weekend. In my heart I know he will explode with anger when I call him with this message. I have been dreading this for the past three days to make the phone call, but it just occurred to me to pray about it when you called. I think God wants you to help me pray about the situation," Grace told her.

"Well, I am glad I walked in obedience and called. God is really looking out for you, and this is nothing he can't take care off, so let's pray now and leave the rest in God's hands," Mercy told her. "What is your dad's name?" she asked her.

"Andrew Vidad," said Grace.

"Father, I am joining my faith with Grace's, and we are bringing this situation before your throne of grace. We ask you to soften her father's heart toward Sam. Fill him with your peace that surpasses all understanding and your love that covers multitudes of sin. Resurrect the love that he once had for Sam as his own son; take away the anger, resentment, and the bitterness he has toward him. Let him see him as a prodigal son who has learned his lesson and is coming back home. Fill his heart with forgiveness so that he will not even remember the reason for his anger toward him. Lord, we know there is nothing that is too hard for you to do. You brought Sam and Grace together again, so we know that you will take care of this situation as well. In Jesus' name we pray, Amen."

"Amen and Amen," Grace said with a shout. "Thank you very much, Mercy."

"You are welcome. Call your dad first thing in the morning and let me know what happens. Relax all is well, okay?" Mercy advised her.

"Okay, I will do that, and say hello to Mr. Yalley for me," said Grace.

"I will certainly do that!" Mercy said and hung up. "Lord, help me always to yield to your promptings so that I don't miss your divine appointments," Mercy prayed silently. Grace, on the other, hand felt very relieved immediately and was ready to call her dad in the morning without any fear.

Grace woke up from a deep sleep and realized if she didn't hurry up she would be late for work. She looked at the clock again, and the time was 6:30 a.m. She immediately picked up the phone and called her dad.

"Hello," said her dad.

"Good morning, Dad. It's me, Grace."

"Good morning, sweetheart. Is everything all right?" he asked.

"We are fine, I just wanted to tell you something," she told him.

"Okay! I'm listening," said Mr. Vidad, anxious to know what was on her daughter's mind.

"Well, Big Sam is planning to come over this weekend to discuss something important with you."

"Discuss something with me, something like what?" he asked in a surprised voice.

"Well, Dad, when he gets there, you will know what this is all about. He said he will try and get there by 2:00 p.m. on Saturday," Grace told her dad.

"Well, he is the father of my first grandson, and if he has requested to see me, I am not going to say no, for the sake of my grandson. I wonder what he has to tell me. Anyway, tell him your mother and I will be expecting him," Mr. Vidad said in a calm voice, to his daughter's surprise.

"Thanks, Dad! I will let him know. I am running late, so tell mom I say hello, bye!"

"I will do that. Kiss my little prince for me, and you have a nice day," Mr. Andrew Vidad told his daughter.

"Thanks, Dad, and you do the same, bye!" Grace said and hung up. She looked up to heaven and said, "Thank you, Lord." She picks up the phone again and called Mercy. *This cannot wait,* she thought.

"Hello," said Mercy.

"Mercy, this is Grace; sorry to call you this early, but I just have to tell you what happened when I called my dad. When I told him about Sam's planned visit, to my surprise he responded calmly and said that Sam is the father of his first grandson and for the sake of that, he is not going to turn him away, so I should tell him they will be expecting him. This is truly the power of prayer. That was not my dad on the phone a few minutes ago," Grace said and paused to catch her breath because she was talking so fast.

"Grace! That's the God we serve. It is our prayers that move him to act on our behalf, so to encourage you, don't allow yourself to worry about anything; just pray about things and leave them in God's hands," Mercy advised her.

"I am so grateful you are part of everything that is happening to me. Say hello to Mr. Yalley, and I will talk to you all again," Grace told her.

"Okay, have a blessed day," said Mercy and hung up.

Grace felt so relieved as she headed off to work. Big Sam called every evening but had not asked her anything about the assignment he gave her, and she really appreciated that. Big Sam, knowing how his father-in-law feels about him, had been praying and hoping he would not say no to his request and also decided that he would not ask Grace anything until she told him something.

Grace, for some strange reason, had decided not to wear

her ring to work yet, but today was different. The morning started so well that she felt like celebrating, and the first thing that came to her mind was to put on her ring and do a little show off at work. She walked into her office with an-air around her, and lo and behold, the eagle eyes in the office noticed it immediately, and before she knew it, she was surrounded, and questions were being thrown at her.

"Oh my God, that is some kind of rock you got on your finger. When did this happen? Is your boyfriend Jesus marrying you?" one of them asked, and they all began to laugh. Meanwhile Grace was sitting down with all smiles and waving her hand in a circular motion.

"Grace, say something. We have work to do," somebody said.

"Okay, my curious co-workers, this is a long story and very personal, so I can't go into details, but I will tell you all this; my ex husband and I have decided to give our marriage a second chance, so we are engaged, and I will let you all know about the wedding date, which will be soon."

"Is this a made-up story, or this is really true?" one of them asked.

"Why would I lie about something like this? I cross my heart, since I don't believe in swearing. I am not joking. I am engaged to Mr. Samuel Luken," she told them with a very serious face.

"Oh, now I understand why. You've been waiting on him to come back. No wonder you never changed your name," one of them said.

"Well, that is not it, but I am glad I didn't, because I don't have to go through that again, with all the paperwork that goes with it," she responded.

With this they all started congratulating her and saying all kinds of sweet things to her and then back to their desk one after the other.

"Well, thank you for your good wishes. I will let you all know about the date soon," she told them once again. *The cat is out of the bag now*, Grace thought as she settled down to work.

The day went on well, and she got a lot done. She was one happy woman, and everything around her now seemed to bring her joy and energy to work.

After work Grace decided to go to a few bridal shops and window shop. She and Sam kind of agreed that it should be a small wedding, but with this kind of engagement ring and its matching band that would soon be added, it called for a very elegant wedding. *How many women get their husbands back after they divorce? I am a blessed woman, and I want to celebrate that day like never before*, she thought as she pulled into the parking lot of Little Sam's school to pick him up.

"Oh! I can't go to bridal shop with Little Sam. He will tell Sam all about it when he calls. Change of plans, I will ask Mercy to go with me whilst Mr. Yalley babysits him on Saturday, good idea," she said as she got out of her car.

"Hey Sam, you ready to go home?" said Grace as she entered Little Sam's classroom to check him out. The look on his face clearly showed that he wasn't himself. Grace held his hand and walked out with him.

"Are you okay," she asked him.

He shook his head and said, "I am very hungry, and I have a stomach ache."

"Sorry you're having a bad day because of your tummy, so now what do you want to do first, take care of the stomach ache or the hunger?" she asked him.

"Hunger," he answered.

"Okay, what do you want to eat then, to kick the hunger out?" she asked him.

"Ice cream," he said calmly.

"Ice cream! I don't think you want ice cream to meet a

stomachache in your tummy. They will become friends and ache your tummy all day long, and I don't think you want that, because that can send you to the hospital," Grace told her son. Little Sam listened to the lecture his mother gave him but was still thinking of insisting on the ice cream, but when he heard hospital that changed his mind immediately.

"I think I will just eat French fries and chicken fingers. Then you eat the ice cream later."

"That sounds like a good idea, and with this we know where we are going, right?" she asked him.

"Yes, Mom," he answered.

"Do you want take out or eat in?" she asked him.

"I don't know," said Little Sam, sounding bored and tired.

"Let's do eat in so that you can play a little after eating," Grace suggested to her son, thinking he would be excited hearing that, but there was no response from Little Sam. As they pulled into the parking lot of the Family Fast Food, Little Sam saw one of his classmates.

"That's Jake, Mommy," he shouted with excitement. Grace looked at him and thought to herself, *Children are very interesting. No wonder they are called children.*

"Let's go in so that you two can talk," Grace told him. He came out of the car quickly and hurried in front of his mother. Jake was excited to see Little Sam. Luckily they were also eating in, so the two boys sat at the same table, and Grace and Jackie, Jake's mom, took the table next to them.

Grace and Jackie carried on a general conversation for a while; the boys finished their food and took off to the playground.

"Be careful," Grace shouted after them.

"So where do you all go to church?" Grace asked Jackie.

"I have given up on that a long time ago," Jackie said.

"Why did you give up?" Grace asked her, sounding a little curious.

"Well, a lot of things happened, but over all it became a very boring place for me, and secondly the pastor preaches one thing and does another," said Jackie.

"Well, with the little that I know about life, anywhere that human beings are gathered there is bound to be imperfection, and the church is no exception, but it is not about them, it is about you and I as individuals. I gave my life to God not long ago, and it has truly been eye opening for me. I realize that a lot of people who call themselves Christians are just playing religion."

"What do you mean they are playing religion?" Jackie cut in.

"You see, religion is man's way of knowing God, and Christianity is God's way of man knowing him; it is having a personal relationship with God and understanding who you are in him. My advice to you is don't allow people to turn you from knowing God, Jackie, know him personally and then you will know the difference," Grace told her.

Just then the boys came back to have a drink, and Grace realized it was time for them to go, so she told Little Sam not to go out again.

"Yes, Mom," said Little Sam.

Grace turned to Jackie and said, "I hope we can continue this someday, but before then I am inviting you to Emmanuel Church of God this coming Sunday."

"Actually, I've heard a lot of good things about them," Jackie told Grace.

"That is good to hear. I don't need to brag about them anymore," Grace responded with a smile.

"Thanks for awakening my conscience about church. Sunday is a couple of days away, so I will think about it," she told Grace.

"Just don't think with your head. Think with your heart, okay? You all have a nice evening," Grace told her and hurried out. She couldn't help wondering how she was able to tell Jackie all that she told her about church, Christianity, religion, and people in general. *God really helped me out with that explanation. Hmm! This is good. I had confidence, and I was talking as if I really knew what I was talking about. I was a preacher woman in there. I hope to experience more moments like these,* she thought with a smile as she entered her car.

Big Sam called a few minutes after they got home to check on them. Grace gave him feedback on how her dad responded when she told him about his visit.

"Wow! God really softened his heart toward me," Big Sam said.

"I have learned that prayers always move mountains," Grace told him without going into any details. "I am beginning to learn that fast," she added.

"Well, I am glad he did not turn me down, and I know with time God will restore our relationship back," said Big Sam. "Grace, there are few things I want you to help me sort out so when I come next weekend, I will discuss them with you," said Big Sam.

"Okay, I will be all ears," Grace responded.

"Let me talk to Little Sam then," he told her. Grace turned to look for him, and she noticed he was fast asleep on the couch.

"Sam, he had a rough day at school today. He is already asleep on the couch," Grace told him.

"What happened? Was he in trouble?" he asked, sounding a little worried.

"No, nothing like that. I think he didn't eat his lunch, and he got very hungry, and then his stomach began to hurt. He looked so pitiful when I picked him up. He told me what was going on and what he wanted to eat, so I took him to the Family Fast Food place. He ate all his food, met a friend, they played for a while, and he was fine after that, but I think he is a little tired," Grace told him.

"Just leave him alone, and I will talk to him tomorrow. Grace, before I hang up, I want you to know that I have realized it is easier to rekindle love than hate, and loving you again has really set me free. I did not know walking out and giving up on our marriage would become a burden I would carry around, and that was killing me slowly. Now I feel so free inside out," Sam told her.

"Sam, that is sweet of you to let me know all that. Coming back together is part of it, but giving your life to God is what really set you free to feel the way you are feeling. I experienced the same feelings, and even my co-workers noticed there is something going on with me. They thought there was a new man in my life, and I jokingly told them yes and that his name is Jesus Christ. There is more to the story, but I will share it with you someday. I am so glad that we are both free from ourselves, and with this new beginning, God being the Lord of our lives and the foundation of our marriage, we are going to be all right, "Grace told him.

"This is so true, and it is a whole new world for me now. Have you heard from Mr. Yalley?" he asked her.

"Not yet, but don't worry, he will take care of it," Grace assured him.

"Okay then! Love you all, and I will talk to you tomorrow."

"I love you too and sleep tight, bye!" said Grace. Grace hung up and couldn't help wondering about the love of God and how it can easily transform one's life.

"Okay, big guy, you need to go to bed now," Grace said as she picked Little Sam up from the couch. She changed him into his pajamas, and he never opened his eyes. "I love you, and your daddy loves you too," Grace said as she planted a kiss on his forehead. As she turned to walk away, Little Sam turned onto his left side and shouted, "Rectangle." Grace turned to look at him with a smile, knowing that he was dreaming. She walked away yawning and ready for a good night's sleep. She entered her bedroom with another loud yawn. "Oh I am so sleepy," she said as she jumped into bed, ready to sleep the night away.

At work the following day, Grace had her first Bible study with her co-workers and other workers from different offices in the building. It was a good fellowship, and she really enjoyed herself. They all wrote their prayer requests and put them in a jar, and before they left everybody picked one and was required to pray for the person, problem, or situation throughout the week. If you happened to pick your own request, you just put it back and picked another one. If a prayer request was answered, a testimony was shared briefly during the next meeting. Grace felt very comfortable and was glad she came. Her prayer assignment was to pray for a six-year-old boy call Aaron who was having terrible headaches almost every day. *That could be my son,* she said to herself. *Lord, teach me how to pray and help me pray seriously for this child,* she prayed in her heart.

Grace turned as she heard her name. It was her co-worker Philip walking toward her.

"What do you think?" he asked her.

"Oh, Philip, I wouldn't miss this for anything. I have been so blessed. Thanks for telling me about this," she told him, sounding very excited.

"You are welcome," he responded as he reached out to give her a brotherly hug.

Grace had never felt so happy in her life like this before; everything in her life now felt so right. As she walked back to her office, she looked up to heaven and said, "Thank you, Lord."

The days went fast, and before they knew it, it was Saturday and Big Sam woke up with one thing on his mind: making it right with his in-laws. He called Grace briefly before heading out. Mr. Sam Luken's moment of truth had finally arrived. He sincerely prayed all the way to his in-laws' house. Mr. Vidad, Grace's dad, opened the door.

"Mr. Luken, we have been expecting you," he said, sounding very formal. "Come in and have a seat," he said as he led him to the living room. "Martha! Mr. Luken is here," he called out to his wife. She quickly hurried to the living room.

"Hello, Sam!" she said as she reached out to shake his hand with a warm welcoming smile.

Mothers, women, they always have a soft heart. They can easily let go. Men, we are another story, thought Big Sam as he sat down.

"You want something to drink?" Mr. Vidad asked him.

"No thanks," he said. *I wish Martha asked me. I would have said yes, but with him asking, I don't feel like drinking anything right now,* thought Sam.

"Okay! Let's go straight to the point. What brings you here?" Mr. Vidad asked him.

"Well, first of all, thank you very much for allowing me to set foot in your house and for warmly receiving me. I know I don't deserve sitting in front of you, based on all the hurt I caused your family, so once again I say thanks for having me.

Before I say anything else, I want to apologize to you and your wife for walking out on your daughter. You loved and accepted me as a son, and I disappointed you. I am truly sorry, and I pray you will find a place in your heart to forgive me," he told them as he tried hard not to cry.

"Why now?" Mr. Vidad asked him with a funny look.

"Well, there is time for everything, and the need had come for me to do this," he answered.

"Okay! Your apology is accepted," Mr. Vidad told him

with a little attitude, without any clue of what he was about to hear next.

"Thank you for allowing yourself to do that for me. It means a lot to me," Sam told him. Mr. Vidad's facial expression remained the same, listening attentively and hanging on every word that Sam spoke as his wife looked on with a smile but wondering where all this was leading to.

Big Sam cleared his throat and continued, "I realize that I was a fool to walk out on the best thing that ever happened to me, my wife and son, over nothing. I became a very miserable man till I couldn't take it anymore. I repented and went to Grace to beg for forgiveness and also asked her to give me a second chance."

With this Mr. Vidad sat up straight and almost said aloud, *She will be a fool to take you back,* but he couldn't, so it become just a thought.

"I gave her time to think about it," Sam continued, "and she decided to take me back and give the marriage a second chance." Mr. Vidad and his wife now had looks on their faces that showed they obviously didn't believe what they just heard.

"I am really surprised, but I know my daughter is a good woman and full of wisdom. I have no doubt she still loves you and am not surprised she has decided to take you back, but I am surprised why you asked her in the first place. She was doing just fine anyway," Mr. Vidad told him.

"Well, I just wanted my family back and am glad I am not going to live in regret for the rest of my life," Big Sam responded.

"Sam, you are adults, and you know what you want. If Grace has decided to take you back, then there is nothing we can do to change her mind. Therefore you have our blessing, and she is all yours once again," Mr. Vidad told him in a very calm voice.

"Thank you very much," said Sam as he breathed a sigh of relief. He stood up and shook their hands in appreciation. "We plan to get married within a month. Grace will tell you the details later," he added.

Mrs. Vidad just sat there as if in shock. Her brain trying hard to absorb all that had just taken place.

"Sam, our lives are full of stories," she finally spoke up, "because it is a journey we are all on. Our disappointments, mistakes, sadness, victories, our joy, accomplishments, sickness, and all that, tell our life stories. You were once a single man. You got married, became a father, and became a divorced man. With all these four stages in your life, I believe you now clearly know which stage you like and want to hold onto till you leave this world. When we learn lessons in life, we try not to repeat them again.

"My husband and I have been married for a little over thirty years, and divorce has never been an option. We have had our share of troubles, but when we said till death do us part to each other, we meant it, and that has given us strength to overcome every problem we have encountered. My advice to you today is that when you stand in front of our daughter again and promise to love her for better and for worse and till death separate you two, please mean it with all your heart and soul and promise yourself you will do whatever it takes to make it work. That is all I have to say to you, Sam, "Mrs. Vidad told him with a very serious face. Mrs. Vidad, unlike her daughter, was a woman of few words, and Sam knew she meant every word she spoke.

When Mrs. Vidad was done with her advice, the room became dead silent, and it took Sam a few minutes to speak up.

"Thank you very much for your advice. I promise you this speech will be a source of reminder, strength, and encouragement for me to press on in our marriage, but most importantly

I want you two to know that Grace, Little Sam, and I have given our lives to God. Jesus is now in our hearts, and Grace and I know that we have access to the Holy Spirit to help us in times of trouble. All that we need to do is to ask for help in prayer," Sam told them.

"We are not churchgoers, but Grace has always known about God," Mr. Vidad responded immediately, trying to downplay what Sam told them.

"With what we both know now, it is one thing to know about God, and it is another thing to have a personal relationship with him," Sam told them. "For example, I can know a lot about Grace, and I will think I know her well but not until I have a relationship with her will I ever understand her or know who she really is, and the same applies to you and Martha. The same way we can know or hear a lot about God but not until we enter into a relationship with him, we will never know what Christianity is all about. This is all new to me, but to tell you the truth something happened to me the day I invited Jesus Christ into my heart, and God has really opened my understanding of him, and I am really amazed about my mentality now. I see Christians and Christianity differently now," Sam added.

Mr. Vidad wasn't interested in any religious discussions, so he decided not to make any comment to encourage Sam to preach to them again, so he turned to his wife and said,

"Martha, is it time to eat lunch?"

"Oh yea! Just give me a few minutes," she said and quickly vanished into the kitchen. In the kitchen as she was getting the lunch ready, she couldn't help thinking about what Sam just told them about God.

Mr. Vidad once again decided not to say anything again to encourage more religious response from Sam, but somehow he had a very good feeling about him. He wasn't the Sam he used to know. He observed that this Sam was full of confidence and boldness and you could see his mind was at peace. *I think my daughter will be okay this time around,* he thought.

All that Martha was thinking about at this point was to find a way to know more about God. *It really makes sense. For all these years, we just knew God from afar. The only time we find ourselves in a church setting was when we attend weddings, baby dedications, or funerals. What Sam said really makes sense, and I am going to ask Grace more about it,* she thought as she carried the food to the dining room.

Mr. Vidad spoke up whilst they were eating and said, "Sam, I have been very angry with you to the extent that when I hear the name Sam, it can mess up my whole day. To tell you the truth, I never wanted to see your face again, but knowing that there is a child between us I know I may have to deal with seeing you during some occasions. I can't explain what happened when Grace called to tell us about your coming. I realized I wasn't angry. Although I didn't know what on earth you were coming all the way down here to tell us, but I was ready to receive you. If somebody told me that I would sit at a table and have lunch with you again, I would have said, over my dead body, but here am I feeling as if nothing has changed between us. Something happened to me to change my heart toward you, but I can't put my hand on it," he told Sam as he looked straight into his eyes.

Sam waited for a while before he responded.

"All that I can say is that God knew we needed forgiveness to be able to embrace the new thing he is about to do in our lives. I have realized that it is only through God that we can forgive and be free from all bitterness, anger, and hurt. Thank you for being honest with me. I know I deserve every bit of your anger, but right now I thank God for what he has done for all of us," he told them.

Mr. Vidad once again decided not to say anything to encourage more religious response from Sam, so he kept quiet.

Martha, on the other hand, really wanted to ask Sam some questions but decided not to because her husband would think her tender heart was blindly believing what Sam was trying to tell them.

Lunch was good, for Martha was a great cook, and Sam was grateful they shared a meal with him. That told him they were really at peace with him. Immediately after lunch he asked to leave, for he had a long drive ahead of him. He thanked them for their hospitality and accepting him back with open arms as their son-in-law. The Vidads gave him a quick hug and wished him a safe journey back. Big Sam sat in his car and breathed a sigh of relief.

"Thank you, God," he said as he looked up toward heaven. "We are left with the final stages of this story," he said aloud as he drove off.

The Dress

"Sam, Mr. Yalley is going to watch you for a while today. Mercy and I have some errands to run in town," Grace told her son.

"Why can't I go with you? I will be good, I promise. I will not run off in the store, please, please, please!" Little Sam pleaded with his mother.

"Oh! Sam, you are always a good boy in the store, and I always love shopping with you, but you know Mercy and I have to do grownup stuff today, and I thought you would love to spend time with Mr. Yalley instead of following me," Grace told him, pretending all that she said was true.

"Okay, Mommy, I will stay with Mr. Yalley," Little Sam told his mom, not really liking the fact that he was being left behind, but he loved Mr. Yalley like his grandpa, so that made him feel better.

They got ready, and mother and son walked

hand in hand across the street to the Yalley's house. Little Sam jumped and rang the door bell.

"Hello, little guy," Mr. Yalley said when he opened the door and saw Little Sam and his mom.

"Come on in. We are going to have fun today whilst the ladies go out and do grownup stuff," said Mr. Yalley as he picked Little Sam up. "You are getting really heavy; does that mean we are growing?" Mr. Yalley asked him.

"Yelp! I am one inch taller now," Little Sam responded.

"Good! That is what happens when you eat your vegetables well," said Mr. Yalley as he put him down.

"Have a seat, Grace, Mercy will be out in a minute," he told her.

"Thanks, Mr. Yalley, for watching him," Grace told him as he sat down.

"I can't believe you are thanking me for this. I should be thanking you for allowing me to experience how to be a grandfather," Mr. Yalley told her with a smile.

"Thanks for being his grandfather then," said Grace.

"You're welcome," Mr. Yalley responded. Just then Mercy came out looking sweet as always.

"I am ready," she said. Mr. Yalley turned to look at her and then saw a bridal store right behind her with the name, We Are His Chosen Ones Bridal Shop. The vision was quick, but everything was clear. *I have to tell them something,* he thought.

Just then Mercy spoke and said, "Honey, we will see you later."

Mr. Yalley knew he just had a vision of the bridal shop they needed to go to so that they didn't have to drive all over town looking for the perfect dress.

"Honey, you two should go straight to We Are His Chosen Ones Bridal Shop," he told them.

"What! That is across town," said Mercy.

"I know it is about one and a half hours away, but that

will save you a lot of time in looking for the perfect dress," Mr. Yalley told her. He didn't give himself away. He made it sound like it was just a suggestion. Mercy, on the other hand, didn't realize it because she was still not used to his gift, so she didn't make the connection when he said something out of the ordinary. Grace had no clue at all, so it was just a suggestion to her.

The two women set off without taking Mr. Yalley seriously. They went to three different bridal shops and came out empty handed. They then decided to try Mr. Yalley's recommendation. They had already spent two hours in vain, and they had to drive one and a half hours so in a hurry they didn't realize they were speeding until a policeman started splashing his lights behind them.

"Oh no! We are in trouble," Grace said.

"Just relax. We will beg him, and if he refuses to have mercy on us, we will face the consequences," said Mercy.

"Ma'am, do you know you were speeding beyond the speed limit? It is fifty-five, and you were doing almost seventy," the police officer told Grace.

"Oh! Officer, we are really sorry. We were hurrying to a shop before they close and didn't realize we were speeding," Mercy told him.

He looked at her and said, "I hear that all the time, but I wasn't talking to you. I was talking to the driver. Let me see your license," he told Grace.

Grace felt there was nothing they could do, so she reached into her purse and gave it to him. As he turned and walked toward his car, Mercy whispered to Grace, "We are in trouble, but there is still hope."

The officer went to his car and did whatever he had to do. He came back, and with a serious face he said, "I decided to let you ladies go, but remember anytime you are on this road, it is fifty-five."

"Yes, sir!" Mercy and Grace responded at the same time.

"Thank you very much, and may God bless you," said Grace as the officer gave her license back to her.

They drove off, wasting another twenty minutes, but by the grace of God they made it to the Trinity Shopping Mall, and We Are His Chosen Ones Bridal Shop was right in front of them, so they packed the car, quickly got out, and rushed into the shop, only to find that the owner was getting ready to close in thirty minutes.

It had been a slow day at the shop for Alice, so she was glad to have two customers anxiously looking for something to buy. She introduced herself and welcomed them with a big smile and told them to let her know if they needed help.

Grace had a look she was looking for, so she started looking through the racks of beautiful gowns. It brought back such sweet memories when she was shopping for her first wedding gown with her mom. It took them three days to find the perfect dress. After each day they would choose a new restaurant and have a good lunch or early dinner. The day they finally found the dress, they called a restaurant that was by reservation only. Mother and daughter dressed up and went and had a good dinner whilst listening to live soft jazz music being played. All these thoughts rushed through Grace's mind, and she found herself smiling. *Oh, mother is a woman of few words, but she knows how to have fun and enjoy life,* she thought.

Mercy noticed the smile on the face so she asked Grace, "Have you found something you like?"

"No, not yet," she responded.

"Then what is that smile for?" Mercy ask her.

"Oh, I was just thinking about my mom," she told her.

"I am glad you have sweet memories of her," Mercy said as she tapped her on the shoulders. Grace turned to smile at her, and right behind Mercy stood this mannequin with this beautiful dress on, exactly the look she was looking for, a simple satin dress with beautiful lace trimmings, making it so simple but elegant.

"Oh my God," she exclaimed.

"What is it?" Mercy asked.

"Over there, behind you, just turn around," she told her as she pointed her finger to the direction of the dress.

"Grace that is beautiful. We have found the dress," said Mercy.

They walked to where the mannequin was and with such admiration in Grace's eyes she said, "I think this is my size."

Alice heard what Grace said, so she came to join them and told them that the dress, the veil, earrings, necklace, pantyhose, and the shoes were all being sold together. Nothing could be sold separately and was being sold for one third of the total price, and that caught Grace's attention, so she asked, "Why? What is behind the deal?"

Alice then told them the mother of a bride who lived in Francia did the shopping for her daughter, only to find out that her daughter eloped and got married. She was so broken-hearted and decided she would help any bride who deserved it. "She brought them in three days ago when I was about to close the shop. She asked me to total the price, and I couldn't believe my eyes when I saw how much she spent. Anyway, when I was done, she told me to sell everything together at one third of the total price. She noticed that I was really surprised, so she made me promise I would do just that. As a Christian my integrity is more important to me than money, so I am doing just that."

"That is sad to hear but very interesting. What size is it anyway?" Grace asked.

"It is a ten," Alice told her.

"That is my size, but I hope it is my kind of ten," Grace said with a laugh.

"Okay then, let's try everything on and see what happens,"

said Mercy. As they headed toward the fitting room, Grace was so amazed about how beautiful the dress and the accessories were.

"I could never afford a jewel like this," Grace said aloud.

"You can't, but God can. When his favor goes before you, everything is possible," Mercy told her.

"You're right, Sister!" Alice added.

The two women helped Grace to dress up from veil to shoes, and when she finally looked in the mirror, she couldn't believe what she saw, too beautiful for herself.

"Oh my! Who is this woman? Do I know her? This is more than I thought. Everything fits so perfectly. I look like a million-dollar bride," said Grace.

"You are more than a million-dollar bride, because your Father in heaven has no name to his wealth, and you deserve every bit of it all," Mercy told her.

"Thanks, Mercy, you are so sweet," said Grace.

"Where do you two go to church?" Alice asked them.

"We go to Emmanuel Church of God, Reverend Maxwell Praise is our Pastor," Mercy answered, feeling very proud about her church family.

"I have heard a lot of good things about him. I heard he is a good teacher," Alice said.

"It is good to know we have a good testimony out there," Mercy responded with a smile.

Grace turned and said, "She and her husband led my son and I to Christ two weeks ago in their living room, and my ex-husband, soon to be my husband again, got saved last Sunday at their church," Grace told Alice.

"Oh! I see, God has cleaned house for you and is restoring all that the enemy tried to steal from you. I am so happy for you. These are testimonies that enable us to know that God is good and how much he loves us. You look so beautiful, girl, go get your man back," Alice told Grace with a laugh.

"Anyway, Alice, I am enjoying every bit of His love. I don't know how I survived all these years without him, but all said and done, I have found the perfect dress and everything else that I will need for my special day. I will take everything from head to toe," Grace told her with a smile.

"That sounds good to me, and Mrs. Crossy will be pleased to hear it went to a well-deserving bride," said Alice.

With everything packed and ready to go, Grace realized she was paying just a fraction of what she budgeted for her dress, so with a grateful heart Grace and Mercy walked out of the shop, happy they had accomplished their mission for the day. As they drove off, it dawned on Mercy that Paul probably had a vision of the exact place to look for the dress. She couldn't say anything to Grace about it, so she just took a deep breath.

Mr. Yalley, on the other hand, had fun with Little Sam all day long; he made sure he kept him occupied throughout. They ate lunch, baked cookies, and ate as much as they could with milk. Little Sam was so happy and with a grateful heart he asked Mr. Yalley, can I call you Grandpa?"

Mr. Yalley looked at him with a smile and said, "I would be honored to hear that from you."

"What is honored?" Little Sam asked, looking a little confused.

"Oh, it means I will feel so special to hear you call me Grandpa," Mr. Yalley explained to his standard.

"Okay, I will call you Grandpa, no more Mr. Yalley," Little Sam told him.

"All right, no more Mr. Yalley," said Mr. Yalley as he made a hand gesture.

"Little guy, it is time to clean up before the ladies come so that they won't think we are messy guys," Mr. Yalley told him with a laugh. Little Sam followed Mr. Yalley to the kitchen to do just that, and in his own little way he helped clean up.

"We are all done!" said Mr. Yalley with a shout.

"We are all done!" said Little Sam with a little dance.

"What are we going to do again?" Little Sam asked him.

"I think I just got an idea," said Mr. Yalley. "Come and sit down and let me teach you how to play chess," Mr. Yalley told Little Sam as they went back to the living room. Mr. Yalley brought his chess box out and began to lay out the pieces.

"The box is very old," said Little Sam.

"Yes, because is over twenty years old, and we have used it a lot. You know what, choose one of your favorite games or toys and take good care of it, and you will have it forever," Mr. Yalley advised him.

"You mean forever," Little Sam asked with a look of surprise on his face.

"Yes, forever, when you take care of things, they stay with you for a long time," said Mr. Yalley.

"Okay! I will take care of my monkey," he told Mr. Yalley.

"That is good to start with," Mr. Yalley told him.

"We are set now, let me teach you how to play," said Mr. Yalley, and Little Sam was ready to learn, but the doorbell interrupted the lesson. Little Sam jumped up and ran to the door shouting, Mommy, Mommy, and Mr. Yalley quickly opened the door, and there stood Mercy and Grace.

"Hey! The ladies are back," he said. Little Sam jumped into his mother's arms whilst Mr. Yalley gave Mercy a hug.

"How did it go?" Mr. Yalley asked them as he closed the door behind him.

"We got the dress, but boy we have an interesting story to tell," said Mercy. The two women slammed their bodies into the nearest chairs.

"You two look so tired. Let me get you something to drink," Mr. Yalley told them. "Water, juice, or ice tea?" he asked them as he stood up.

They both responded, "Water!"

"At your service," said Mr. Yalley as he brought them the water.

"So what happened?" he asked and sat down beside his wife.

"Well," said Mercy, looking at Grace, "we did not take you seriously with your recommendation, so we went to three shops and came out empty handed. We then decided to try the shop you recommended, and in a hurry we were speeding without knowing, and a policeman stopped us, but God bailed us out," Mercy told him.

"You mean he let you go?" Mr. Yalley asked in surprise.

"Yes he did, with warnings, we were surprised ourselves because he looked and spoke like a no-nonsense guy, but somehow his heart softened toward us, and he let us go. That is why we felt it was God who bailed us out. After wasting twenty minutes, we got to the shop only to find out it would close in thirty minutes, but the lady was sweet and waited on us.

"You two were really lucky," said Mr. Yalley.

"It was more than luck. It was God's favor," Mercy responded.

"You're right, honey! There is no such thing like luck to us believers. It is always God's favor," Mr. Yalley quickly said, correcting himself.

"Grace, continue from there," Mercy told her.

Grace with all smiles told Mr. Yalley the story behind the dress and how she ended up paying a fraction of what she budgeted for her dress alone.

"Thank you very much for your recommendation," Grace told him.

"You're welcome," said Mr. Yalley. *Thank the Holy Spirit, not me,* he thought.

"By the way, Reverend Praise call, and he said he has no problem marrying the two of you. The only thing is he has to meet with you two before the big day. Secondly, he suggested you can choose Saturday afternoon or Sunday after the service for the ceremony, but if you wouldn't mind he would prefer Sunday after the service because he wanted the whole church to witness the ceremony, but it is up to you two to decide what you want. He also said he asked the wedding committee to take care of the reception except for your wedding cake."

"Oh my! Are you serious?" Grace asked, sounding surprised.

"Yes, I am serious, discuss it with Sam and let us know a week to the wedding," Mr. Yalley responded.

"Thank you very much, and I will let you know what we decide. Mercy, thanks for taking the time to help me out. I really appreciate that," said Grace.

"Oh, come on! I need to thank you because I felt so honored to help a sweet and beautiful bride like you to look and find her perfect dress," Mercy responded with all smiles.

"We are grateful, and I am very flattered, thanks. I think we will call it a day. Little Sam looks so sleepy. You two have a nice evening, and we will see you tomorrow at church," Grace told them.

"All right! Goodnight," Mercy responded. Grace picked up Little Sam and carried him as they stepped out of the Yalley's house. *What a blessing to have the Yalleys in my life. God really handpicked them to be my neighbors,* Grace thought as she opened the door to her house.

The phone started ringing the moment Grace opened the door, and she quickly put Little Sam down and picked it up, knowing it was Big Sam.

"Hello," she said.

"Hi, honey!" came Big Sam's voice.

"Oh, hi! How are you doing?" Grace asked him.

"I am doing fine but suffering from the missing-you disease," said Sam.

"Poor you. I am sorry to hear that, but don't worry, your cure is on the way," Grace responded with a laugh.

"So where have you all been?" he asked. "I called several times and there was no response," he added.

"Mercy and I went out looking for my dress. I wanted it to be my little secret. That was why I didn't mention it to you yesterday," Grace told him.

"Oh, I see! Did you find anything?" he asked her.

"Yes, I found the perfect dress, all the accessories that I need for one third of the total price," she told him. Grace then proceeded to tell him all that took place and the story behind the dress.

"That is an interesting story, but I am glad your search is over, and I can't wait to see you in it," Sam told her. Grace then told him about Reverend Praise's offer as well.

"That is very generous of him. We said we don't want a big wedding. What do you think?" he asked.

"Well, I thought about it, but the point is we didn't invite all those people. They will just be there to support us, which I think will be nice because you got saved before them, apologized, and proposed to me before them as well. So there is nothing wrong with them seeing the end of it all," Grace told him.

"Well then, we will do it on Sunday before the whole church," said Sam.

"Honey, can you hold on for me for a second. Somebody is coming on the line," Grace told him.

"Sure! I will hold on as long as you want me," Sam said with a laugh.

"Silly you," Grace said with a laugh as she changed the line.

"Hello," she said.

"Hello, Grace, this is your mom."

"Oh hi, Mom! How are you and dad doing?" she asked.

"We are fine, honey! And how is my grandson doing?" she asked her.

"He is doing fine", Grace told her mom.

"Anyway, I called you several times today, and no one picked up," Martha told her daughter.

"Sorry about that. We were out of the house for a while," Grace answered.

"Okay! Well, we were just calling to let you know we are happy for you once again. Sam is like a son to us, and we are glad he has realized he cannot do without you and Little Sam. Your dad was great. Somehow he was not angry at Sam anymore, and I was very pleased about that," Martha told her daughter.

"Mom, I am glad you all treated him well. It is a blessing everything worked out this way and we are going to be a family again. Actually, he is on the line. I put him on hold to take your call. I am sure he was about to tell me what happened when he visited. Tell dad I say hello, and I will call to give you all the details later," Grace told her mom.

"Okay then, tell Sam I say hello, and kiss my grandson for me, bye!" Martha told her daughter.

"Bye, Mom," Grace said and immediately changed the line.

"Hello, Sam! Sorry, that was my mom," said Grace.

"Really! I bet she called to tell you about my visit," Sam said.

"Not really," Grace answered. "All she said was she was happy for me and she was glad you have realized you cannot do without us. She was also pleased about the way my dad received and treated you. I could sense she was surprised my dad wasn't angry at you," Grace told him.

"I told her you were on the line and that I would call and

give them the details later," Grace added. "Those are her comments and how she feels, so what is your story?"

"I will summarize mine just like your mom did. God went before me and took care of a lot of things, so everything went on well. Your dad played it cool, accepted my apology. I then told him of my mission. He told me he was surprised I asked you to take me back, but he wasn't surprised about your answer, and that you are a good woman full of wisdom. He said we are adults and that there is nothing he can do about our decision except to give us their blessing.

"Your mom gave me a speech on the different stages of my life, single, married, father, divorce, and she believes that among the four stages I know which stage I like best now, so I should do whatever it takes to make that stage work out. All that she told me was full of wisdom, and I hanged on every word till she was done. I thanked her for the advice and promised them her advice would be a source of strength and encouragement for me to press on in our marriage. I then told them how we gave our lives to God and how he is now going to be the foundation of our marriage. Your father quickly responded by downplaying what I said about our faith. Your mom, on the other hand, was very interested, and I believe she will be asking you some questions later. I was glad we had lunch together. That made me feel they have really accepted me back. I left there with a thankful heart and a good feeling about myself. Sorry I said I was going to summarize my story like your mom's, but I guess I have to get it all out," Big Sam told her with a laugh.

"Sam, I am glad to hear that, and I have no doubt we are on the right track this time. Now we know who we are in Christ, and we understand what he expects of us as a couple. The best part is, he is helping us all the time to do our best. With this we are going to be fine," Grace responded.

"I am so anxious to start loving you all over again, waking

up with you every morning, and hearing your voice," Sam told her.

"Me too," Grace said and then gave out a loud yawn.

"Somebody is sleepy," Sam said.

"Yes, I am. It's been a long day," Grace told him.

"Okay then, let me leave you so that you can get ready for bed. Goodnight and I love you," Sam told her.

"I love you too, bye!" Grace responded and hung up the phone.

Tori View Meets Mr. Right

"Hello, Mr. Yalley," came Tori's voice when Mr. Yalley picked up the phone. "This is Tori from the gas station."

"Oh! Hello, lady, how are you doing?" Mr. Yalley asked her, sounding very excited. "Has the godly young handsome man shown up yet?" he asked her with a laugh.

"Oh yea! He has. That is what I am calling to let you know."

"Oh! I am excited already," Mr. Yalley cut in.

"Two days ago, which is exactly one month you gave me that word. Just to start from the beginning, the owner of the gas station passed away six months ago, and I learned he was a very strong Christian. His oldest son, who is thirty years old, took over the business. They have a chain of them, so he decided to visit each one of them. His secretary made a schedule for him, and they called to tell me when he was visiting ours. Two days ago I came to work and completely forgot that was the day he was coming; around. At 12:30 p.m. a young man walked in and wanted to see the manager. They showed him the office, and he walked in. He then introduced himself as David Strong and said he was the new managing director for the Zion gas stations. 'Please have a seat,' I said after I shook his hand. He sat down and began to ask me questions about our sales. Delivery, workers, etc. I noticed that anytime he asked me a question he would look so deeply into my eyes, and that made me very uncomfortable, but he had such beautiful eyes that I couldn't help but admire.

"After a little while he looked at his wrist watch and said he was very tired and needed a little rest. He apologized for cutting the meeting short. He told me he was lodging at the Maxwell Hotel. He then looked at me and said, 'Will you mind having dinner with me at 7:00 p.m. so that we can finish this business discussion, because I leave tomorrow morning for another appointment.' I looked up and said, 'Sure.' When he was about to walk away, he turned and said, 'This is business, but don't forget it is after work.' Somehow I knew what he meant immediately; it is business but dress for the evening. 'I will wait in the lobby,' he added and walked away.

"Mr. Yalley, after work I quickly went home and got myself ready. I put on a pair of jeans, a nice blouse, a jacket, and high heels. I got there, and he was in the lobby waiting. He had on a pair of jeans, a nice shirt that matched my blouse, and a jacket. When I saw him, my heart began to beat so fast that I thought I was going to pass out. He told me he learned they served good meals at the hotel restaurant, so if I didn't mind we should just eat there. I told him I didn't mind.

"They showed us our table, and we sat down. He looked around and said, 'Nice restaurant, what do you think?'

"'I am impressed,' I responded. We ordered our food, and within fifteen minutes we were eating. He asked me a few questions again, and then the conversations become personal.

Oh! Mr. Yalley, I hope am not taking too much of your time with this story."

"No! Not at all. If I don't have time to listen to what God is doing, what else will I have time for?" Mr. Yalley responded.

"Well, thanks for listening, so like I said the conversation become personal.

"'Where do you go to church,' he asked.

"'Well, I got saved about five weeks ago,' I said, and I told him the whole story, about you and Mercy as well.

"'That is very interesting,' he said. He told me he got saved when he was thirteen at a summer camp. He asked me whether I was married. I answered by showing him my ring less finger. He laughed and did the same to me. He then asked where my ex-husband was. I said I'd never been married, and he looked at me and asked again, 'What about your boyfriend?' With this I became very uncomfortable, and I think it showed on my face.

"He looked at me and said, 'its okay, listen, you can trust me with that. You don't know what this question is going to lead to.' The way he said it just did something to me, and I knew I could trust him, so I told him I never had a boyfriend.

"'A beauty like you!' he said, sounding a little surprised.

"I then told him about my life. He listened attentively, and when I was done he cleared his throat as if he were choking with tears and said, 'Tori, what you thought was working against you is now going to work for you. A lot of girls would love to be in your shoes right now, but it is too late.' He then told me about his life, how when he was twelve he had a crush on a girl and wanted to kiss her so badly. He knew at age ten that there are certain things you don't do before marriage. Being the first born, his parents made sure they preached that to him so that he didn't not set a bad a sample for his siblings. That was always at the back of his mind, but he had his own plans. He decided to tell the girl how he felt so that they could be 'special, secret' friends when they went to camp the next summer, because he would be thirteen and a teenager with a little mature look, but unfortunately for that idea and fortunately for him, he got saved during that summer camp and experienced a real encounter with God.

"The desire to do all the things he thought about vanished, and he realized how important it was for him to keep himself pure for his future wife. It was hard, but with the help of the Holy Spirit, he was able to flee from temptations that would lead him into losing his virginity. He started working with his father straight out of college after graduating with honors in business management. All he does is to love God with all his heart, work hard, and have fun with family and friends. He said for the past one year he has been praying for a wife that has also kept herself pure for God and her husband so that the two of them could appreciate what they have. 'I knew I was so ready to love a woman now,' he said.

"He took my hand into his and told me to look in his face. 'Tori, this is my story, and I have no doubt in my heart I have found that wife,' he said.

"'What!' I said with a little shout and nearly stood up from my seat, for I was not expecting that at all.

"'Calm down,' he said. I took a deep breath and said I I'm okay.

"'I am not saying this because I know now that you are also a virgin. To tell you the truth, the moment I walked into your office and laid eyes on you, I knew in my heart that you were the one. I am leaving tomorrow morning, and I know I have to spend a little time with you, to know more about you. That is why I came up with the story that I was tired and needed to go and rest,' he said with a laugh.

"'Tori I don't want to date you. I want to marry you,' he told me with this look in his eyes that made me fall in love immediately. I quickly searched my heart to see whether there was anything that would make me refuse his proposal, but Mr. Yalley, there was nothing, everything felt right, so I told him I would be his wife. He took my hand and kissed it and then prayed a prayer of thanksgiving to God. I couldn't believe my ears, but I was grateful. He said he has two more weeks of traveling, and when he is done, he would like to visit my parents and officially ask them for my hand in marriage. Oh! Mr. Yalley, I love my dad, but I wish you were my dad for him to come to."

"Tori, I'm glad to hear that, but God didn't give you to me, and nobody can ever replace them. They are your parents, and I know they will be very happy for you," Mr. Yalley told her.

"Mr. Yalley, everything happened so fast that it took all my hurts away and filled me with pure joy," said Tori.

"That is the God you serve, Tori. Sometimes his blessings come so swiftly that before you realize it, all your frustrations were over nothing," Mr. Yalley told her.

"He promised to call every day, and I thought that was so sweet. We will probably start planning the wedding after we visit my parents. He planned to come and pick me up, so I would love to come and introduce him to you and Mercy."

"Tori, you are now our little sister in Christ, and we are so happy that God has kept his word for you, and here you are with a man who has it all: God, the looks, character, education, fun loving, and money. We truly serve a God who gives us the very best. We are excited for you, and we can't wait to meet Mr. Right," Mr. Yalley told her with a laugh. "Mercy went out, and when she gets back I will tell her all about how Tori met Mr. Right," he added.

"Mr. Yalley, thank you very much and I will be in touch, bye!" Tori told him.

"Bye, lady, and take care of yourself," said Mr. Yalley.

Mr. Yalley hung up the phone and began to worship God for his goodness. He remembered that three days after he gave

Tori the word of knowledge, he began to doubt whether it was God who had spoken through him or just his flesh, but he quickly told Satan to get behind him because he knew it was God and refused to entertain such thoughts. He felt so humbled, and the only thing to do was to worship his God, so he sat there and just worshipped from the depth of his soul.

Shortly after that Mercy came home. She noticed he had a big smile on his face so he asked him, "What is that smile for?"

"Guess," he answered.

"Seeing my sweet face," she told him.

"Heaven knows I will never get tired of seeing your face and the sight of you always melts my heart, but this is not about you. Just guess again," he told her.

"I am too tired to guess anything right now. Just tell me what it is," said Mercy.

"Just heard the most exciting news a little while ago," said Mr. Yalley.

"What news?" Mercy asked.

"Okay, let me give you a clue," he said.

"Oh, Paul! Just tell me what it is, and stop keeping me in suspense," said Mercy, sounding a little frustrated.

"I still have to give you the clue, but before that just sit down and relax so that you can enjoy this good news," he told her with a big smile on his face.

"Hurry up then, "she said as she sat down, sounding more anxious.

"Here is the clue: Ruth's husband came back home, and Tori, dash, dash, dash," said Mr. Yalley.

"Tori met Mr. Right," Mercy answered with a shout.

Mr. Yalley just kept nodding his head with a big smile on his face.

"Am I right, am I right?" Mercy asked him anxiously,

"Yes, you are right! She called a little while ago to tell us."

"Thank you, Jesus," Mercy shouted with her hand lifted toward heaven. "Tell me more, what did she say? How did it happen?" Mercy asked her husband impatiently.

"Tori told me everything. I'm going to try my best and do the same," said Mr. Yalley.

"I am all ears, but let me get a glass of ice tea first. You want some?" Mercy asked her husband as she stood up.

"Just give me water," said Mr. Yalley.

"Here you are, dear," said Mercy as she gave him the water.

"Thanks," said Mr. Yalley. He took a sip and said, "God is really good, and he really wants the very best for all of us. He has blessed Tori with a husband who is a Christian, a virgin, well educated, rich, and I am sure he is good looking too. His father owns the gas station where Tori works. He died six months ago, and he is in charge of the business now, so he decided to visit each one of them. He came to Tori's, and the rest is history," Mr. Yalley told his wife.

"Just like that! This is love at first sight," said Mercy.

"He told her the moment he laid eyes on her he knew she was the one. He invited her to dinner that evening, and after knowing each other's backgrounds, he told her he didn't want to date her; he wanted to marry her, so she agreed to marry him," Mr. Yalley added.

"Oh, Paul! We serve a good God. This feels like God just dropped the blessing on her lap, or the blessing found her. Isn't that something? You are minding your own business, and your blessings come looking for you. Oh! We truly serve a good God, and I pray everybody will come to know him. I am so happy for her, and I can't wait to meet him. Father, thank you for doing this for her," Mercy said with a prayer. The Yalleys sat down in the living room for a long time just talking about the goodness of God with gratefulness.

Divine Surprises

Grace and Little Sam were ready for church on time, and as they stepped out of the house, the Yalleys were also walking toward their car.

"Hello!" said Mercy with a wave.

"Good morning, neighbors!" Mr. Yalley said with a smile. "Come, let's ride together."

"Okay," Grace said as she hurried across the street, holding Little Sam's hand.

"Good morning, Grandpa," said Little Sam as he sat in the car.

"Where did that come from?" Grace asked in a surprised voice as she turned to look at her son.

"Oh! Yesterday Little Sam asked me whether he can call me Grandpa, and I told him I would be honored to hear him call me that," Mr. Yalley told them.

"I see," said Grace.

"That is so sweet of you, little guy," Grace told her son as she ran her fingers through his hair. Little Sam just looked into his mother's face and gave her one of his sweet warm smiles without saying anything.

Little Sam has given us a taste of being Grandpa and Grandma since the day we met him," said Mr. Yalley. "Is everybody buckled up and ready to go?"

"Yes, sir!" said Little Sam with a shout with his hands lifted up, knowing that Mr. Yalley was talking to him in particular.

"Okay then, let's pray. We always pray before we drive off. Mercy, will you pray for us?" said Mr. Yalley.

"Sure!" said Mercy. "Father, we thank you for this morning. It's a privilege for us to join millions of your children today just to acknowledge who you are. I pray that you will anoint Reverend Praise, the leaders, and the choir so that all that they will do today will go forth to accomplish its purpose. Cleanse our minds so that we can hear and understand the message you have for us today. Open our hearts to receive it and cherish it as a precious jewel. No plan of the enemy will prosper during the service. Give us traveling grace, as well as all those who will be heading there today. In Jesus' name, I pray. Amen!"

"Amen!" they all responded.

"Let's go now," Mr. Yalley said as he drove off. When they got to the parking lot, the Holy Spirit whispered in Mr. Yalley's ears, *today is going to be a day full of surprises.*

"Hmm, I wonder what it is going to be." Mr. Yalley said under his breath. "I am all for it, Lord," he added.

As they walked into the hallway of the church, Mr. Montey, a business man who owned a hardware store, waved at them with a big smile. Mr. Yalley walked over to him.

"Hello, Brother," he said and stretched out his hand to give him a handshake.

"Hello, Mr. Yalley," Mr. Montey responded as he shook Mr. Yalley's hand.

The moment his hand had contact with Mr. Yalley's hand,

Mr. Yalley saw beneath his clothes, and what he saw really shocked him, but he couldn't show it. Mr. Montey was a man who knew how to dress up and be a clean gentleman, but his secret was known to Mr. Yalley within a split second.

When Mr. Montey was a young man he was somehow drawn to ladies' underwear. He felt ladies had the most comfortable underwear, so he decided that would be his preference. When he was single, he would go and buy them, pretending he was buying them for his wife but because of this unusual behavior, he didn't have a girlfriend.

He kept to himself for years until he met Katie, a sweet Christian girl he couldn't let go. Well, through Katie he came to know the lord, and eventually they got married, but he never told her about his unusual desire to wear the same underwear with her. Two years into the marriage Katie caught him wearing one of her pieces of underwear.

"That is funny, Jim!" she told him, laughing. Little did she know that her husband couldn't pretend any longer, and that was the icebreaker for him. It was funny at first, but when he asked Katie to buy him new ones, she became very concerned. That was eight years ago, and she was now used to it. Her husband wore the finest silk and lace underwear every day.

Mr. Yalley started laughing in a funny way as he released Mr. Montey's hand. He immediately realized that Mr. Montey was surprised about the way he was laughing, so he quickly said jokingly, "Brother! This is the day that the Lord has made, let's rejoice and be glad. Enjoy the service."

"Thanks, and you do the same," Mr. Montey responded with a look on his face.

As they went their way, Mercy tucked him in the side with her elbow and asked, "What was that laugh about?"

"Mercy! You don't want to know right now. Your mind will be better off without it," Paul told her.

"Okay! If you say so," she responded as they entered the sanctuary.

During the praise and worship, Mr. Yalley found his eyes fixed on the choir and couldn't naturally take his eyes off them. He was wondering what was going on when the Holy Spirit spoke again and said,

You see Brother Peter? Although married barely six months ago, he has a crush on Annabelle, and during choir practice he really struggles to keep his mind on the songs. It is affecting his marriage. He loves and adores Tina very much, and he is embarrassed to tell anyone. Tina is already sensing there is something on his mind but can't put her finger on it; he denied there is anything bothering him when she asked him about it.

Annabelle was into a lot of things before she came to know me. She is a talented singer, and I have anointed her voice so that she can minister to souls in songs, but the spirit of seduction is operating through her. She has no control over it, and Peter happens to be one of her victims. I want her to be set free so that Peter will be free as well. Your assignment is pray for her till next Sunday.

Immediately after worship Mr. Yalley sat down, took out his prayer journal, and wrote a prayer for Annabelle's seductive spirit.

Elder Samson gave the announcements, and at the end he said, "Do you all remember Mr. Luken, who gave his life to God two Sundays ago, apologized, and proposed to his ex-wife?" Some people nodded their heads and some said yes. "Well, for your information, after the main service next Sunday, you are all invited to stay for their wedding ceremony."

With this everybody began to clap their hands and cheer them on.

"For the sake of those who weren't here that Sunday, will you please stand up, to be Mrs. Luken?" he added. Grace stood up, and there was more clapping. "Thank you Grace. We are all happy for you. Satan's assignment failed on this marriage," Elder Samson said with a shout of halleluiah!

A family was late coming in, and as they were being seated on the far right of the Yalleys, one of them dropped their Bible, and Mr. Yalley turned to look, as a lot of people did. His eyes caught a glimpse of Pearl's face, a sixteen-year-old straight-A student sitting beside her parents. *She seems to be sad,* he thought.

Yes, she is sad and very worried, came the voice of the Holy Spirit. *She put herself in a very compromising position and didn't flee from temptation, so now she is pregnant.*

Mr. Yalley sat up straight and gasped. Mercy turned and looked at him but couldn't say a word.

The only person who knows is the boy in question, but he has denied he is the one out of fear, the Holy Spirit continued. *He feels very guilty because he knows he was her first and in his own way made her feel so special, and when it was over, he promised his love forever, so for him to deny the whole thing is like a stab in her tender heart. She is planning to confide in a friend who is not a Christian and seems to know it all, how to help her abort the pregnancy. Every child is a gift from me regardless of how they enter this world; they are all my precious little ones. That child has a destiny that needs to be fulfilled on earth, and secondly, that is going to be her only child. I want you to pray on her behalf so that my peace that surpasses all understanding will fill her afresh. Pray that my joy will be her strength because she is going to need divine strength to go through the coming months. Pray that she will repent of fornication and ask for forgiveness, which I will give her, but also she can forgive herself and the father of the child. Pray that her parents will not feel ashamed of the situation but rather embrace her with the supernatural love that I have enabled them to have. Nothing moves in heaven when my children don't pray. When you pray she will tell her parents within three days. It will be announced to the church, and she will ask for forgiveness. That child will be loved by all, and her parents will get all the help they will need. She will finish her education and become whatever she desires to be. The boy in question will eventually marry her, but I will take care of that part personally.*

The presence of the Lord was all over Mr. Yalley. He felt weird, but at the same time he was so much at peace. He took his journal and wrote a prayer for Pearl and for the parents. As he was writing the Holy Spirit spoke again, *pray that none of the church members will gossip among themselves and with people outside the church when they hear the news. I love Pearl, and she is the apple of my eye.*

Mr. Yalley's flesh wanted to feel sorry for Pearl, but he couldn't. Rather he felt such love toward her. He was humbled by all this. *Even in the midst of our disobedience God takes time to look out for us with love and compassion. What kind of God is this? He* thought. *Only God can give us this kind of love,* he concluded.

When it was time for the offering, Mr. Yalley noticed that the youth were on duty this Sunday. The church had a very good program that groomed the youth gradually into leadership. Reverend Praise was thinking of having a preaching contest for them. They would be told to read a passage and preach a twenty-minute sermon on it. To him it would show their understanding and how God ministered to them through the passage. It would be done twice a year, and one person would be selected as assistant youth pastor for one year. When Mr. Yalley heard about it, he was so excited because to him that was a great idea. It would enable them to have a serious Bible study and prayer life. *I can't wait for that contest to start,* he thought.

When the offering plate was being passed around, he noticed that Joshua was nicely dressed, and he was really impressed, but he had a haircut that wasn't his style at all. Joshua had gone through a lot of changes the past few months, but this new haircut really surprised Mr. Yalley. He kept looking at him. *This boy needs some serious prayers,* he thought. He had the kind of parents who think that everything their child does is cute until they are in trouble, then you will hear them say, "He or she is a good boy or girl, but we do not know what happened."

Mr. Yalley was about to say a quick prayer for him when he heard the Holy Spirit say, *Hold it! Not yet. He needs more than you think. He is under serious peer pressure. Instead of desiring to fit into what he has been taught as a Christian, he is trying to become what his worldly friends are telling him. They've been teasing him about his haircut, so he cut his hair to look like them. Now they are teasing him because he has never smoked pot. He knows it is wrong, but because he is not standing up for what he believes in, they thinks he is like one of the many Christians out there who are holy on Sundays, and Monday through Saturday they live like the devil is their best friend. I was giving him the opportunity to minister to his friends, but because he has been denying me with his actions for the sake of worldly friendship, the power I gave him to resist temptation is weak, so he is gradually becoming one of them, and because he is my child, Satan hates him more than he will ever know. He is planning to smoke the pot with them, but if he does that, it will become a stronghold, and Satan will make sure it destroys his life eventually. The gift of prophecy is going to be birthed in him, and Satan does not want him to walk into his destiny. He is busy robbing my people of the gifts I have birthed in them because they are not right with me.*

Pray that he will be convicted of that desire and repent of wanting to abuse the temple of God. Pray that he will understand that he is not equally yoked with those friends, and he has to draw a line, how far he will go with them. Pray that his faith will be strengthened, and he will rise up in his spirit to be the light he is supposed to be among those friends.

When you pray he will go and hang out with them, but he

will not smoke. One of the boys who they all thought has mastered pot smoking is going to react badly after he finishes smoking, and it will become a scary situation. He will appear to be dying. I will then fill Joshua afresh with my power, and he will rise up in faith, lay hands on the boy, and pray for him. I will say everything through him, and the boy will be free and okay. They will become amazed and gradually through that one incident they will all come to know me. So now Joshua's life, future, and that of those boys' depend on your prayers.

Mr. Yalley took his journal and wrote a prayer for Joshua, who was about to smoke pot with friends.

Mercy sat quietly and still, wondering about what her husband had been jotting down. She turned and whispered in his ear, "What are you writing?"

"I will tell you later," he whispered back.

Mercy turned her head without saying a word. Reverend Praise came forward to deliver the message for the day, but before he did that he always asked the congregation to stand up and take the hand of somebody other than a family member and say to them, "You are about to hear the absolute word of God. It is the truth yesterday, today, and forever. You are blessed to be here today."

Mr. Yalley took the hand of a woman sitting behind him; beside her was a young man who seemed to be her son. When they finished saying the proclamation, as Mr. Yalley was about to release her hand, he felt a tingling all over his hand. It felt very weird, but he gave the lady a warm smile and sat down. He was still thinking about his hand and was wondering whether it was a sign from the Holy Spirit. Just then the Holy Spirit spoke again.

You were right. That was a sign from me. Her name is Angel. She is visiting with her middle child. Her husband travels a lot for his company, and she gets very lonely sometimes, so her children are everything to her. When she was growing up, her parents were very strict, so she became a conservative Christian throughout her college years, and she is still the same until recently. As a matter of fact, she is too hard on herself just to please me and that is robbing her from truly enjoying who she is in me. She attended a family friend's birthday party three months ago. She was served a glass of red wine, which she refused to accept because she had never tasted alcohol in her life, and this was a birthday party for a Christian woman whom she admires and respects so much.

"Angel come on, a little bit of wine is not going to send you to hell," Auguestina at her table told her. Everybody was in a party mood, giggling, laughing, and having a good time, and she felt left out, because she was the only one who seemed to look uptight. So when Auguestina pressed her a little more, she accepted the glass of wine. She told herself, I will just take a sip, and that will be all, *but before she knew it her glass was almost empty.* I was wrong by thinking that anything alcohol tastes awful, *she thought. She started feeling light headed but felt bold and a sense of happiness. She began to socialize freely and found herself having a good time like everybody else.*

Auguestina noticed her change of mood so she asked her, "Angel, how is it going?"

"Great! I am having fun, and it is good to be out of the house," she responded with a big smile. "Let me ask you something," Angel told Auguestina.

"What is it?" she asked her.

"What is the name of the wine you served me?"

"Oh! I bet you like the smooth ride down your throat, ah?" said Auguestina. "Well, it is called Red Rose wine," she told her. Just then the server was passing by, so Auguestina took two glasses off the tray and said, "Here, have your seconds. I could see your glass is empty," she said as she handed the glass to her. Angel took it and without a question took a sip immediately.

"Hmm, this is good!" she told herself.

"*Enjoy yourself,*" *Auguestina told her, winking her eyes at her as she stood up to talk to a friend.*

Three days after the party she couldn't get the taste and the feelings the wine gave her out of her mind, so she went out and secretly bought herself two bottles of Red Rose wine and hid them somewhere in the house. She secretly started drinking one glass a day, but now she is on three glasses a day, and sooner or later it will be the whole bottle within a day. She has forgotten that I am the source of her joy, happiness, her boldness, her confidence, her laughter, and smile. Satan has her in his trap. I know her future, but this drinking is going to turn her into an alcoholic, and it will cause so much pain in her life and her family. She has decided not to drink on Sundays because it is the Lord's Day.

Pray that the desire to drink and the taste of that wine will vanish from her system, as well as the feelings it gave her will be erased from her memory forever. She will try it again, which will be for the last time, and I will use that to bring her healing. When she drinks it, it will taste like water and will have no effect on her. She will be surprised, and in the midst of wondering about what is going on, I will minister to her and convict her. She will then cry out to me with regrets and a repentant heart. I will forgive her and restore her back to me; she will have victory over alcohol, never to touch it again. I will make her relax and enjoy herself in me, and she will become a brand new woman in me. I would have wanted this to be between me and her, but some people have bore witness to her first drink ever, so because of that I will make her confess to her husband and children, and I will use that to minister to her husband to set his priorities right. Pray without ceasing, and I will do the rest.

Mr. Yalley took his journal again and wrote a prayer for Angel and Red Rose wine. He was surprised he listened to all that the Holy Spirit told him and listened to Reverend Praise's message at the same without being distracted in any way. *It is only God who can allow me to experience something like this.*

It feels like I'm serving two masters, but both have my undivided attention, he thought with a smile.

Reverend Praise's message was so timely. Never doubt what God can do through you or for you. Mr. Yalley was so blessed because God had been manifesting Himself through him in a very awesome way since he came to church. *I am surely a living testimony to what God can do through you,* he thought with a grateful heart and a humble spirit. Mr. Yalley listened attentively but at the same time expecting the Holy Spirit to speak any moment.

Grace was blessed with the message as well, because God had restored her family back to her, and within a few weeks she had over and over seen the love and goodness of God in her life. *He is really the one true God, and when you experience his love for yourself, you cannot help it but give him all the glory,* she thought.

Reverend Praise asked them to stand up. He prayed over them, and they all said the benediction. As they filed out of the pews, Mr. Yalley thought to himself, *what a morning in the presence of God. I am a very blessed man.* As they neared their car, Mr. Yalley realized the Guides were parked next to them. They were a family of five, but today Mrs. Guide was not among them, and that was very unusual.

"Hello, Guide family!" Mr. Yalley said, and Mercy waved at them. Mr. Guide looked back and saw the Yalleys.

"Oh, hi!" he responded.

"I took off without realizing that was your car I was parking next to," said Mr. Yalley. "How are you all doing, and where is the lady of the house today?" asked Mr. Yalley.

"Oh, she is under the weather today, so she couldn't make. Pray for her when you think about her," Mr. Guide told them without having real eye contact with them. The Holy Spirit spoke immediately and said, *that is a lie, he yelled at her this morning over nothing when they were all getting ready for church. She felt humiliated before the children and cried her eyes out. Her eyes looked swollen, so she decided to stay behind. The kids are sad and are going home with heavy hearts.*

Mr. Yalley wanted to tell him, "Tell Lilly we will be praying for her," but because he was so shocked about what he had just heard, when he opened his mouth what came out was, "She will be fine when the yelling stops."

Mr. Guide's face changed as if he had seen a ghost. He quickly turned around to see whether the children were listening, but they were talking among themselves in the car. He turned around again and asked Mr. Yalley, "What did you say?"

"Oh, never mind, I don't know why I said that, but anyway, tell her we will be praying for her," said Mr. Yalley.

Mr. Guide was confused about what Mr. Yalley said, but he managed to say, "Thank you! I will tell her," several times, which made him, look stupid.

Lord, am sorry for letting the cat out of the bag," Mr. Yalley apologized as he drove off.

Oh no, Son! You didn't do anything wrong. I planned it that way, said the Holy Spirit.

Mr. Yalley breathed a sign of relief as the Holy Spirit continued.

Mr. Guide loves me dearly. He is very sensitive in the spirit, and he knows when I speak to him or through any means. His impatience and anger is a stronghold in his life, and I know he wants to be set free. He has prayed about it several times, but failed all the tests I gave him to do, so I have decided I will just deliver him and set him free tonight. He knows I spoke through you, and he is repenting again and asking for forgiveness right now. When he gets home, he will break down and weep at the foot of their bed like a baby and apologize to his wife, asking for forgiveness and that of the children as well. The tears are going to cleanse his soul, and when he is down, he will feel like a brand new man inside out. By my power, grace, and mercy he will become a man full of patience and understanding, he will love deeply, and experience how love covers a multitude of sin. There will be no room for him to dwell on anything that is negative. Lilly will accept his apology, but she will still not be herself. Just to cheer her up, he will take the family to her favorite restaurant for lunch, which she will go to reluctantly. During lunch Mr. Guide, who is now a free man from his strongholds, will stand up and say, "Everybody, this is my wife of fifteen years, and I love her very much. She has made me the proud father of three beautiful children. I have been a jerk and hurt her emotionally. I have turned on a new leaf today. I apologize to her and ask her to forgive me, but right now in front all of you all, I want to tell her one more time how much I love her and how sorry I am to walk all over her emotionally."

He will then take her hands and say to her, "Honey, you are the love of my life. I am really sorry for doing the things I did to you. I now know how much you have endured my stupidity all these years. Thank you for your patience and grace. With the help of God I promise you this will never happen again, and we are yet to have the best times of our lives."

Lilly at this time will be crying, and her heart will be healed immediately. He will give her a hug and kiss her on her forehead. He will turn around and with a wave he will say, "Thanks to you all for listening. Everybody in there will start clapping for him, for the fact he was trying to make things right. You don't need to pray about this. I will take care of it, Son. You are a blessed man.

Mr. Yalley drove in silence for a while as he listened to the Holy Spirit.

I wish I could take the ladies to lunch, but all that I want to do right now is to go home and absorb all that just took place, Mr. Yalley thought. Mercy was thinking the same thing but she wanted to go straight home so that Paul can tell her what was going on. Grace, on the other hand, somehow felt the

Yalleys would probably want them to go to lunch, but she had made up her mind she would say no, because they had already planned what to eat for lunch. The three of them were busy with their thoughts, and none of them could say anything, except for Little Sam, who kept singing "Jesus Loves Me."

Grace breathed a sign of relief when they got to the house, as she came out of the car she spoke up and said, "Thanks for the ride."

"You're welcome," said Mr. Yalley.

"Let's ride together more often," Mercy suggested.

"That will be nice, I will take you up on that, thanks, and you two have a wonderful afternoon," Grace told them.

"You do the same. Have a playful afternoon, Little Sam, but take a nap and be good to your mom, okay!" said Mr. Yalley.

"Yes, Grandpa," Little Sam answered.

"Oh, that is so sweet. I really like this Grandpa thing," Mercy said with a smile. Hand in hand, mother and son walked across the street to their house.

Mercy followed her husband silently as they entered the house. Mr. Yalley went straight to the bedroom and lay prostrate on the bed. Mercy came in shortly after that, to change her cloths. One look at her husband on the bed and she knew there was something serious going on with him. She quickly went and sat near him on the bed. She put her hand on his back as she asked him, "Honey, what is going on, are you okay?"

Mr. Yalley flipped over and pulled her to lie beside him. He then gave her a kiss on her forehead.

"Hope I wasn't making you worried with all my interesting behavior at church," he said.

"Not really, knowing what God is doing through you, but I couldn't help wondering what was going on," she responded.

"It has been a very interesting day, but to tell you the truth I am humbled, for I have been in the presence of God, taking instructions from him from the moment I set foot on the church grounds till I left," Mr. Yalley told his wife.

"Hmm! What did he tell you, and what was that funny thing you laughed about when you were talking to Mr. Montey?" Mercy asked her husband.

"I will let that be the last story to tell you," he answered.

They laid beside each other on the bed as Mr. Yalley told his wife all the things God revealed to him and the instructions he gave him. "He asked me to pray for Annabelle, Pearl, Joshua...with Mr. Guide he said he would take care of him himself, but he told me about everything that will take place in their house this afternoon."

Mercy listened attentively without blinking an eye. She was not surprised but humbled about what God was doing in her husband's life once again.

"Now about Mr. Montey, this is what God showed me about his private life; he loves to wear ladies underwear."

"What?" Mercy said as she sat up in bed.

"Well, as a young man, he thought ladies have the most comfortable and beautiful underwear, so he chose to join the ladies club when it comes to underwear. His wife is now used to the fact that she wears the same underwear as her husband, so it is not a problem at all for her," Mr. Yalley told her. Mercy began to laugh so hard that tears started running down her face. "This is why I decided to save this for the last," said Mr. Yalley.

Mercy, knowing the way Mr. Montey carries himself around, couldn't imagine him in silk lacy underwear, so the more she thought about it, the more she found herself laughing. She laughed till she fell off the bed. She got up from the floor to a kneeling position and then crawled back into the bed, all along laughing.

"Paul you should have told me this first, now I don't feel holy anymore," Mercy said, still laughing.

"You would have been laughing so hard, and you wouldn't be able to listen to the rest of the story," Mr. Yalley told her.

"Well, you're right!" she responded as she wiped her face with a tissue. "Oh my God! I couldn't remember the last time I laughed so hard like this. This is really funny. I wonder whether there are women out there who prefer men's underwear," said Mercy.

"You never know what is beneath people's clothes," Mr. Yalley responded. "Now back to business," he told her. Mercy wiped her face once more and sat down at the foot of the bed, ready to hear what her husband had to say next.

"You will support me, and we will pray without ceasing. We will go through the list and pray for them during our morning and evening devotion. Throughout the day those prayers will continue to be on our lips. I want us to do three days fasting together as we pray," Mr. Yalley told his wife.

"That is fine with me, for where you go, I go. We are in everything together, and together we will stand in the gap for them," Mercy told her husband with all sincerity of her heart. "Satan will be disfigured, and all his little demons will not recognize him by the time we are done with him," Mercy added with a laugh.

"Are you hungry?" Mercy asked her husband as she stood up to change her clothes.

"No, Honey, my stomach feels like I just finished eating my favorite food," said Mr. Yalley.

"I know what that feels like, satisfied in the spirit," she responded. "I will just go ahead and eat something light now and wait till we eat dinner together," Mercy told her husband.

"Go ahead, but make sure light didn't turn into heavy because I know how that goes," Mr. Yalley told her as he started laughing.

Mercy turned, gave him a look, and walked out of the bedroom. In the kitchen Mercy figured out what she wanted to eat when she opened her fridge, a small plate of fresh salad, one apple, and a glass of water. She sat down to enjoy her light lunch, but she felt a little lonely eating all by herself. *That was the result of doing everything together as a couple,* she thought.

She remembered when they first got married. Paul was always home by 6:00 p.m., but she would work up till midnight some weeks. Paul would get home and snack on things till she got home for them to sit down and eat a meal.

"Paul, go ahead and eat, don't wait for me," she would call and tell him.

"I never enjoy my meals without you," was always his response.

"It is not good to be eating so late," she would remind him.

"Oh! We will be fine. We are doing it out of love," he would tell her.

Mercy got tired of the situation, and at the same time worried about her husband, so she made arrangements with her supervisor to take her break around 6:30 p.m. when she has to work up till midnight. She will rush home have dinner with her husband and go back to work all within one hour. Paul was so glad she did that for him, so to show his appreciation, he started doing things to surprise her during those times, and it became such a fun moment for them.

All these memories flashed through her mind as she sat there by herself. *I don't know which of us would go first, but I don't think I will live long without him,* she thought.

Yes you can, Christ bore that on the cross, and you can do all things through Christ who strengthens you, came the voice of the Holy Spirit in her heart.

"That is so true. I don't want to think about this anymore," she said aloud as she stood up to take her plate to the kitchen.

I would just read to while away the afternoon and get my mind off everything, she thought.

Mercy went back to the bedroom to get her book, and to her surprise Paul was fast asleep. She stood there looking at him with such admiration and love. *I am a blessed woman to be loved by this man,* she thought. She looked up to heaven and said, "Thank you, Lord." She quickly picked the book she had been reading and walked out of the room to the living room to read.

Mercy was beginning to enjoy her book when the phone rang. She quickly picked it up so that the ringing wouldn't disturb her sleeping husband.

"Hello," she said.

"Hi, Mom, it's me!" came her son's voice.

"Hello, Son! How are you?"

"I am doing well, and everything is fine," he told her.

"I am glad to hear that," Mercy told him.

"How is Dad doing? Are his eyes still seeing beyond?" Paul asked his mother.

"You know, he is a vessel that God has chosen to use, so he is really using him. God reveal a lot to him during church service this morning and ask him to pray without ceasing. I was really humbled when he told me how the Holy Spirit spoke to him throughout the service, and he was able to listen to the message as well. He said it was like serving two masters, but they all had his undivided attention," Mercy told her son.

Paul listened attentively but couldn't find words to make any comments. "Where is he," he ask his mom.

"He is taking a nap," Mercy told him.

"I was missing you all, so I decided to call and hear your voice," said Paul to his mom.

"We miss you too, Son, why don't you come down next weekend? Grace and Big Sam's wedding is next Sunday."

"I wish I could, but I am studying for my finals, and I have a lot to deal with," said Paul.

"Oh! I forgot. How it is going?" Mercy asked.

"Very well, I will say," he told her.

"The Holy Spirit is always there to help you, so as you study, don't forget to rely on him for clarity of mind and a sharp memory to remember all that you have studied," Mercy advised.

"Thanks, Mom, for your free advice," Paul said, laughing.

Mother and son carried on a conversation for almost an hour. Mercy realized he called just to talk and feel at home, so she gave him her undivided attention. He told her so many things that were going on in his life and on campus, some were so funny. He told her about how he had constipation for three days and when he finally went, the whole room smelt like rotten eggs for a long time. Despite the fact that he had sprayed the room with air refresher. Mercy found herself laughing aloud with him.

"Paul, that is terrible! I told you to eat something with fiber every day and drink water instead of the sodas you've been drinking," Mercy reminded her son.

"I do that, Mom, but I don't know what happened," he responded.

"Well, we all do go through that sometimes. It's one of those things in our lives," Mercy responded. He then told her about how he nearly missed an important class by going to the wrong class and how a girl in one of his class was being extra nice and sweet to him.

"That is the love of God she is showing toward you," Mercy teasingly told him.

"I don't know about that, Mom!" Paul responded.

"I don't want to ignore her, but knowing what she is up to makes me want to run when I see her coming," Paul told his mom.

"Paul, just continue to be nice to her, and gradually tell her about your faith. That could make her run if she is up to no good, or she could become interested in knowing more about your faith, but importantly you have to be praying for her. God probably just put her in your way so that you can lead her to the cross. The best place she will ever be in her life," Mercy advised.

"You're right, Mom," he said, agreeing with all that his mother told him.

"I think I will invite her to the Wednesday Bible study that I attend, pray for me so that I will walk in grace and not be irritated by the sight of her and my attitude toward her will not hinder the power of God that will enable me to touch her life," said Paul.

"We will, Son!" Mercy promised.

"Thanks, say hello to Dad when he wakes up, and I will call again," said Paul.

"I will do that, we love you and say hello to Tete, and you two take care of yourselves," Mercy told her son.

"All right! Bye, for now!" Paul said and hung up.

Mercy hung up and just sat there with a smile on her face. "Thank you, Lord, for the life of our only child; he is such a good boy. It is not anything that we have done, but because of all that you have enabled us to do," Mercy prayed. Treasured memories ran through her mind about Paul, and she realized she didn't feel like reading anymore, so she sat there and allowed her mind to recount a lot of those treasured memories. In the midst of all that, her parents flashed through her mind, and she decided to call them immediately. *Good relationships with your children will always create a strong family bond that will last forever,* she thought with a smile as she reached out for the phone to call them.

The Lukens' Wedding

Grace opened her eyes, looked at the clock, and realized that she overslept.

"Oh my God! What happened to me?" she said as she jumped out of bed and hurried to Little Sam's room to wake him up, but she was surprised to see him all dressed up and ready to go.

"Hi, Mom, I'm ready. I already had breakfast," he told her.

"Oh! Sam, I am so proud of you for finishing first, now let me hurry up and get ready, or else we are going to be very late today," Grace told her son as she hurried off to get ready.

"I have a Monday morning staff meeting at 8:00 a.m., and it is already 7:25 a.m. I have to drop Little Sam off first, oh! Help me, Lord," she prayed as she quickly got dressed. Within twenty minutes they were out the door, but Grace was twenty minutes late when she finally made it to her work place. As she walked the hallway to her office, she started dreading how she was going to open the staff room door and how the inquisitive ones would turn to see who just entered, but when she entered her office, she noticed that everybody was at their desk. *The meeting can not be over so soon,* she thought.

"Good morning, Grace, they decided to change the meeting time to 9:00 a.m.," one of her co-workers told her. Grace breathed a sign of relief as she sat down.

"Good morning! Thanks for letting me know," said Grace with a smile. It then dawned on her that God had been really looking out for her today, starting from Little Sam. He has never got up from bed on his own during school days, but he did it today, and that really saved her time to get ready herself. She made it to work, and the meeting time had been changed. She couldn't help but marvel at the goodness of God. "Thank you, Lord," she said.

Later on during the day, Big Sam called her just to say hello. He told her he had taken two weeks off and that he would come on Wednesday to help with the preparations for their big day. Secondly, he asked her to try and see whether they could have their meeting with Reverend Praise on Thursday. She told him it will be really nice having him around till the big day and that she would call and make the appointment.

"You know, Sam, this is very interesting, although we have not discussed this yet, I had also taken two weeks off starting on Wednesday," Grace told him.

"That is great, Grace!" Sam responded. "I was thinking and wondering whether you would work up till Friday and then take next week off. I am glad you did that," he told her.

"I didn't know I could take off like that, knowing my workload, but the favor of the Lord went before me, and when I spoke with my boss, she agreed," Grace told him. "Let me tell you what happened this morning," said Grace. She took her time and told him what happened, starting from the time she got out of bed, and how God was looking out for her till she made it to work and how the staff meeting time was changed to her surprise.

"Wow! Sam got up and got himself ready for school, my son is maturing," Sam said. "Well, I prayed that this would be permanent for him, because I was getting tired of dragging him out of bed every morning. He was very proud of himself, so I hope this will make him want to continue doing that," Grace told Sam.

"Have you told your co-workers yet?" Sam asked her.

"Yea but not about the date. I promised them that later, so I intend to do that before I leave today," said Grace.

"Well, I told mine, and Clement, John, Fred, Moses, Katrina, Clara, and Karen said they will carpool and come," he told her. "You know what Fred said when I told them? He came to my office and whispered in my ears, 'I am glad you've come back to your senses; you nearly threw away the best thing that ever happened to you. Thank God no one snatched her before you came to your senses.' I looked at him and said, 'You are perfectly right, and I owed it all to God for having mercy upon me and restoring my marriage. This does not happen to a lot of people, and I feel really blessed.' He tapped me on the shoulder and said, 'Then you stick to that God with everything you got, congratulations! I will certainly be there to cheer you two on.' That is Fred, he says it as it is," Sam told Grace.

"I'm glad he said it to your face instead of somewhere else, as you've always said, he is one of the honest people in the office, and do you think he is a Christian?" Grace asked.

"I don't know, or I'm not sure I should say, but he is a good man," Sam answered.

"Well, we have our work cut out for us to be praying for them," said Grace.

"I agree with you, God help us do our best," Sam responded.

"Well, honey! I got to go, and I will talk to you in the evening, have a nice day, and I love you," Sam said as he made a kissing sound on the phone.

"Love you too, bye!" Grace said and hung up.

Later on during the day, Grace decided it was time for her to announce her upcoming wedding, so she stood up and said, "I have an announcement to make." Everybody turned and looked at her. "You are all invited to my wedding ceremony on Sunday, 12:30 p.m., at Emmanuel Church of God," she told them with all smiles.

"Grace, we all know that you have a new boyfriend call Jesus Christ, but we didn't know you would marry him so soon," one of her co-workers said jokingly with a laugh, and everybody joined in the laugh.

"I am not joking," she told them firmly. "I am marring my ex-husband, the details are none of your business, but all that I can say is God has given me back my family. Jesus Christ is the center of this upcoming wedding, and we are going to live happily ever after, and you are all invited," she told them and sat down.

Her Bible study group already knew about it, but she told them not to tell anybody until she announced it. Philip stood up and started clapping, and to her surprise everybody joined in. Congratulations! Were coming from every corner in the room.

Grace stood up again with a smile and a wave and said, "Thanks!" as she turned her head around in all directions in the room. "I hope to see you all there, now go back to work," she told them jokingly as if she were the boss.

As she was clocking out for the day, a few of her co-workers came around to congratulate her personally and ask her whether there is anything they can do to help.

"Thanks for your thoughtfulness, this wedding actually has no detailed human planning, that is why I don't even have invitation cards. It looks as if God planned everything before bringing us together again, so we are just flowing into it. The most important thing is to see you all there," she told them.

Grace noticed that Abina, one of her co-workers, had stayed around till everybody left her alone. She came closer to her and said, "Grace, have you ordered your cake yet?"

"Yea! My parents are ordering it for us as a wedding gift," she told her.

"What about finger foods?" Abina asked.

"Well, the church ladies are blessing us with that," Grace told her.

"Well, with such an open invitation, there will never be too much food. You don't know this, but I do a little catering on the side," Abina told her.

"Really! I didn't know that," said Grace, sounding surprised.

"I hope someday it will become a real business with a name out there," Abina said with a smile.

"Have faith, anything is possible, and before you know it, you are living that dream," Grace encouraged her.

"Anyway, I wanted to bake you one of my favorite cookies," she offered.

"Are you sure? You don't have to do that," Grace told her.

"I know I don't have to, but I want to bless you as the church ladies are doing," Abina told her.

"With that I can't argue with you. I can't turn down a blessing. Thank you very much, and I pray that your kindness will bear fruit in an area of your life that you thought you would never see happen," Grace told her.

"Thanks," said Abina. "I know where the church is, so I will certainly see you on Sunday," she added and hurriedly left. As Grace drove off to pick up Little Sam, she couldn't help but wonder how Psalm 23 was becoming so real in her life, especially where it said goodness and mercy shall follow you all the days of your life. "Goodness, you are really chasing me down," she said aloud. "Anyway, thanks for everything," she added as she pulled into the parking lot of Little Sam's school.

Big Sam called Grace around 11:30 a.m. the following day and told her he had arrived.

"What? I thought you said you were coming on Wednesday," she asked, sounding surprised but excited.

"Yea, that is what I said, but I tricked yah!" he told her, laughing.

"Where are you now?" she asked him.

"I'm almost at the house," he answered. "I nearly call off my trick when I realized I couldn't let myself in the house and surprise you when you get home, but I decided that a half surprise is better than none," Big Sam added.

"Well, you really got me on this one; I was expecting you tomorrow, but it is good to have you a day early. I will see you in a little bit," Grace told him. Grace took her lunch break and hurried home to let Sam in.

"What a pleasant surprise!" Grace said as she hurriedly got out of her car. Big Sam hurried to her side and gave her a hug.

"It is good to be back," he said. Grace looked in his eyes and gave him one of her warm smiles. She snacked on something quickly and went back to the office to clear her desk before starting her vacation.

Big Sam settled in, and after a while he decided to cook a surprise dinner with anything that Grace had in the freezer or fridge. Luckily there was everything he needed to cook a balanced dinner, so he immediately put himself to work. He knew Grace and Sam would be in by 5:30 p.m., and the surprise would not be perfect if they came in and he was still cooking. He hurried up like a professional chef in a cooking competition, and he was glad by 4:20 he was done. He laid the table for three, cleaned up the kitchen, and put everything away, he then sat down to relax and watch the news.

Grace got to the house around 5:26. She told Little Sam to wait in the car because she wanted them to eat out but she had to get something from the house. She wanted to surprise him, but she forgot that Big Sam's car was parked in front of the house and Little Sam could see it. Just then he noticed his dad's car and started shouting, "Dad is here, Dad is here, Dad is here!"

Big Sam was beginning to relax when he heard the door-bell. He got up to open the door and wondered why Grace didn't use her keys.

"Sam, let's eat out, Little Sam is in the car," she said when he opened the door. The aroma of what happened in her kitchen met her at the door; she sniffed the air without paying attention.

"That makes me hungry," she said and then realized that Sam had been cooking.

"Oh! Sam, you've been cooking," she said, looking into his face. Sam nodded his head with a smile.

"Go get Little Sam so that we can have dinner," he told her. Grace ran down the stairs, back to the car.

"Little Sam, I have changed my mind, come and let's go in first," she told her son. Little Sam knew his dad was home, so he was glad to get out of the car.

"Is Dad coming to stay with us now?" he asked as he followed his mother up the stairs.

"Why are you saying that?" Grace asked her son, pretending she did not know what he was talking about.

"Mom, that is Daddy's car, he is in the house," said Little Sam, pointing at his dad's car with a look of surprise on his face.

"Are you sure that is your dad's car?" Grace asked him.

"I am very sure, Mom," said Little Sam.

The door was still open, and Big Sam was hiding behind it. Little Sam entered the house still talking.

"I am very sure, mommy." Grace still pretended she did not know what he was talking about. Little Sam was about to make a turn into the hallway when Big Sam came out of his hiding place with a shout and grabbed him. "Mommy! I told you that was Dad's car, Daddy!" he said as he gave his dad one of his best squeezed hugs.

"You're right, Little Sam, that was your dad's car, and he was in the house all along," said Grace. Big Sam looked at her, and they both started laughing, somehow Little Sam knew immediately that his mother was tricking him.

"Mommy! You tricked me," he shouted.

"Tricked yah! Tricked yah!" Grace said as she began to tickle him. He started wiggling and laughing in his dad's arms.

"Are you going to stay?" Little Sam asked his dad, immediately he put him down.

"I am staying all the way through Sunday," Big Sam told his son.

"All right!" he Little Sam responded with a shout. "You promise?" he asked his dad with a serious look on his face.

"I promise," Big Sam told him as he lifted his right hand up.

"Okay! Then let us do the pinky thing," said Little Sam. Big Sam stuck his big pinky out, and Little Sam stuck his little pinky out, the two pinkies gave each other a hug and sealed the promise.

Children are so pure in heart, and I wonder what fatherless and motherless children go through emotionally, Big Sam thought as he noticed how happy Little Sam was.

Grace kicked her shoes off her feet at the door and said, "Little Sam, Dad has a surprise dinner for us. Go and wash your hands and come and let's eat. No wasting of time, for am hungry," Grace told her son as she walked to the dining table. They took their places at the table, and Sam said let's pray.

They reached out held each other's hands and with their heads bowed he prayed with the thought that this is the beginning of their dinnertime together as a family.

"Father, thank you for today, and this moment in our lives as a family. We are together and it is all because of your mercy. I pray your blessing upon us. Keep us together and always watch over us. Thank you for being our provider. We thank you for the dinner. Bless it and let it nourish our bodies. We invite you to dine with us. In Jesus' name we pray, Amen."

"Amen!" Grace and Little Sam responded.

"Oh! That looks yummy," Grace said as she took the lid off the dishes. Wild rice, baked chicken, steamed carrots, sweet peas, and dinner rolls. "Sam, you really got yourself busy," Grace said. She couldn't believe he did all that cooking. With a grateful heart she affectionately took his hand and squeezed it gently. Sam squeezed hers back; in their hearts they knew what that meant. They were happy at the table, and everybody ate to their fill. Little Sam of all people did not have room for ice cream. Out of joy he ate till he couldn't eat any more.

After dinner Big Sam told Grace to relax and that he would do the cleaning up.

"Oh no! You did the cooking. I should do the cleaning up," she told him.

"That sounds fair, but I insist, just relax. I will clean up," he responded.

Grace saw he was really serious, so she took the offer, but after a while she decided to go and keep him company in the kitchen. Big Sam was washing the dishes with his legs spread apart, shoulders straight up as he stood behind the sink. Grace entered the kitchen, noticed his posture with admiration, cleared her throat, and said, "I am feeling guilty letting you do all this, two hands are better than one you know, let me help," she said as she picked up a clean kitchen towel to dry the washed plates and dishes.

"I told you to relax, woman," Sam said with a smile. "Allow yourself to be a queen for a moment," he added.

"Well, the queen wants to help a little so that she can be near her king," she told him.

Upon hearing that, Big Sam turned and with such affection in his eyes he said, "The king is honored to have the queen in his presence," and then he bowed a little before her. Grace thought that was funny, so she started laughing, and Big Sam joined in the laughter. Little Sam heard the loud laugh and rushed to the kitchen.

"What is funny, Mommy?" he asked.

"Your dad was being silly," she told him.

"Did he tickle you?" he asked.

Grace, not wanting to go into any details, said, "Yes, he tickled me." Big Sam then took a step toward his son as if he was going to tickle him as well.

Little Sam seeing that, took off laughing and shouting, "No, I don't want to be tickled.

Well, Sam was glad to have her Grace standing next to him, and Grace was happy to have him home. They worked together, and in a few minutes the kitchen was back to normal. They both joined Little Sam in the living room, and the three of them had a good family time together. Grace couldn't help thinking how much Big Sam had changed. He has loosened up a lot and seemed to have a smile on his face all the time. Serious Sam is now a smiling Sam; rigid Sam is now a playful Sam. She loved him with all that, but now she knew that with this change they were going to have a lot of fun and laughter.

"Hey, little guy, it is time for your bath," Grace told her son with a tap on his back.

"Do I have to go now?" he asked, not wanting to interrupt the fun he was having.

"Yes, you have to, tomorrow is a school day," she told him.

"Come on, let me help you do that," said Big Sam to his son.

"Are you going to take a shower or bubble bath?" he asked him.

"Shower," he answered.

Big Sam helped his son with the water temperature and gave him a back scrub, tickling him in between. This made Little Sam laugh his head off, and when his dad turned on the shower, he was one happy naked boy in the shower. After the shower he put on his pajamas and he was ready to go to bed.

"Dad, I am going to tell Mom goodnight, and I will be right back," he told him and walked away sluggishly. He came back after a while, and Sam helped him up the bed, as he was tucking him in, Little Sam spoke and said, "Dad, will I get a divorce when I grow up?"

Oh God, help me to address this unexpected question well, Big Sam prayed immediately in his mind.

"Well, little guy, when God created marriage, he did not add divorce to it, and so he does not like divorce. When you become a child of God, he loves you forever, and the same way when we fall in love with somebody and marry them, God wants us to love them forever, but because we don't obey God and walk in his ways, we divorce, like your mom and I did. We told God we are sorry, so he forgave us and is helping us to get married again.

"Now listen carefully, Son, you have Jesus in your heart, and as you grow up, your mom and I will help you to know more and more about this. You will become responsible to obey him and walk in his ways as you understand who you are in him and what he expects of you. With that he will direct your steps, and you will meet a Christian girl who will be the right wife for you. By the grace of God, the two of you will not repeat the mistakes your mom and I made. When you allow

God to be part of everything that you do, he will direct your steps, and you will do the right thing.

"The love of God is unconditional, so he does not stop loving you when you make mistakes. I want you to remember that, but there are consequences for our actions and mistakes. There are a lot of mommies and daddies out there who didn't get a second chance like your mom and I, but God still loves them."

"Dad, are you going to sleep on mommy's bed today?" Little Sam asked his dad, interrupting the speech as he looked sternly in his face.

"Boy! You are full of questions today, but that is a very good question, so I want you to listen to my answer very well. I am going to sleep in your room again today, because your mom and I are not married yet."

"But you said you and mommy are back together, and her bed is bigger than mine," Little Sam cut in.

"Son, you are one smart boy. That is why I said you should listen carefully."

"Okay, Daddy," said Little Sam as he straightens himself on the bed.

"You remember your mom and I are divorced; that is why we live apart, but your mom and I will be really back together on Sunday when we stand before God, the pastor, and everybody and the pastor blesses us then we are permitted by God to sleep on the same bed, so we are waiting for that," Big Sam explained to his son.

"Oh Daddy, so when you are not married, you cannot sleep together?" he asked.

"That is right!" said Sam, not wanting to explain it further.

"Okay, I promise I will marry and won't divorce," said Little Sam to his dad with quite a serious face as if he really understood all that his dad told him.

"Anyway, enough of these conversations. Get some sleep, okay?"

"Okay! Daddy, I love you, goodnight," said Little Sam as he gave his dad a squeeze.

Back in the living room, Sam told Grace about the questions their son asked him and the response he gave him. She was really surprised to hear that.

"He asked you that? This child is really observing things and thinking with his little brains," Grace said. " I am glad you gave him a little preaching, and I know that will go a long way in his spirit," she added.

"God really helped me to pull the talk off, and I hope he will always remember it. He is a very smart boy," said Big Sam.

"You want something to drink?" Grace asked him after a little while.

"What do you have in mind?" Sam asked her.

"Tea, juice, chocolate drink, whatever," she said.

"Let's do chocolate drink then," Big Sam suggested.

"Right up!" Grace said as she stood up.

Grace filled two long glasses with the drink and put a straw in one because she knew Sam loved the sipping sound through a straw. Like he always said, "It is a childhood feeling that never went away." They sat beside each other on the sofa, enjoying the drink.

"That is so refreshing," Big Sam said after along sip.

"I'm glad you like it," said Grace with a smile.

Big Sam cleared his throat and said, "Grace, where do you want us to go for our honeymoon?"

"You know, I have not thought about that, do you have any idea or any place in mind?"

"As you know, I still live in the house we bought together. I have done a few changes and it looks different from the last time you saw it. I feel it will be nice to start from there to rekindle the good memories we had there, then we can go somewhere else after that.

Grace thought about it for a few minutes and said, "I think that is a good idea, so honeymoon at 1962 Korkor Lane, settled," she said, nodding her head.

"You are in for a big surprise," Sam told her.

"We will see how that is going to knock my socks off," Grace responded with a laugh.

They sat there chit-chatting about anything they could think of, trying to catch up with time lost, but before they knew it, it was twelve midnight and Grace began to yawn.

"Sam, I think I will call it a night," Grace said as she stood and picked up the two empty glasses. She took them to the kitchen and came back to the living room, bent over, and gave Sam a quick hug from behind.

"Goodnight, honey, see you tomorrow," he said.

"Goodnight," Grace said and walked away. Big Sam sat there and watched the night news till he fell asleep on the couch.

Grace woke up in the morning and quietly walked into Little Sam's room, not wanting to make to any noise to disturb Big Sam, but to her surprise he was not in the bed. *He fell asleep on the couch. Well, I hope he slept well,* she said to herself.

Big Sam heard a little noise a round and woke up only to realize he fell asleep in the living room, so he quickly stood up and went and lay down. Grace brought Little Sam in to help him get ready for school, and to her surprise Sam was lying in the bed.

"Oh, somebody made it to the bed," she said.

"Well, as you know, certain things never change, and sleeping on the couch is one of them," Sam responded, still sounding sleepy.

Little Sam looked at his dad and asked, "Daddy, did you forget to bring your pajamas?"

"No, Son, I didn't forget. I was just too tired to change," Sam told his son.

"Next time don't fall asleep in your clothes, okay?" Little Sam told his dad.

"Okay, I will remember that, little guy," said Sam.

By the time Little Sam was ready to go his dad was fast asleep. He couldn't tell him goodbye, and that nearly upset him, but his mother found a way to cheer him up before they left the house.

Grace bought a box of donuts on her way back, because she knew Big Sam loved coffee with cream and two donuts in the morning. Big Sam was awake but still lying down when Grace came back.

"Are you back?" he shouted from the room.

"Yes, I am back," Grace answered. She quickly went to the kitchen and started brewing a pot of coffee. Soon the smell of fresh brew coffee was in the air, and that brought Big Sam out of the room.

"Hmm! I smell something good," he said as he walked toward the kitchen. He walked in and saw the donuts and said, "As if you read my mind, when I woke up and I realized you were gone, the first thing I said was, oh! I should have told you to buy some donuts on your way home."

"That means we are thinking alike," Grace told him. The coffee was ready, so they served themselves and had breakfast together sitting on the kitchen counter chit-chatting. Big Sam got down to pour more coffee, and as he walked toward the coffee pot, Grace noticed he looked a little taller, she wasn't sure if it was her imagination or not.

"Have you grown a little taller?" she asked him.

"Not that I know of," he said.

"You seem to be a little taller, or is it my imagination?" she told him.

"I think it is because I lost some weight," said Sam.

There was a look of surprise on Grace's face as she asked, "How much have you lost?"

"Well, the last time I weighed myself it was about a half pound," he told her with a serious face. Grace fell out laughing,

"That is so funny, Sam," she said. "I have never seen you lose weight or gain it," she added. "You have been at the same weight for how long?"

"Eight years," he said. "So losing a half pound was really hard to do," he added with a nod of his head.

"Are you serious about the half pound?" Grace asked him.

"I'm dead serious," he responded.

"Okay, losing a half pound has made you taller, Sam, and I think that is great," Grace told him, still laughing.

Sam stood up and began walking around the kitchen on his toes and making himself look much taller. Grace sat there with her eyes, following his movements, laughing and admiring him from head to toe. Husband and wife to be were beginning to have a taste of what life would be like together again after Sunday. Grace had a good feeling about everything, and she knew they are going to be all right.

Grace made a few phone calls and made some hotel reservations for their parents and few relatives who would prefer to spend the night after the wedding. She decided to clean house after that, because her house was going to be full of people over the weekend. The cleaning went well with Big Sam helping here and there. Before she knew it, it was time to pick up Little Sam. Big Sam decided to go along, so he hopped in the car, and off they went.

"So we have three more days to go, then we can call ourselves Mr. and Mrs. Luken again," said Sam.

"Yelp!" Grace responded. "This is the easiest wedding anybody could plan. The only thing I have done was to look for my dress, everything is being taken care of," Grace said. "It feels kind of weird because there is nothing to get stressed about, this is all the goodness of God," she added.

"I have realized that if you do anything Gods way, there is no stress, frustration, headache, or whatever. I have never felt so happy in my life like I am feeling now. Sometimes I feel like standing on top of my roof and shouting, 'Jesus loves me! And I love him too!' You really miss up on life when you don't know him, and somehow you wouldn't be aware of it until his light shines in your heart," Big Sam told Grace with sincerity.

"I bet you the Jesus thing does something to you. No one can explain it to your understanding unless you experience it yourself," said Grace. "I pray that all our family members will come to know him," Grace added.

"Amen to that," Sam said as they pulled into the parking lot of Little Sam's school. "Let me go and check him out," Big Sam suggested.

"Okay! He will be excited to see you anyway," said Grace.

Little Sam and his classmates were in a line walking to a common area where they will be checked out. He happened to turn and saw his dad walking toward them in the hallway, so he started waving his hand to draw his dad's attention. They've been told not to talk, so he waved without opening his mouth. Big Sam caught up with him and held his hand. Just then the teacher turned and saw Big Sam. He stopped and asked, "Who is that, Sam?"

"That's my dad," he answered with all smiles.

"I'm Mr. Luken and am picking him up today," said Big Sam.

"Oh! Mr. Luken nice meeting you finally. I'm Mr. Wheatthin," the teacher said as he stretched out his hand to shake Big Sam's hand.

"Just sign here, and he will be all yours," said the teacher. Big Sam took the pen and did just that.

"Are you ready to go?" Big Sam asked Little Sam as he gave the sheet back to Mr. Wheatthin.

"Bye! Sam, see you tomorrow, and have a good day, Mr. Luken," Mr. Wheatthin told them.

"Nice meeting you, have a good day," said Big Sam.

Little Sam held his dad's hand and started skip-walking beside him as they headed out. *Oh God, thank you for giving me the chance to be part of this again,* Big Sam silently prayed when he noticed how happy his son was walking beside him.

Grace noticed the same thing from afar. *Oh Lord, thank you for bringing us together,* she prayed silently.

"Hi Mom," Little Sam said as he hopped into the back seat.

"Hi, Little Sam, how was school today?" Grace asked her son.

"We had field day today. We had a lot of fun outside," said Little Sam.

"Oh I see. You took a little break from studying. Good for you all," said Grace. "Let's plan something fun to do to while away the afternoon," Grace suggested.

"I know what we can do," Little Sam quickly responded.

"We are listening. Bring your ideas," said Big Sam as he had eye contact with Grace. "Let's have a picnic at the park," said Little Sam.

"That would be fun. Good idea, Little Sam. We haven't been to the park in a while, and the weather is just perfect for it," said Grace, sounding excited.

"Well then, let's go grab some food and drinks and head off to the park," said Big Sam.

"All right!" Grace shouted.

They quickly did a take out, grabbed some blankets from the house, and headed off to the park. The park was less crowded than they expected, so they got a nice shady spot to spread their blanket. Little Sam was in a hurry to play, so he quickly ate his food and took off to the playground. *After all his playing at school today, this child still has the energy to run around,* Grace thought. Big Sam and Grace noticed a homeless man sitting on a bench who kept looking in their direction.

"I'm going to invite that guy over there to join us. He looks okay, what do you think?" Big Sam asked Grace.

"I noticed he kept looking at us. I'm sure he is hungry. Go ahead and let's bless him," Grace told him. Big Sam beckoned the man to come. He hesitated for a while, as if he wasn't sure about the invitation, but he probably realized he had nothing to lose, so he made his way toward them.

He stood a few yards from them with a look that said, *what do you want from me?*

"We want you to join us, if you don't mind," Big Sam told him.

The man's facial expression changed suddenly, and a warm smile broke out on his face. He sat down at the edge of the blanket without saying a word.

"My name is Sam, and this is my wife, Grace," said Big Sam.

There was a look of surprise on his face after the introduction. He spoke up and said, "My name is Samuel, but my folks call me Sam."

"That is interesting. I'm glad we have something in common already," said Big Sam.

After the introduction, Samuel felt more comfortable with his newfound friends. Grace quickly fixed him a plate and told him to feel free to help himself. He thanked them and starting eating like there would be no tomorrow for him. Big Sam and Grace watched and felt sorry for him. What was his story, Grace wondered.

Samuel opened up to them after a while. He told them he was once a married man with two children. He lost everything due to gambling three years ago and became homeless shortly after that. He had tried everything but had not been able to get his life back. He had not seen his children in two years, and that was so hard on him.

"I just don't how to make this right," he told them.

"The only person who can help you is God; trust me, that is your way out," Big Sam told him.

"No one had told me this before. What do I do?" Samuel asked.

Big Sam in a simple way preached the gospel of Jesus Christ to him, and before they knew it, they led Samuel to Christ. It was a very beautiful moment to watch Big Sam and Grace holding hands with Samuel, helping him to surrender at the foot of the cross to say yes to Jesus.

Little Sam came back, thirsty for something to drink.

"Little Sam, we made a friend. This is our son," said Grace.

"Hello," said Little Sam with a smile. Samuel just smiled at him as if he couldn't find words to say anything. "Little Sam, it is time to go, so don't go back to the playground. Let's pack up," Grace told her son. They all stood up and packed. Big Sam chitchatted with Samuel for a few minutes, just encouraging him, while Grace looked on with all smiles. They gave all the leftover food and drinks, including the blanket, to Samuel. He thanked them and was sad to see them go but glad he crossed paths with them. Samuel stood there and waved at them till their car was out of sight.

"Going to the park was not about us at all. This was all about Samuel," said Grace.

"It is humbling to be used like this," said Big Sam. "A day well spent because another soul has made it home," Big Sam added.

Little Sam was ready to go to bed by the time they made it home. He took his shower and went straight to bed. Grace and Big Sam watched a movie together and called it a night after that.

Big Sam and Grace woke up with one thing on their mind: their 12:30 p.m. meeting with Reverend Praise. After Grace dropped off Little Sam, they sat down to eat breakfast.

"I wonder what kind of questions Reverend Praise will be asking us," Grace said.

"We will find out when we get there," said Big Sam. The hours went quickly, and before they realized it, it was time for the meeting. They hurried out and made it there at exactly 12:30.

After welcoming them he told them that, as the policy of the church says, before he marries any couples, they have to go through four counseling sessions with him, but since they had a unique situation, one session was okay and very important. He said a short prayer and asked the Holy Spirit to come and take control over the meeting.

"Did you all go through a counseling session before you got married?" he asked them.

Sam looked at Grace and they both said, "No."

Reverend Praise was not surprised because, a lot of people don't.

"I'm glad you two have given your life to the Lord before marrying again. He will be your helper, and that will make a whole lot of difference," he told them. "So how did you two meet?"

"At a party," Sam answered.

"Do you want to tell me more?" he asked. Sam and Grace looked at each other for a moment.

"Okay, I will tell my side first," said Grace.

"Stephen was my first boyfriend; we started dating in the

eleventh grade. After high school we went to different colleges, but we continued to see each other. At the end of our second year, he met a girl in his English class, so he dumped me. I was broken hearted, so for the remaining two years of college, I decided nobody was going to touch my heart again.

"The summer after my graduation, I went to a friend's birthday party, and I was seated at a table where I was the only one without a partner. It happens that one of the guys knew Sam, and I heard him say, 'Sam Luken, come over here.' When he saw him come in, I looked up, and I saw this nerd walking toward us. Everything about him was singing nerd, nerd, nerd! His hair was out of shape, the funny beard, the loud colored shirt, his pants were a little short, showing his white socks, and the boot like shoes he was wearing, plus a big wrist watch..." With this they all started laughing.

"He was really dressed up to impress the ladies," said Reverend Praise, still laughing.

"You're right, Reverend!" said Sam.

"Well, I will never forget that first impression," said Grace.

"Anyway, he came over to join our table and began to talk to the guy. I think his name was Chris—"

"Yes, you're right!" Sam cut in.

"I noticed that he had a nice face despite the funny beard; he was soft spoken but had a deep voice that came out so beautifully when he laughs. We became like a little family around the table, so Chris introduce him to us as a good friend of his. He joined us in the conversation and felt comfortable with all of us. After a while the live band started playing, so the people around our table all moved to the dancing floor to dance, and Sam and I were left behind.

"What is your name?' he asked after a while to break the silence.

"Grace,' I said.

"Do you live around here?' he asked.

"Yes, about thirty minutes drive from here,' I told him without looking in his direction. He sat there for a while and said, 'Let me guess, you live in Lazarus apartments.' I was so surprised to hear that because that was where I lived. I turned slowly and faced him.

"Have you been stalking me or what?' I asked him. He laughed a funny laugh and said, 'That is where I live and I'm hoping you live there too.'

"How long have you been living there?' I asked, and he said two months, and I told him the same applied to me.

"He then asked me what block I was on. Reluctantly I told him 600, his face lightened up, and he said, "Me too.' *This is getting interesting,* I thought.

"I hope your apartment number is not 602,' I told him.

"No, no it is actually 605,' he said. This made me stand up from my chair. 'I couldn't believe this,' I said. 'You are the guy who lives opposite me, you leave home early, come late, and play classical music all night long.'

"He smiled and said, 'I'm glad you know a little bit about me, with this it wouldn't be difficult to strike out a conversation out of friendship. After all, we are next door neighbors.'

"Just then the music stopped because the band took a break, so they all returned to the table. He immediately told them how we just found out we were neighbors living opposite from each other. With this information Chris calmly said, "I don't know how you got here, but I know you don't need a ride from me to go home. You got somebody to take you right to your door.'

"*What makes you think I want to give this nerd a ride home? I'd rather be caught dead than to be seen riding with him,* I thought and then forced out a little smile.

"'Let me make sure she will do that before you can be free of me," he told Chris and then turned to me and said,

"Neighbor, would you give me a ride home?" looking straight into my eyes. Before I could respond, everybody at the table started shouting, 'Yes! Yes! Yes!'

"So I said, 'Okay, I will give you a ride home based on the fact that I have a lot of witnesses.'

"'Thanks, you are safe in my company,' he said.

"Chris tapped me on the shoulder and said, 'I would bet my life on that.'

"Well, I gave him the ride home, and the following day when I got up in the morning I saw a note tucked under my door. He was thanking me for the ride and wished me a nice day. I stood there looking at the note, and all that I could think of was, that was so sweet of him, but he was a nerd.

"A few days after that I got a card in the mail inviting me to dinner at his place, which was four days away, and he gave me his number to call and let him know if I would make it. The funny thing was, in the card he drew two doors facing each other and a road linking them. When I finished reading it, I tossed it on my dining table, thinking about the kind of menu he would come up with. *Frog legs and cow tongue or whatever a nerd would serve if he wanted to impress a girl. Why not take her out to a nice restaurant and save yourself from disgrace,* I thought.

"I decided I was not going to call. Silence means no, but to my surprise a day before the dinner, I was watching a movie when my door bell rang around 10:00 p.m. I wanted to ignore it, but it kept ringing, so I looked through the peep hole. I didn't recognize it was him at first because he had shaved his beard and also had a haircut. I opened the door because somehow I felt he was the one, and there stood Mr. Handsome. The look on my face immediately gave me away. He smiled and said,

"'Yea, my new look is blowing everybody away; I think it is a good change, and I'm enjoying it. Anyway, sorry to bother you this late. I am now coming in, but I want to know whether you are joining me tomorrow evening or not?' I could tell he was trying to read my facial expression.

"I wanted to say, 'Dummy, the silence means no,' but I couldn't. Here I was standing in front of Prince Charming, so I found myself saying, 'Oh! Yea, I will be there.'

"'Good! I will see you around 7:00 p.m. Goodnight,' he said and walked to his door. The whole night I couldn't get him off my mind. What a transformation. I would rather be caught dead than with him, and now he was Prince Charming. I had closed my heart to love, but I think it was about time I opened it up again. It was not just about the look. I felt he was a good human being hiding behind the nerd look. I didn't know what he was up to, but I was just going to relax. I wondered how a nerd's apartment would look. 'God help me,' I said with a laugh.

"The following day was quite an interesting day for me, because I became very anxious and restless as the hours passed by. I was so tired and mentally drained by the time I got home around 5:30 p.m. I took a quick shower and felt better. I sat down to while away the time by watching TV, but I fell a sleep. When I woke up, I felt very refreshed. I looked at the clock, and I had fifteen minutes to get ready and get out the door. When I finally came out of my apartment, I told myself I would go with an open mind and just have fun. I rang his doorbell and heard him shout, "Is open, come on in." Which I thought was rude, but hey, that's a nerd's way of welcoming a lady, so I kept my cool. When I entered his apartment, the first thing I noticed was how clean the place was, everything was at its place. *He is a neat freak kind of nerd,* I thought.

"We went straight to the dinner table because the food was ready. Buttered white rice with a touch of black pepper, steak and mixed steamed vegetables, and cheesecake for dessert. I remember the dinner like it was just yesterday. To confess, I was really impressed. We ate mostly in silence. I was busy thinking about his motive with all this. After dinner he wouldn't let me help him clean up, he told me to sit down and relax. I didn't want to be nosey looking around, so I sat down still till he was done. I didn't think cleaning up immediately was necessary, but nerds do things differently, so I had to respect that. He washed everything and put them away before settling down.

"We began to talk, and I realized that although he seemed to be rigid, there was a side of him that was very playful. We played cards, drank some kind of black tea he introduced me to. We watched a movie, and before I knew it, it was 1:00 a.m. I started yawning, so I asked to leave. He was so polite and nice, and I truly had fun. He saw me to my door and thanked me for coming and said he really enjoyed my company. I told him the dinner was really good, that it was the best dinner I had eaten in months. He smiled, but I felt he thought I was lying. I looked at him straight in the eye and said I really meant it. He smiled again and said, 'Thanks, I am glad you came and shared dinner with me. Can I have your number?'

"'Sure,' I said and gave it to him without any hesitation.

"We became friends after that. He would call to check on me or knock on my door to chat. I remember one day I was about to eat dinner when he knocked on my door, so I invited him to join me, and we had dinner together. After that he said he had some dessert, so we went to his place and ate apple pie and ice cream.

"When you look forward to somebody calling you or knocking on your door and you can't get them off your mind, it means you like the person and somehow are falling in love, so when he told me four weeks after our first encounter that he liked me very much and wanted to know me more—not as friends but beyond the friend thing, to quote his words—I agreed, and we started dating. Six months after that he proposed, and we got married within one year of our first meeting. We had a lot of differences in our way of thinking, doing things, personality, our social life, etc., but the love we had for each other over shadowed all our differences, to me he was the nerd who became my Prince Charming. And despite everything that has happened, he is still my a Prince Charming," said Grace

"When it comes to love, women have such good memory for detailed recollection, and that is so wonderful," said Reverend Praise.

"You're right about that, that is why we need to treat them right, and I have learned this the hard way," said Sam. "Anyway, honey, thanks for bearing with me and being so sweet," Sam told Grace as he tapped her on her shoulder. "With my side of the story," said Big Sam as he turned to face Reverend Praise, "I was a nerd all right, the funny kid on the block. I become a real nerd when I was in high school. I was not in any sports, but you will find me in anything academically. Debate club, science club, spelling B, poetry club, writers club, you name it, and I would be there, and I was good in all, so I got the girls. The beautiful ones that the athletes were supposed to get. I was helping them with homework and teaching them as well. I became popular among them although I did not look it, and that led me into doing things that I'm not proud of today.

"In college it was a different ball game. The girls were too embarrassed to be seen with me, so I was quite a loner, but it did not bother me at all. I just studied and was always on top of my class. I briefly dated a girl in my second year. She was a nerd as well, but to me to be a girl and a nerd is a wrong combination. When that ended I never bothered myself to look for a girlfriend till I met Grace at that party, to me there were too many coincidences to let her slip away. I knew immediately that my appearance was a turn off for her, so I decided to cut my hair and shave my beard, and guess what? It worked. I was not looking for a wife, but meeting her that day was the best thing that ever happened to me, and then I nearly messed up for good."

"Well, well," said Reverend Praise with all smiles, "that is interesting to hear. I love the way love came slowly, and it wasn't like you were all over each other, rushing into everything. Friendship came, love followed, and then marriage, this always creates a solid foundation for marriage. I want to ask you two something very important but very sensitive. I know that whatever you did when you were divorced is in your past and you have forgiven each other and that is why you are sitting before me today. But sometimes our past comes to haunt us, so I want to ask you two whether there is anything you did that you would like to bring it in the open now," Reverend Praise asked them.

Sam cleared his throat and said, "Three months after our divorce I met a lady at work and we dated for almost four months. Frankly speaking I thought I was ready to start dating, but I was always feeling guilty when she was around me. As if I were doing something wrong and was being watched. Unfortunately, she picked up on these feelings, and she kept telling me that she felt I had a wall around me and is hard for her to get in. My response was always, 'I don't know what you are talking about.' Finally, I guess she felt she was wasting her time, so she dumped me. I felt sorry for her, but there was nothing I could do. She was hired for a six months contract, and when it ended she just vanished," Sam told them.

Reverend Praise turned to Grace. "How do you feel about that?" he asked. Although that was the first time she heard about the woman who came after her, she was not moved in any way.

"Nothing, I feel nothing, we were divorced and that was expected, and secondly, he has apologized and asked for forgiveness, and to me it includes all that," she told Reverend Praise with all sincerity of heart.

"Grace, I know what you just told us is the very truth, and I am glad God has enabled you to walk in such forgiveness. It is a good place to be in one's heart," Reverend Praise told her. Grace had nothing to say, so she just smiled and her face looked so radiant as if God was telling her, *Good job, Grace,* with his presence.

Grace felt it was her turn to say something about her single life, so she spoke up and said, "With me I did not date anybody; as a matter of fact, I did not want to date anybody because I love my life that way. I was just allowing myself to open up a little bit when he showed up. I thank God that he is the one anyway. I got back what belongs to me and am please and thankful to God," Grace told them.

Sam turned and took her hand and said, "Honey, I am truly sorry for allowing another woman to have a link to me. I pray God will blot this from our memories."

"Honey! When we confess our sins to God, he forgives us and does not hold it against us, and if God has forgiven me so much, who am I to hold this against you? I am so glad she did not go through the wall," Grace responded with a little laugh.

Sam squeezed her hand and said, "I love you."

"I love you too," Grace responded.

"All right! That is taken care of," Reverend Praise said. "What do your parents feel about all this?"

"My parents are very excited, and as they put it, 'We are glad you came back to your senses,'" Sam said with a laugh.

"My parents were very angry with Sam, especially my dad, when Sam divorced me. It got to a point he couldn't call Little Sam by name. He would say how is my prince, my favorite grandson, or big boy doing? After Sam and I talked things over and decided to marry again, he made a trip to my parent's house to apologize and tell them personally about our decision. Prayers went forth for that meeting, and God honored our prayers, so when he got there everything went well. They even shared a lunch with him, and he said he was able to share the gospel with them somehow," Grace told Reverend Praise as Sam looked on, nodding his head.

"I am really thankful to God for their reception and willingness to accept me back. As he said, we are adults, and they could not stop us from doing what we decided to do, and if that was what their daughter decided to do, they would give us their blessing. This taught me that the evidence of forgiveness cannot be postponed but has to be shown immediately for more healing to take place," Sam said in response to what Grace said.

"We have no secrets, parents are happy, and I'm honored to be part of it all," said Reverend Praise. "Is there anything special like a message you two would want me to share before the marriage ceremony?"

"Yea! We would say preach the message of salvation," said Sam, and Grace nodded her head in agreement.

"Both our parents don't know the Lord, as well as a lot of ours family members and friends who will be there to support us. Now we know that some of them have been exposed to the Word of God over the years, and so we pray that those seeds will bear fruit this time," Grace added.

"Are you going to have a rehearsal on Saturday?" Reverend Praise asked them.

"No! We have decided just to talk about it when everybody gathers at my house. We want to keep it real simple; we are going to ask Mr. and Mrs. Yalley this evening to be our best man and matron of honor. This is how I have planned our entry. Mr. and Mrs. Yalley will come in first. Mr. Yalley will go to the right and Mercy to the left when they get to the altar. Followed by Little Sam, the ring bearer, and Nelta, the flower girl. Little Sam will join Mr. Yalley and Nelta, joining Mercy. We will then walk in hand in hand with my parents on our left and Sam's parents on our right. When it's time for the rings, Sam's dad will step forward and help little Sam give them to us," Grace told Reverend Praise.

"I think that will be so nice and beautiful. I can't wait to see it unfold," Reverend Praise told them. "Okay then, I think we are set for Sunday, we have covered everything we need to cover so far. I am so excited," he added as he rubbed his two palms together.

"We want to thank you for all that you are doing for us. I'm so humbled when I think of how God is blessing us through so many people," Sam said as he choked back tears.

"He just wanted to let you know that he is real, and when he said he will bless us to be a blessing, he meant it. We are a blessed church, and we are honored to be a blessing to others. He said goodness and mercy shall follow you all the days of your life, and we are just one of the many ways he is going to use to bless you two, so just receive it, enjoy it, and pass it on," Reverend Praise told them.

"We got everything covered, so let's pray and thank God for a wonderful meeting and call it a day," he told them. "Father, I thank you for the life of Sam and Grace, thank you for rescuing them on their way to hell and clothing them with your righteousness. Thank you for making them a testimony, that you are a God who restores. Where there was bitterness, you brought forgiveness. I thank you that Sam and Grace have experienced your forgiveness and are able to forgive each other. Let them be the couple that brings hope to a dying and confused marriage. We are going to rejoice on Sunday, and Satan will finally be put to shame.

"We pray for all those unsaved family members and friends who will be there on Sunday that your presence will clothe them and destroy all the strongholds and bondages that will prevent them from saying yes to you when you come calling them to your table of salvation. Create a strong desire in them to say yes to you when the altar call is made.

"I pray your blessing on all the ladies who will be baking and doing all the finger foods, the decorations, and any other things that they will do to make Sam and Grace's day beautiful. Bless them beyond their expectations. In Jesus' name we pray. Amen and Amen."

"Amen! Amen!" Sam and Grace responded.

"Thank you very much," Sam said as they both stood up.

"You are both welcome," he told them as he stretched out his hand to give them a handshake. After that he walked them to the door and bid them goodbye.

"Thank you, Lord, for your goodness," he prayed as he closed his office door.

Sam and Grace decided to go home and pay the Yalleys a brief visit before picking up Little Sam from school.

"There is somebody at the door," shouted Mercy from the kitchen.

"Okay! I will get it," Mr. Yalley said as he rushed to the door, but for a moment he saw Sam and Grace standing there. He thought he had opened the door, but to his surprise the door bell rang again and Mercy shouted, "Get the door!" He then realized he just saw a vision of who was behind his door. *There goes my divine gift in action. I wonder why they are here,* he thought. As he reached out to open the door, he saw Mercy dressed up nicely in a dress she bought three months ago, and she looked so beautiful. *Oh, they are coming to ask Mercy to be their matron of honor, that will be so nice. It is so wonderful to know the future,* he thought as he opened the door with a big smile on his face.

"Surprise!" said Sam and Grace when he opened the door.

"Oh my goodness! What a surprise. Look at the two of

you, so dressed up. What is the occasion?" he asked them. "Come on in and feel at home."

Mercy heard their voices and came out of the kitchen.

"Hello! What a nice surprise," she said with all smiles as she walked toward them. "May I offer you something to drink?"

"No thanks, we are fine," said Grace.

"Okay, then," Mercy said as she sat beside her husband ready to hear what the Lukens had on their minds.

"Is everything all right with you two, and how is the wedding preparation going on?" Mr. Yalley asked, pretending he had no idea why they were there.

"The days are really numbered now," Mercy said with a smile.

"Well, we just came from Reverend Praise's office for our one-day counseling section," Big Sam told them.

"All right! How did it go?" Mercy asked them.

"It was wonderful," Grace responded. "He asked us how we met, and bringing all those memories back to life was just wonderful," she added.

"I remember mine like it was just yesterday," Mercy said as she looked into her husband's face. Mr. Yalley gently tapped her on the shoulder in agreement because to him it was like beating all odds and winning the lottery; she had been untouchable because her dad was very strict with his girls, but in his heart he knew that she was his girl. *This memory will forever be special to me,* thought Mr. Yalley.

Big Sam cleared his throat and spoke up, "Well, the reason we stopped by is to ask the two of you to be our best man and matron of honor."

The Yalleys sat there for a few minutes without saying anything.

"Are you sure?" Mercy finally responded, sounding very surprised.

"Yes! Yes! We are sure!" Sam assured them. "Our parents are still together, and that is a good thing to see, but when it comes to the godly part, we have nobody out there we want to emulate like you two, and it would be our pleasure to see the two of you standing beside us with your support," Sam told them.

"We are so honored to hear that, and we will gladly do that," Mr. Yalley told them as Mercy looked on with all smiles.

"Thank you very much," said Grace.

"You are welcome," Mr. Yalley responded.

"I think I know what to wear already," Mercy said.

"I bet is one of those dresses that have the tag on for two years in the closet begging to be worn," Mr. Yalley said, laughing.

Mercy playfully hit him with the sofa pillow and said, "Don't be silly." Sam soon joined in the laughter.

"They are good at that, but they always don't have anything to wear," Sam said.

"You two are ganging up on us, but you have forgotten that is why we are called women," Grace said, and they all started laughing again.

"Mercy doesn't go to the extreme to confess. If you are raised by Pastor Matthew, you will learn to be modest," Mr. Yalley said, defending his wife.

"Thanks, honey!" Mercy said, smiling.

"I don't have anything to say about that," Sam said, sounding funny.

"I know, it is because of the old Grace you knew, but you are looking at a new Grace," Grace responded with pride.

"Let me hear more," Sam said in a teasing way.

"Well, you know I love to look good, so I shop to keep up with myself, but when I became a single mom, I realized I could not live like that anymore. It was difficult at first, but I was committed to the change and now I'm free of unnecessary shopping," Grace told them. "As a matter of fact, for the past eight months, I have bought two blouses, one pair of pants, one pair of shoes, and one much needed jacket as compare to, so to me that is a big accomplishment," she added.

"Honey, I am so proud of you, although that was not a problem when we were married, because I admired the way you dressed up and carried yourself all the time. Eventually I learned from that, especially how to coordinate colors whether dressing up or down. You remember how I didn't care and you used to say, 'Sam, for heaven's sake, it's a dinner party. Please don't wear that,' and I would say that is my style. Eventually nobody had to tell me to pay attention to my clothes, so I give you the credit for being the fashion lady, but with this new attitude toward spending, I think I will join you so that we could save more and do better things with the money, for we are not growing younger," Sam told her.

"You know, as Christians God expects us to be good stewards of the things that he blesses us with, and that include the money that comes into our hands. I'm glad the two of you are going to start your new life on that note. Well, well. Life is full of lessons, and we will all continue to learn till we leave this world," said Mr. Yalley.

"Anybody want fresh-baked cookies?" Mercy asked.

"No, thanks, it is time for us to go and get Little Sam," Sam said.

"You sure you don't want to try even one?" Mercy persisted.

"Okay! We will," Grace said. Mercy went to the kitchen and returned with a tray full of cookies and paper napkins.

Big Sam reached out for the napkin first and said, "One for me, one for Little Sam." He quickly put one in his mouth and started eating it up. "Hmm, yummy! That tastes good, what kind of cookie is that?"

"My grandma's shortbread cookies," Mercy told him.

"This is a killer cookie," he jokingly said as he put another one in his mouth.

"Can I have another one?" he asked.

"Help yourself," Mercy told him.

"Okay then, two for me and two for Little Sam," he said as he helped himself again.

Meanwhile Grace was standing there admiring his playfulness.

"What about me?" she asked. Sam turned and looked at her and said, "Have you changed your mind?" he asked her.

"Changed my mind about what?" Grace asked him with a look of surprise on her face.

"I thought you said you had stopped eating cookies?" Sam asked her, looking serious. Grace realized he was playing a game with her, so she responded and said, "Oh yea! I remember telling you when I was sleep walking the other night." They all started laughing, including Mr. Yalley, who was still sitting in the living room listening to them.

"Please, help yourselves, or else I will be eating grandma's cookies for dessert for the next two weeks," Mr. Yalley told them as he stood up to join them, and they all started laughing again.

Mercy turned toward him and said, "You're right about that, Paul, you better convince them to help you out, because that is exactly what is going to happen for the next two weeks or more," Mercy told her husband, and that brought more laughter.

Grace reached out for a napkin and helped herself with six cookies. "Thanks, Mercy," she said.

"You are welcome," Mercy responded.

"Sam, we need to go now," Grace said as she reached out for her husband's hand. Hand in hand they said their good-byes and stepped out of the Yalleys' house.

"I'm so happy for them," Mr. Yalley said as he closed the door behind them.

"Oh, honey, we got to be their best man and matron of honor," Mercy said, sounding excited.

"I will finally wear that dress I bought three months ago on sale, although for nothing and for no reason, it now has a purpose, Mercy added.

"I will say the Holy Spirit knows the future and got you prepared for this day," Mr. Yalley told his wife without saying anything about the vision he saw.

"I agree with you and I'm so grateful he is always looking out for us," said Mercy. I can't wait to dress up on Sunday. I love weddings. They always bring tears to my eyes. I can't wait to see my Paul take a bride one day," Mercy added with a sweet smile on her face.

"We have to wait till he meets Joyce first."

"Well, you're right! I wonder how he is dealing with the fact that he knows her name. Do ask him about that sometime," Mercy told her husband.

"No, I have decided not to bring it up anymore till he does that. I know emotionally he is very stable, but this is new to him, and I don't want him to experience any emotional rollercoaster when it comes to it."

"You're right about that, let's just keep on praying for him, and when the time is right, the chosen Joyce will show up," Mercy told her husband. "I will call him this evening and just love on him," she added with a smile.

Mercy called Paul, and they stayed on the phone for over one hour just fellowshipping. He was happy to hear his mother was going to be Grace's matron of honor.

"Mom, remember to take some picture, okay?" Paul said.

"I will do that and print them out before you come home," Mercy promised her son. Mercy went to bed that night with plans to go to the beauty shop to get her hair done. *I wonder whether my hair dresser will still be there. I will call first thing in the morning to find out,* she thought and drifted off to sleep.

Grace, on the other hand, stayed up late with Big Sam just talking. It was past midnight before they finally went to bed. Grace fell asleep immediately as she settled into bed.

———————————

Grace got out of bed with one thing on her mind. *Today is my last day as a single woman.* But she quickly realized it was going to be a very hectic day. *I didn't go through the traditional wedding planning, so I am not stressed out, but to have a houseful of people today is going to be another story.*

When she finished getting herself ready for the day, she went straight to the kitchen to start cooking, and to her surprise Sam was already fixing breakfast.

"Oh! You are up. I was going to bring you breakfast in bed," he told her with one of his big smiles.

"That would have been really nice. I missed being waited upon like a queen this morning," Grace said jokily. Just then Little Sam walked into the kitchen with a look of hunger on his face, and it was clear that he was not in the mood to talk to any of them.

"Hi, Little Sam, you are up early today. I thought Saturdays were your sleep-in days," Grace asked her son. Big Sam picked him up, pretending he was heavy just to put a smile on his face.

"Little Sam, you weigh about a thousand pounds; you are growing so fast and getting too heavy for me. Oh my goodness, I'm about to break my back," Big Sam said as he put him down slowly.

"Daddy! You are just pretending. I am not that heavy," Little Sam said, giggling.

"Breakfast is ready. Go and brush you teeth so that we can

eat together," Big Sam told him with a playful smack on his back.

"Okay, Daddy," Little Sam said as he rushed to the bathroom to do just that.

During breakfast Sam and Grace made their final plans for the day and Sunday. By 6:00 p.m. her house would be full with family members—Sam's parents as well as her parents and a few relatives from both sides. They decided that Sam would sleep in the hotel that night and Grace would join him on Sunday after the ceremony, and on Monday they would travel to Sam's place to spend the remaining days of their honeymoon. Sam's parents would do the same, as well as two relatives. Grace's parents would spend the night in Little Sam's room, and the remaining relatives would sleep anywhere they could lay their heads in the house. Sunday night his parents would move from the hotel into Little Sam's room and her parents will move into her room with Little Sam, they will stay on to watch him till she is back from her honeymoon.

She was surprised when her dad offered to stay and watch him. She felt he wanted to seize the opportunity and make up for not seeing his first grandson as much as they wanted to. It really worked out well because Little Sam would not miss a day of school. He adored his grandparents, and they knew he was going to have fun with them around him for a week. Sam's parents would leave on Monday morning, as well as the few relatives who spent the night because they didn't want to drive in the night.

After their discussions Sam told Grace they should pray, so they held hands, and he prayed, "Father, we now understand you are the giver of every good thing. Something good is happening to us, and we thank you for it. I am so grateful for giving me back my family. We pray for all the people who will be traveling here to support us. Watch over them and bring them safely here. We pray that there will be peace among all the relatives who will gather here. Let there be joy, laughter, and celebration.

"I pray that Grace and I will have a good night's sleep, so that we will wake up tomorrow morning full of energy for our big day. Thank you for new beginnings, and we know that with you on our side everything will be all right, thank you Jesus. In the name of Jesus we pray, Amen."

"Amen! Amen!" Grace and Little Sam said. Little Sam took off to watch his favorite Saturday morning show, and Sam and Grace cleaned up and started cooking immediately so that they could all eat together in the evening.

"This is going to look like we are having pre-wedding party," said Sam.

"We prayed for joy, laughter, and celebration. We are in for an unplanned party then. We will just flow into whatever this dinner turns out to be. Grace said laughing. They decided to cook a couple of dishes to stuff the fridge and freezer so that her parents wouldn't have to cook for a few days.

When they were done cooking, the kitchen looked like a tornado had just passed through. They took their time and cleaned up and put every pot and utensil in its place.

"Two hands are better than one," Grace said with a grateful heart as she looked around the kitchen one more time before stepping out. Sam enjoyed every bit of their time together in the kitchen, especially when they bumped into each other as they move around. It became a game of expectation for him as he looked out for that moment again, and he was full of gratefulness and joy that when Grace said, "Two hands are better than one." He couldn't find words to respond, so he just nodded with a smile. *If only she could see or feel how I am feeling right now, she would understand why I couldn't find words to respond,* he thought.

They both changed their cloths and freshened up; they came to the living room to relax before their visitors started walking through the door. They were able to relax for two hours before they heard a car honking outside. Little Sam rushed to the window and started shouting, "Grandpa! Grandma!"

Grace and Sam looked at each other, and the look on their faces clearly said which grandparents he was talking about. Grace looked at the clock, and it was 5:00 p.m. Little Sam by now was struggling to open the front door so that he could run out of the house into the arms of his grandparents.

"Sam, relax, let me open it for you," Grace told him with Big Sam right behind them. When she finally opened the door, there were her parents coming up the stairs.

"Hi Mom and Dad!" she said.

"Welcome," said Big Sam. Little Sam was jumping up and down in front of his grandpa, shouting "Grandpa! Grandpa! Grandpa!" His grandpa picked him up and walked into the house with him. Shortly after that Sam's parents also arrived. After they settled in, Sam and Grace quickly took them across the street to introduce them to the Yalleys. The Yalleys were so pleased to meet them. They chatted for a while, and Grace said, "Sorry, we have to go, we have a few more relatives coming."

"You are going to have a house full, do you want me to help you with some cooking, you know I will love to do that," Mercy told Grace.

"Thanks! you are always so thoughtful. Sam and I did a lot of cooking today, so don't worry about that, but my parents will stay on to take care of Little Sam, so you can get together with them whilst we are gone," said Grace.

"Well, that sounds good to us, and we will get to know each other more," Mercy responded.

"You both have wonderful children and is been such a blessing to know them. We are so happy for them, now they can grow old together just like us," Mr. Yalley said with a little laugh.

"Thank you two for being a good neighbor to them for us," Mr. Luken Sr. said.

They said their goodbyes and left. Before long Grace had a house full of relatives with few children included. Little Sam was glad to have them to play with, but because he was used to being by himself, he soon got tired of them and started complaining about everything.

Dinner was served around 7:00 p.m. Eating, talking, and catching up with each other as well as teasing here and there brought laughter all over the house. It created an atmosphere of joy, laughter, and celebration just as they had prayed for. It was such fun, laughter, and merrymaking that Big Sam wished he could be part of it all night long, but he had to take his tired parents who were already dosing off after the big dinner to the hotel.

Big Sam was getting ready to leave when Grace said, "Honey, wait a few minutes. I need to tell them how we are going to walk down the aisle."

"Attention, please! I have something to tell you all." Everybody turned to give her their undivided attention. "This wedding is going to be a simple but blessed wedding you can ever imagine. As you all know the wedding will be immediately after the main service. I learned they will reserve a few pews in the front for us, so I will advise you to be there by 9:30 a.m., the service will start at 10:00 a.m. When the service is over, remain in your seat unless you have to use the bathroom, the service will end at 12:00 p.m., and we will walk in by 12:30 p.m."

When she finished explaining the rest of the order of events, she asked, "So, what do you all think?"

"I think that is great," one of Grace's aunties said, and everybody agreed with her. She later on thanked Nelta's mother, for preparing her from head to toe to be her flower girl even though she didn't ask her.

"Thank you all for coming to support us, and it is really good to see you all again. I hope you will have a good night sleep and be ready for our big day tomorrow," Grace told them with a little shout. Sam stood beside her with his left arm around her shoulder, supporting her in every way. After a little while, Grace began to feel the warmth of his arm and wished her speech will not end so that she can continue to enjoy the closeness. *It is only a couple of hours away, and this strong arm will be all mine again,* she thought as Sam removed his arm.

"We will not miss this for anything," Aunt Power told her.

"Thank you Aunt Power. I really appreciate that," she responded.

There is something about her that Grace never liked, but she was the only one who kept in touch with her after her divorce and always had something comforting to tell her. *I don't know why I never liked her. I guess is one of those things that you just don't like somebody for no reason. Lord, if there is nothing in her that I should be careful about, please help me to like her,* she prayed.

Finally, Sam and his parents made their way out, Grace walked them to the car, and for the first time Sam pulled her close and gave her a squeeze, planted a kiss on her lips, and whispered, "I love you," in her ears as he pulled away from her.

"I love you too, sleep tight and see you tomorrow morning," Grace told her with one of her warm smiles. *Oh, I can't wait for tomorrow,* Grace thought.

Back in the house, Grace brought out all the pillows, bed sheets, and blankets she could find in her house to be used. She helped Little Sam get ready for bed, and she went in and took a long warm bath. After that she felt calm and relaxed, before she jumped into bed, she took her dress out of the bag and hung it on the closet door, the veil on top and the shoes in front of the dress. "This is the first thing I want to see tomorrow morning," she said. She quickly got into bed and lay there day dreaming about how lucky she was to be in this position and all that will take place tomorrow. She and Sam decided to write their own vows, and she can't wait to read it to him and hear his as well. As she drifted off to sleep, her last thought lingered on the fact that in a couple of hours she is going to walk into a world that she is very familiar with but this time with new beginnings and God Almighty as the foundation, Jesus as their mediator, and the Holy Spirit as their helper. *Who doesn't want this?* She thought as she drifted off into a deep peaceful sleep with a smile on her face.

Mr. Yalley was able to fast for three days with Mercy supporting him. They prayed without ceasing for all the assignments God gave Mr. Yalley. As they were having their evening prayers, Mr. Yalley saw a vision of a woman driving a green car who had Grace and Sam's names written in red on a black paper. She was driving fast and chanting at the same time. She would call Grace and Sam's names in between the chanting. *Who is* this *woman?* Mr. Yalley thought. The Holy Spirit spoke in his spirit and said, *she is one of Grace's aunties. She is coming to the wedding tomorrow. As a matter of fact, she was the negative force behind their break up. She was surprised to hear they were getting married again, so she is coming with an evil intent to bring confusion between them. She bought Grace one of her favorite perfume and wants to find a way to be part of her dressing team so that she can give it to her. She will then insist she put a little on, and the intention is to cast a spell on her that will make her regret what she is doing. When it is time for them to exchange their vows, Grace will be full of regrets and sadness and will become very angry at Sam. That will be the beginning of their nightmare.*

What she doesn't know is that Sam and Grace are my children now, and I am the foundation of this marriage. Greater is he that is in them than he that is of the world. No weapon formed against them shall prosper. She thinks they are the same old Sam and Grace; she doesn't know that they have been redeemed by the precious blood of my son, Jesus Christ, and I have put a wedge of protection around them.

Sam and Grace are baby Christians, and there are doors that are still open in their lives for the enemy to come in, but I know their hearts, and sooner or later they will come into full knowledge of what they are up against, as well as the power within them to overcome any plan of the enemy.

Pray that Lucinda will not have access to the dressing room in the church. Pray for her soul, for she will be one of the people who will come to know me during the ceremony.

One look at her husband, and Mercy knew something was happening in the spirit, so she kept quiet and prayed silently for him.

"Wow! That is interesting," Mr. Yalley finally said.

"What is it, honey?" Mercy asked him calmly.

"The Lord just showed me that Grace has an aunty call Lucinda who was the negative force behind Sam's change of attitude that led to their divorce. She is surprised they are getting back together, so she is coming to the wedding to cast a spell on Grace so that she will regret her decision to marry Sam again. At this point there is nothing she can do, so she will say her vows with such anger toward Sam, and that will be the beginning of their nightmare," Mr. Yalley told his wife.

"What? I can't not believe this. Satan is really busy," Mercy said loudly.

"Yes, he is really busy, that is why we can not relax in our prayers at all," Mr. Yalley responded. "The Lord said they are baby Christians and still have some open doors that Satan can use to bring a level of confusion in their lives. He said I should pray so that Lucinda does not make it to her dressing room. She bought Grace her favorite perfume, which she mixed up with a spell and plans to give it to her as a gift before the ceremony. She will encourage her to use some, and when Grace sees that bottle of perfume, she won't be able to resist it, and that is how her troubles will begin," Mr. Yalley added.

Mercy stood up and was ready to wage a war in the spirit. "Father! In the name of Jesus, we are bringing Lucinda before your throne; you said everything that has a name will bow to your name. I command the evil spirit in Lucinda to bow right now. I command the spell or the potion to bow in the name of Jesus. You said that prayers of the righteous avail much; we stand in the gap for Sam and Grace. At your own time you've made all things beautiful for them, and it is only by your grace and mercy that they've found love in each other again. Satan has been defeated in every area of the lives; we arrest every plan of the enemy and wrap it in the blood. Satan, you have been exposed, you are a liar and once again you have been defeated!"

Mercy prayed as she walked up and down in the living room with her husband following and shouting, "Amen! Amen! In Jesus' name! Oh! Thank you, Lord," affirming what Mercy was saying. When Mercy stopped Mr. Yalley picked up from there.

"Father, thank you for enabling my spirit to see beyond what my eyes cannot see, thank you for revealing this to us and using us to stand in the gap for them. You said anything that we bind on earth will be bound in heaven, so we bind every plan of the enemy. I bless them with your peace, joy, and calmness as they go through tomorrow. Grant them such peaceful sleep so that they will wake up refreshed and ready for the day. With this we pray in Jesus' name, Amen," Mr. Yalley prayed.

"Amen!" Mercy said with a shout.

They sat down in silence for a while because the presence of God was so strong on them. "Oh! God is good," Mr. Yalley said finally, breaking the silence. "Moments like this make me want to stand on my rooftop and shout, my God is real, he is tangible, and you can feel him, people are really missing on who God really is, all the funny ideas they have come up with," he added.

"If you go on that roof top, your neighbors will think you are getting crazy," Mercy said, laughing.

"Only the religious people will think I'm crazy, but those who have been born of the Spirit and have experienced His presence will know what I am talking about," Mr. Yalley responded. "Religion has done so much harm to Christianity. God have mercy on us," he added.

"Hey! That is my name, you know, I cannot give it out like that," Mercy said with a serious face and then started laughing. Her husband looked at her for a while and said, "That is funny," and started laughing as well.

Mercy looked at the clock. It was 10:00 p.m. "Well, it is time to get some sleep, for we have a big day tomorrow," said Mercy as she stretched her arms on the couch. Mr. Yalley stood up, went to the kitchen, and drank a tall glass of water.

"You were really thirsty," Mercy told him as he put the glass down.

"I think so, water is the best fluid for your body anyway, and I thank God I still have the taste for it, there are a lot of people out there who cannot stand the taste of water, and they continue to poison their bodies with all kinds of liquids," said Mr. Yalley.

"You are a hundred percent right, honey," Mercy responded. Hand in hand they walked together to the bedroom to catch a good night's sleep.

Grace woke up around 5:00 a.m. and stayed in bed thinking about nothing in particular. As she lay there it dawned on her that this was the last time she would wake up by herself in the morning. She remembered Sam's funny way of snoring sometimes and started laughing. This always made her laugh, because his snoring sounded like somebody playing the organ on a high pitch. *Sam has never accepted the fact that he snores. I guess anybody who snores never admits to it,* she thought.

She turned on her side and looked at her wedding dress for a long time, admiring everything about it. The other day she realized from her engagement ring box that it was the same designer who designed her dress. The ring was very expensive, and she can imagine how much the dress could have cost, she lay there just being thankful.

She looked at her clock again, and it was 6:15. She prayed and thanked God for the day and asked him to watch over all of them. "Time to get up! " She told herself as she quickly pull herself out of bed and went straight to the bathroom to take a shower. She turned her shower on and was beginning to enjoy the warm water running all over her body when she heard her phone ringing. She knew it was Sam, so she wiped her left hand and quickly reached out and picked up her bathroom phone.

"Hello, Sam, how are you, did you sleep well, and are you ready for your big day?" she asked him, excited to hear from him.

"How did you know I was the one calling?"

"The power of love helped me," she said with a little giggle.

"I like that. Anyway, I was just calling to let you know how much I love and adore you. I can't wait to take my Gracy home," he told her.

"Well, thank you, my one and only Sam," she responded.

"Listen, one of my friends has offered to pick you up to the church in his brand new car, by the way his name is Dan. I have given him the address and your telephone number, so be expecting him," Sam told her.

"Do I know him?" she asked.

"No, you don't, that is why the name didn't sound familiar to you, but trust me he is one of the good guys in the office. I was always avoiding him, but now I know it was because he was a Christian, you are in good hands, so just enjoy the ride," said Sam.

"Okay, honey, love you and see you soon," Grace told her husband-to-be.

"Love you too," he responded and hung up.

Grace hung up her phone, and it started ringing again. Grace picked it up, and it was Mercy.

"Hi Grace, I was just checking on you," she told her. "Did you have a good night's sleep and ready for your big day?"

"Oh! Mercy, that is so sweet and thoughtful of you. I slept well, and I have been up a little over an hour now. I kind of laid in bed for a while, just enjoying my last hours of sleeping by myself as a single woman," Grace told her with a laugh.

"Well, I hope you enjoyed every bit of it, but you know it is wonderful the other way round too," Mercy told her.

"I know what you mean, if you have tasted a good marriage before, it is no fun being single, so I am really looking forward to becoming Mrs. Luken in a few hours," Grace responded with a laugh.

"Take care, and I will see you at the church," said Mercy.

"Thanks, Mercy, and see you later," Grace said and hung up.

Grace quickly finished taking her shower and got dressed. She helped Little Sam get ready as well. Everybody in the house did the same; they all had breakfast and were ready to get out the door by the time Grace's ride arrived. Her parents and Little Sam rode with her.

Mr. and Mrs. Yalley had a good night's sleep, and they both woke up looking forward to a wonderful day. They ate a light breakfast and then dressed up, looking their very best for the occasion. Mr. Yalley gave his wife a lot of compliments. It had been a long time since he had seen Mercy dressed up and looking so gorgeous.

———————

When the Yalleys came out of their house, they were surprised to see the number of cars lined up in front of Grace's house.

"I didn't know there were going to be so many people like this. I would have insisted to help her with something," said Mercy.

"That would have been nice but am sure they got everything under control," Mr. Yalley told his wife.

As they drove off, Mr. Yalley wondered about how everything went with the assignment he was given last Sunday. He knew in his heart that God has taken care of every one of them, but there is this longing in his heart to know the end results.

Good job, my son, the Holy Spirit spoke up.

"What?" Mr. Yalley said, thinking Mercy was telling him something.

Mercy looked at him and asked, "Did you just say something?"

Just then he realized it was the Holy Spirit.

"Never mind, honey," he told her. Now he is all ears to listen to the Holy Spirit. Five minutes passed without a word, and it felt like he had been waiting for one hour, then he spoke again. Mr. Yalley breathed a sigh of relief, because he thought that not recognizing his voice immediately made him miss God.

Good job, Son, you stood in the gap and prayed without ceasing, Satan has been defeated. Mr. Montey is a godly man in heart; he loves me with all his heart. Wearing ladies underwear will not take anything away from who he is in me. It is just his choice and preference.

Mr. Yalley caught himself laughing; he immediately stopped and said, "Sorry."

"What is funny, and why are you sorry?" Mercy asked him.

"Honey, the phone lines are busy," he told her. Mercy immediately knew he was talking with the Holy Spirit, so she began to pray quietly for him.

Annabelle has been set free from the seductive spirit and Peter is a relieved man. His wife has already noticed the change.

Pearl told her parent, and they embraced her with love. They have already had a meeting with the pastor; he decided they should announce it next Sunday instead, because of what is going on at the church today. Continue to pray for Pearl, she is still dealing with the betrayal and hurt.

Joshua didn't smoke the pot and two of the boys he hangs out with are in church with him today. One of them will respond to the altar call, and he would lead the other one to Christ in two weeks. Eventually a Bible study group would come out of that.

Angel realized where she was heading and that scared her, so she confessed to her family. They are all praying and looking out for her. Her husband realized that too much traveling on his part somehow had contributed to the situation, so he is making other arrangements to reduce the number of days he travels in a month.

Mr. Guide became very scared because he knew he had been exposed, so with a humble heart he repented, apologized to his wife. Just as I told you, in a restaurant full of people he apologized once again. I delivered him from the spirit of anger, and immediately he did that. I have filled him afresh with understanding, toler-ance, patience, gentleness, and laughter. He is amazed about the way he feels free inside-out and how he is not making big deal out of everything. He has realized how my joy is his strength and how laughter is truly medicine to the bones. You are going to meet him in the hallway, and with all smiles he will give you a firm

*handshake and say, "Thanks, Mr. Yalley." That is all he is going to
say, because he knows you will understand what that means, and
your response will be, "You are welcome, brother, enjoy the service."
Good and faithful servant, your prayers went forth and did their
work.*

*The next thing I want you to do is to pray for Theresa and
Pat. You know they've been friends for a long time and have truly
been there for each other all these years. Theresa as you know has
been wheelchair bound for years and Pat has been confined by her
daughter's situation for years as well. I never reveal the future to
my children, but that which I have spoken about them will come
to pass. Pray that they will both hold onto the fact that I know the
plans I have for them, to give them a future and a hope. Pray that
my joy will always be their strength. Pray, pray for them, for there
are times they become weary in their situation and the enemy seizes
the opportunity to steal their joy. Pray that they will always hold
onto the fact that I have not forgotten about them and never will
I. I just want them to be still and know that I am God. Enjoy the
day; all will be well with the Lukens.*

With these there was silence, and Mr. Yalley knew the
Holy Spirit was done with him. *They are so beautiful inside-
out, such sweet ladies,* he thought as their faces flashed through
his mind.

Mercy advised herself not ask any questions, so when they
got to the church, she came out of the car smiling and ready
for the day. Just as the Holy Spirit said, Mr. Yalley met Mr.
Guide in the hallway of the church; he walked toward them
with all smiles and gave him a firm handshake.

"Thank you, Mr. Yalley," he said.

"You're welcome, brother, enjoy the service," Mr. Yalley
responded just as the Holy Spirit instructed him to do. Mr.
Guide quickly vanished into the crowd. *Is a blessing to know I
have a direct line to heaven and the lines are so clear,* Mr. Yalley

thought with a peaceful smile on his face as they made their way into the sanctuary.

Mr. and Mr. Yalley quickly found a place to sit and joined in the worship. The praise and worship team were singing their hearts out, and a person would be dead not to feel the presence of God. The joy of the Lord was on everybody's faces because what was happening in the spirit realm was very contagious.

Lord, thank you for blessing us with your presence. Thank you for making your presence so tangible and real to us. We are truly a blessed church. Anything that is not of you would either bow to the name of Jesus Christ or flee. Thank you, Lord; you have power to overcome all things both in the natural and in the spirit. I know right now that whoever Lucinda is, you are delivering her from her evil ways, Mercy found herself praying silently.

The moment the praise and worship ended, the groom and the bride and their team quickly left to start getting ready. Grace was tempted to stop by the fellowship hall to see what the women were up to, but she talked herself out of it, because she wanted it to be another surprise.

Aunt Lucinda, on the other hand, was in haste to go and do evil and didn't pay attention to her gas gauge. She took off speeding as fast as she could, and thirty minutes into her driving the empty tank light came on. The worst part was she was in the middle of nowhere and she was so dressed up that she was too embarrassed to come out of her car and wave for help. She sat in her car frustrated for almost thirty minutes, finally she came out, and the first car she waved at stopped. It was an off duty police officer who luckily had a gallon of gas he was going to use for his lawn mower. He quickly gave it to her as a Good Samaritan, and Lucinda thanked him for his kindness.

"Oh! It's good to be kind or do what is right. It makes you feel good about yourself, and you are blessed in return. For anything we do, whether good or bad we will reap a harvest of good or bad," the officer told her without knowing what she was up to.

Lucinda started feeling very uneasy about all this long talk, but with a straight face she managed to say, "You're right officer, thanks again. Sorry I have to leave now, for I'm running late to a wedding." With that she quickly got into her car.

The officer waved and said, "Have a nice day, ma'am." Lucinda waved back and drove off feeling a little guilty because of what the officer said, but she quickly suppressed the thought. Little did she know what awaited her at Emmanuel Church of God.

Lucinda finally arrived at the church very late; she put her nicely wrapped gift in her purse and rushed to the church. The bridal team was already in the changing room getting ready. An usher greeted her at the entrance.

"Hello, and welcome to the house of God," he said.

Lucinda looked up and said, "Thanks, I'm here for the wedding."

"Okay! Follow me then," he told her. He walked quickly in front of her and ushered her through a door that brought her to where the groom's and the bride's families were seated. She found herself seated among some relatives that she had stopped talking to.

Reverend Praise was preaching about loving your neighbor as yourself, and that really made her very uncomfortable. On top of that she couldn't turn her head to look left, right, or behind her without having eye contact with some of her enemies, so she kept her head straight with her eyes fixed on the pastor.

The church service was over within thirty-five minutes after she was seated, and she was glad it was over but very angry about the message she just heard. *Who can love his or her neighbor as themselves? Crazy neighbors, annoying relatives, back-biting friends, hypocrites all over the place? I have no time for that,* she thought.

Little did she know that the love of God can enable a person to love his or her enemies. He paid the ultimate price for the sins of everybody, and no one can hold anything against her neighbors, friends, relatives, or anybody else. But Lucinda had no idea about this.

"After the benediction I want you all to remain in your seats unless you have somewhere to go or you have some other personal reasons to leave. We are going to have a wedding ceremony. If you stay you will find out who they are and more about them. There will be refreshments for everybody in the fellowship hall immediately after the ceremony, thank you all for being part of this special day in their life," Reverend Praise told the congregation.

A handful of people left, but it didn't make any difference at all; the church was still packed full.

Grace looked so beautiful in her simple but elegant gown; words could not describe how she was feeling inside standing next to Sam and waiting to walk in together.

Mr. Yalley couldn't take his eyes off his wife; she looked incredibly beautiful in her dress, which was just perfect for the occasion. It has been a long time since she dressed up like that, a long satin skirt with a split at the back and a beaded top. Her pearl necklace was a gift he gave her two years ago on their anniversary, and she always said she looked overdressed anytime she tried to dress up with it. Today was just a perfect day to show them off, and you could see she was enjoying every bit of the attention she was getting. Mr. Yalley squeezed her hand and whispered in her ears, "Honey, you look so gorgeous."

"Thanks, and you also look like the real Prince Charming," she responded with a smile and admiration in her eyes.

The choir started singing "Great Is Thy Faithfulness" as requested by Sam and Grace. When they started on the second verse, as planned, the Yalleys walked in and parted ways at the altar. Little Sam and Nelta followed, looking so cute, everybody started cheering them up as they walked down the aisle. As instructed they parted ways at the altar, Little Sam joining Mr. Yalley on the right and Nelta joining Mercy on the left.

Everybody gasped when Sam and Grace walked in, she looked so beautiful from head to toe, and Sam looked like a movie star. Mrs. Jackson, the children's ministry coordinator asked Mrs. Zinak sitting next to her, "Is the matron of honor her sister?"

"Mrs. Jackson, I think you need your glasses. That is Mercy. Don't you see her husband standing over there as the best man?" she told her with a laugh.

"I recognized him, and I was wondering where she was, knowing how inseparable they are. Oh my God, she looks so beautiful, elegant, and breathtaking. She seems to be tall as well," said Mrs. Jackson with a look of surprise mixed with admiration.

She is a beautiful middle-aged woman, but now she looks ten years younger. She looks taller with her heels on and is just breathtaking to look at her, she thought.

Mrs. Jackson was not alone; a lot of people couldn't believe their eyes when they recognized Mercy. Mercy could feel all the admiration that was going on, and she was really enjoying every bit of it.

Sam and Grace stood before Reverend Praise with both parents standing beside them. When the song ended, Reverend Praise spoke up and said, "Don't they look beautiful?"

Everybody started cheering and clapping their hands upon hearing that. This brought Sam and Grace nearly to tears, because they felt so honored and were full of the joy of the Lord, they found themselves smiling with gratitude.

"What is happening here today is a testimony to the body

of Christ. Sam and Grace were once married; Sam got bored with the marriage and divorced her. They both moved on, Grace relocated with their only child, but a little over a year after that he came begging for forgiveness. Before Grace could respond, she gave her life to the Lord, as well as their son, and because of the grace and mercy of God, she gave him the second chance, he asked for.

Sam followed her to church the following Sunday and gave his life to God as well. They found love again in each other. God has restored what Satan tried to destroy, hallelujah! Praise the Lord for his goodness," Reverend Praise told them with a shout. There was hallelujah response here and there in the congregation, and some stood up to clap their hands.

"No weapon formed against these two shall prosper because Jesus Christ is in their hearts now, and God is the foundation of this marriage," said Reverend Praise. A few people shouted Amen! Amen! In affirmation to what he just said.

Lucinda was getting very irritated, the demons were tormenting her for bringing them to a place where the name of Jesus Christ is mentioned, so anytime the name Jesus Christ is mentioned they pinch her, and she will feel this explosion in her head, and then she will start having a terrible headache. She wanted to leave but couldn't make herself get up, so she started fidgeting all over the place, looking into her purse every second. A woman sitting next to her asked her whether she was okay. She looked at her but couldn't say anything. The look on Lucinda's face told the woman there was something wrong with her.

Lord, help this lady, if is deliverance that she needs, please don't let her leave without your touch, she silently prayed for Lucinda.

The praise and worship team started singing again, and the whole atmosphere was electrified with the presence of the Lord. Lucinda was forced to stand up and clap her hands as everybody else, she couldn't understand why she is having chills all over her body, but one thing she noticed was that when the chills starts the headaches stops. Little did she know that the demonic headaches were bowing to the presence of God, the worship team sang two more songs as requested by the Lukens and everybody was touched one way or the other.

"Praise the Lord!" shouted Reverend Praise.

"Hallelujah! " They all responded.

"Praise the Lord!" he shouted again.

"Hallelujah!" they all responded with a shout.

"Isn't God good?" he said. "Give the worship team a clap for blessing us with their angelic voices," he added.

When the clapping stopped, Reverend Praise began to pray, "Father, we thank you for this moment, thank you for your presence, we are bless to have you on our side. I declare right now that, that which you have spoken concerning each person here today will come to pass. I pray your blessing on the rest of the program, and I pray that everybody will leave here blessed, in Jesus' name I pray, Amen."

"Amen!" they all responded.

"Sam and Grace asked me to tell you about the love of God, because is that super natural love that made it possible for them to be here today," Reverend Praise told them.

Reverend Praise is anointed to preach the gospel of Jesus Christ that lead men unto salvation. Anytime, anywhere he preaches, stony hearts turn to God, so he knew that something wonderful was about to happen in the lives of some people. This is the day they will be called sons and daughters of God.

Reverend Praise preached the gospel of Jesus with passion, and there was no way anyone wouldn't be moved hearing this anointed man of God talk about his God and what he did for him and how he paid the ultimate price for everybody.

Lucinda was really touched by the message, her stony cold heart began to feel, and the spirit of awareness over shadowed her conscience, and for the first time in her life she realized what a horrible person she was. She doesn't even have to look far; evidence of her evil ways was in her purse. Instead of being happy for her niece, she found herself on a quest to ruin her life the second time. *Only a horrible person would do things like this. I was not like this when I was growing up. How and when did all this start?* she thought, searching her mind for answers. The demons realized that the light of the Holy One was beginning to shine on her conscience, and her heart and her mind were beginning to feel, so they got busy torturing her physically. Headaches, out of breath, numbness in her leg, on and off sharp pains in her abdomen, Lucinda was a stubborn woman, so she just stayed put.

The demons thought with all this torturing she would be forced to get out of there and the moment she steps out outside, they've got her where they wanted, but little did they know that the Holy Spirit was at work giving her the strength to endure.

"God loves you, and he wants you to come just as you are, today is your day, and this is your moments to say yes to Jesus," Reverend Praise appealed to the soul that God is touching. The worship team began to play "I Surrender All to Jesus" softly in the background.

"If you want to say yes to Jesus, don't let anything stop you, for your soul is at stake, heaven or hell, there is no in between. If you are ready to do that, just get out of your pew and make your way to the front. Jesus is waiting at the altar with open arms to make you his very own," Reverend Praise appealed to them.

People began to stand up and walk to the front, in all, forty-four people from both sides of their family, including Big Sam and Grace's parents came forward and a few from the congregation. Words could not describe Big Sam and Grace's joy when they saw their parents holding hands and ready to say yes to God. Lucinda was one of them and family members who knew her well were so happy to see her in the front. Sam and Grace couldn't believe their eyes; they were so happy and excited for the wonderful things God had in store for their family through this encounter.

"This is a walk that I personally can assure you that you will never regret you took, for your real life is about to begin," Reverend Praise told them. He thanked God for giving them the opportunity to know who he is; he then asked them to repeat after him.

"Father, I have realized that I'm a sinner, and I need a savior. I ask you today to forgive me. I know now that no man can come to you except through your son, Jesus Christ. I believe you sent your only begotten son to die for my sins so that I can have eternal life. I surrender my life to you, and I invite you into my heart, be the Lord of my life from now onward. Help me to become all that you want me to be, Amen."

"Amen!" they all said.

"Father, they are yours now. I pray a wedge of protection around them as they begin to take baby steps in you. Satan, you have been defeated in their lives, and every hold you have on them has been broken in Jesus' name. I speak to every stronghold, bondage, habit, addiction that Satan has enslaved you with to leave right now in the name of Jesus. They are no more yours, and you have been made their footstool now, who the son sets free is free indeed, and they are free emotionally and mentally. I pray that your blessing will always be upon them, and they will know that you are the one true God yesterday, today, and forever, in the name of Jesus, I pray, Amen."

Tears were running down a lot of faces, but they were all tears of joy. Lucinda was so subdued but felt such a relief, as if a burden have been lifted off her shoulders, and she was enjoying every moment of it. Silently she asked God to forgive her evil intention without knowing that God has just done that.

Sam's parents are very religious, but they realized that there was more to it than being religious. No wonder all their children repelled against Christianity without knowing the difference. They knew they had to make things right, so they both surrendered their lives to God. Grace's mother made the first move, and her husband followed. It was just beautiful to see them holding hands as a sign of unity and giving their lives to God. Sam and Grace held each other's hands tightly, thanking God silently for what he was doing right before their eyes. Their parents, family members, and friends coming to know the Lord at their wedding. *What more could we ask for,* they both thought.

"Welcome to the family of God. We have a gift for you all to give you a head start on this journey. After I finish marrying this beautiful couple, make sure to go through the door on my right before heading off to the reception. Somebody will be waiting in that hallway with something special for you. You can all be seated now," Reverend Praise told them, and as they walked back, he said, "Clap for them, for today they've been born of the spirit, today is their spiritual birthday."

Everybody began to clap, some people stood up as they clapped. Lucinda felt very special, and somehow she knew that this new life was going to be a good one. With a sweet smile on her face, she went back to her seat and sat down. She told herself that after the ceremony she would make sure she talked to everybody she has not spoken to in years.

"Well, well, we are now ready to marry these two," said Reverend Praise. Sam and Grace came forward once again, holding hands and with their parents standing beside them. Reverend Praise watched them as they said their vows.

Big Sam took Grace's hand. Looking into her eyes and with a shaky voice he read his vows.

"Gracy, I'm blessed to be standing in your presence. Before I experienced the love of God, you enabled me to experience the love of my fellow human being. Your smile, your gentle spirit, your patience, the simplicity of the way you embrace life is a source of inspiration to me. I was dying in my own selfishness, and those qualities brought me back to life.

"Your forgiven and selfless heart made it possible for us to be standing here today, and to that I will ever be grateful. I stand before God and my fellow men, and I promise to love you till death separates us. I promise to honor, respect, and cherish you for the rest of my life. You are my soul mate, and you will always be the love of my life." Big Sam became emotional at the end. He was shivering, and his palms became very sweaty.

Grace was really touched by his brokenness. It was now Grace's turned, so she held Big Sam's right hand with her right hand and with all smiles she poured out her heart to him.

"Sam, we are standing here today because of the grace of God. I'm so grateful because you listened to your heart and did what was right. I'm a blessed woman to have you as my husband once again. Our all-knowing, all-seeing God knew I couldn't live without you, so he worked it out and gave you back to me. I stand before God, our parents, our relatives, our friends, and our fellow men with these promises. I will love you with every fiber in my being. Every breath I take I will take one for you. I will honor and respect you as the spiritual leader of our home. I will cherish our relationship as best friends and lovers. I will support and help to bring the best out of you. My Sam, till death do us part, I will love till then."

"That was wonderful, love is in the air," Reverend Praise jokingly said after Big Sam and Grace exchanged their heart-warming personal vows, which meant so much to them. They exchanged their rings and promised each other a love that will last till death do them part. After that they took communion and lit the unity candle.

After that Reverend Praise asked everybody who wanted

this marriage to last till death separate them should stand up and stretch their hands toward them. He prayed over them and also a special blessing from a Jewish book for newlyweds.

"You may kiss your bride," he told Sam.

They gave each other a hug, and Sam gave Grace a kiss on the forehead.

"Ladies and gentlemen, is my pleasure to introduce to you Mr. and Mrs. Luken," said Reverend Praise as he began to clap his hands.

Everybody joined in the clapping; some were making noise just to cheer them on. Sam and Grace gently waved at them with sweet smiles on their faces. They slowly made their way out of the sanctuary to the reception.

"We are married, we did it," Grace said as she squeezed Sam's hand.

"Yes! Honey, we did it, and I am the happiest man on earth right now," Sam said as he gave his bride a sweet smile.

One of Sam's co-workers is a professional photographer, and he offered to capture their special day for free, so he quickly went to work when they came out. He took as many as they wanted, and after that they all made their way to the reception. The hospitality team did a wonderful job, they decorated the room so beautiful, and Grace was so amazed when they entered the room.

"Wow!" she said as they all started looking around and admiring everything around them. They were greeted by the ladies with cheers of congratulation, they led then to a long table with a beautiful center piece that matched the tablecloth. Sam, Grace, their parents, Reverend and Mrs. Praise, the Yalleys, and three elders of the church with their wives were seated around the table, and single chairs were all over the place for anybody who wanted to sit down. Their wedding cake was so beautiful. It was four tiers high, alternating between round and square shapes. The flowers on the cake were so well sculptured that at first glance one would think they were real lavender flowers. In between the flowers and all around it were small cake-top figures with different characters. Happy couples, proud father, pregnant wife, crying wife, dinner time, and many others. It became the center of attraction because everybody seemed to like the unique decorations. Grace's parents were happy their gift was drawing so much attention.

There was so much finger food that if you could selectively eat well, that would be lunch for sure.

Abiana came with her cookies earlier on; the women were so impressed and asked her whether she was a caterer.

"Yes, but I do it as a hobby," she told them.

"Girl! You need to be out there doing this," one of the ladies told her. Abiana put them in small goodie bags that had "We thank you for coming. Be blessed, Sam and Grace," written on them. She tied them with different colors of ribbon and then arranged them on a large tray. Not knowing one of the hospitality ladies had a small baking business. She kept admiring the artistic touch she put in the whole thing. *I need this girl to work for me,* she thought. When she became less busy, she cornered her and offered her a job. Abiana knew that will be a good opportunity for her to start from, so she accepted the job offer on a part-time basis.

Reverend Praise stood up, prayed, and blessed the food. "Eat, make merry, and have fun," he told them. The ushers came and served all the people on the bride and groom's table, and the fun began. Lucinda, on her way to the fellowship hall, went to the bathroom and emptied the perfume in the sink and threw the bottle in the trash. *This is the end of this part of my life,* she thought. As Lucinda was coming out of the bathroom, she saw May, her first cousin, one of the many relatives she had stopped talking to, and with all smiles she said, "Hello."

May wasn't surprised she greeted her because she saw her

standing in the front giving her life to God. They had been praying for her, and it was a blessing to witness that moment in her life.

"Hi, Lucinda! It is good to see you, and I'm really happy for you. We are no more relatives but sisters in Christ," May told her as she gave her a hug.

That move really brought tears to Lucinda's eyes.

"Thanks a lot. It's so good to hear that," Lucinda told her.

"Come on! No crying now, although I know they are tears of joy, but we are here to celebrate what God has done, so let's go in and have fun," May told her as she put her arms around her shoulder. "My number is still the same," she added.

"Thanks, I will remember that," Lucinda told her. She was surprised how easy it felt to connect again with May, and she was really happy to talk to her. *I guess God has really done something in my heart,* she thought as she walked into the reception area with May.

The food was good, and everybody ate their fill. Sam and Grace were happy, enjoying all the love being showered on them, and they were surprised people brought them gifts, a whole table full of beautifully-wrapped gifts.

"Wow! They brought us gifts too," said Grace.

I am humbled by all this kindness. I guess this is what the love of God is all about. I wonder if every church out there walks in this kind of love. It looks as if I may have to move eventually to join Sam, but until then I am going to be a member of this church so that I can learn more about this love and it will forever be my church, Grace thought with a look of appreciation on her face.

They were playing soft praise music in the background, and everybody was having a good time fellowshipping with one another. Every few minutes somebody will come over to talk to them. Among them was this elderly couple who came to fellowship with them. They introduced themselves as Mr. and Mrs. Samson, and although they were very old, the man really looked like Samson in the Bible, tall and strong looking. He told them his wife divorced him after six months of marriage because she couldn't stand his attitude. She moved back home to her parents and vowed never to marry again. He became very miserable to a point where he couldn't eat. His next-door neighbor, who they thought was one of those crazy Christians, noticed how fast he was losing weight and started reaching out to him. He ended up going to church with them and gave his life to God.

That night he told God how he still loved his ex-wife, and if God brought her back to him he would serve him with everything he had. The following day was his birthday, and the first person who called him was his ex-wife. He was surprised, but he knew God was about to answer his prayers. Through that phone call the door of communication was opened, and they ended up marrying again after six months of divorce; they have been married for forty-six years and had been blessed with six wonderful children and twelve grandchildren.

"Wow! That is a wonderful, sweet happy ending story to hear," said Sam.

"We are happy for you, and we wish you all the best with God's blessing," Mrs. Samson said with a shaky voice.

"Thank you very much for telling us your life story, and we are looking forward to many years together just like you two," Grace told them.

"Everybody has a story to tell about their life, full of life lessons," said Sam.

"Divorcing within six months of marriage will be very devastating, but here they are today, loving each other for forty-six years, all because of the grace of God," Grace said as she looked into Sam's face with a sweet smile.

As the saying goes, everything has an end. People were beginning to leave, and Abiana was standing at the door, handing them a give-away cookie. Sam decided to thank everybody before they all leave, he stood up and shouted, "Attention please!" Everybody turned to look at his direction. "My wife and I want to thank you all from the bottom of our hearts for all that you've have done. We have never felt so loved and blessed in our lives like this. We are so grateful for your love and kindness and to the ladies who labored to feed us all this afternoon, may God bless all of you, thanks again," Sam told them, almost choking with tears.

Finally it was time for them to leave. Grace saw Abiana at the door, and she gave her a big hug and then took their share of the give-away cookies.

"That is so nice and thoughtful of you," she told her with a smile. Grace called the photographer to take one more picture, Abiana in the middle holding her tray of cookies with a big smile on her face.

"I will give you a copy, please remind me after two weeks," Grace told her.

"Thanks and enjoy your honeymoon," Abiana told them as she waved goodbye.

They decided that the bridal team will all go to the hotel and spend some time with the bride and groom so that Little Sam will not feel ignored. That really worked out. He was happy and talking a lot, and when it was time to leave, he gave his parents a hug and was happy to leave with his grandparents.

Sam and Grace found themselves alone at long last.

"It's been a long day full of joy," said Sam.

"Oh! I am so happy this is behind us now," Grace said as she collapsed on the bed, not out of exhaustion but being playful. Sam came and sat gently on the bed beside her.

"Mrs. Grace Luken, my beloved wife, are you ready to introduce those arms I miss so much to me again?" he asked his newlywed wife as he gazed deep into her eyes with love and affection. Grace sat up with her arms wide open and stretched out toward Sam.

"Come, my love, they miss you, and they are all yours now and forever," she told him.

Sam Luken's love was home, and he would be forever grateful for the guiding lights that led him there. They hugged each other tightly and stayed in that position for a while till their heartbeats began beating as one. The warmth of their bodies began to open the doors of the sacred love they once shared all over again. They walked boldly through the door and surrendered their minds, hearts, and bodies completely to each other. A new day had truly begun for Big Sam and Grace.

The Yalleys were so happy to be part of all that had taken place, and they couldn't stop talking about everything that happened. Mercy had not worn high heels in a long time, so by the time they got home, her feet were sore and aching. She quickly kicked the shoes off her feet and sat down with her legs stretched out on the couch.

"You really pay a price to be a glamorous lady," she said.

"Here, let me give them a little massage," Mr. Yalley told his wife as he sat down and put her feet on his thighs. They sat silently for a while as Mr. Yalley did his massaging job.

"Those magic hands always do the job," Mercy told him with a smile as she began to feel some relief.

"They are anointed hands, and that's why," Mr. Yalley responded.

"Oh yea! I know that, that is why I can always count on them," Mercy told him, laughing.

"I wonder who Lucinda was?" said Mr. Yalley.

"I saw her," Mercy told him as she sat up.

"Really! What does she look like? Mr. Yalley asked, sounding very surprised.

"I went to the bathroom, and when I was coming out,

somebody called her name, so I turned immediately to see who she was. She was the lady wearing the lavender suit with the matching hat," said Mercy.

"Oh my! I noticed her among the people who went forward to receive Christ. I thought she was going to look kind of ugly. I guess that reminds us again that Satan comes in all forms," said Mr. Yalley.

"She is a very attractive woman, and you will never think she is capable of anything like that, but the good news is that by the grace and mercy of God, she is a free woman. God will use the passion she had to do evil to do good now for his glory," said Mercy.

"I am so glad God used us to stop what Satan planned to do through her. Is so amazing how God shielded us from things. Grace will never know how God stopped the devil in his tracks at the very end of her story," said Mr. Yalley.

"I am so happy for them and am glad she asked us to be part of their special day, you know? It brought a side of me that I think I have kind of suppressed or ignored. You know what I mean?" Mercy asked her husband.

"I have no idea what you are talking about," Mr. Yalley responded, pretending he had no clue what she was talking about.

"I mean, I mean, dressing up good and looking just gorgeous," Mercy finally spilled it out.

"Oh! That's what you meant," Mr. Yalley said, laughing.

"I know you were pretending you didn't know what I was talking about," Mercy said as she playfully threw a pillow at him.

"You are beautiful dressed up or not, it does not take anything from the fact that you are my girl," Mr. Yalley told his wife as he winked at her.

"You look so funny when you do that," Mercy said, laughing.

"Anyway, it was so funny when I realized people didn't recognize me. Those who did were too surprised and speechless, that is not good, so I promise I will step up a little bit into the fashion world," Mercy told her husband.

"Honey, whatever you decide to do, you will always be beautiful to me," Mr. Yalley assured her.

"Thanks, you are so sweet," she responded with a smile.

Just then the phone rang. Mercy quickly looked at her watch. "It is five o'clock. I hope its Paul so that I can boss him a little bit about today," Mercy said.

Mr. Yalley picked up the phone. "Hello!" he said.

"This is Tori, Mr. Yalley."

"Hello, lady, and how are you doing?" Mr. Yalley asked her.

"I am doing fine," she answered.

"How is Mercy doing too?" Tori asked Mr. Yalley.

"She is doing fine, we just came back from our next door neighbor's wedding at our church, and she is sitting right here relaxing her feet," Mr. Yalley told her.

"Well, I just called to tell you I don't work at the gas station anymore. Ruth is now the manager, I handed over to her."

"Oh! That's wonderful," said Mr. Yalley. "How is she doing anyway?"

"She is doing fine; she told me she owes you a call last week. Billy gave his life to God, and she is so happy and thankful to God," Tori told him.

"Oh! Hallelujah! Thank you, Jesus, for that," Mr. Yalley cut in with excitement.

"I know she is very busy because of the new position, it comes with a lot of responsibility, but she is learning fast and doing a good job," Tori added.

"I'm glad to hear that, and I know she will call someday," said Mr. Yalley.

"Well, the second thing I called to tell you about is that David and I are visiting my parents tomorrow so that I can introduce him to them. I want to introduce him to you two first before we head off to my parents," Tori told him.

"Oh Tori, that would be great, we would love to meet him," said Mr. Yalley. "What time do you think you two will make it over here?"

"We want to set off early, so we hope to get there by 11:00 a.m."

"That will be great; we will just eat lunch together then?" Mr. Yalley told her.

"We will love that, thanks a lot," Tori told him in a sweet voice.

"We will be looking forward to seeing you two tomorrow," said Mr. Yalley.

"All right, I'm excited already. Tell Mercy I say hello."

"I will certainly do that, and you two drive safely tomorrow," Mr. Yalley told her.

"Okay, bye!" she said and hung up.

Mr. Yalley went back to sit on the couch near his wife and told her about the visit.

"That is so sweet of her to do that. I can't wait to meet Mr. Right. I am so excited," Mercy said with a laugh. Mercy noticed that her husband became very quiet after telling her about the visit. She allowed him to sit still for a while and then asked him whether he was okay.

"When I was talking to Tori, I saw a vision that was very disturbing. I saw a dwarflike man chasing her and shouting, 'You are my wife, you are my wife!' She looked very scared and tired because she had been running for a while," Mr. Yalley told his wife.

"What! This is joy-killer information. What does that mean?" Mercy asked.

"I don't know, but it's very disturbing, and I have no doubt Satan is up to something," said Mr. Yalley. "I don't feel like praying about it right now. I believe there will be more revelation to it, so let's put it at the back of our minds," he added.

Mr. and Mrs. Yalley sat beside each other lost in their thoughts and a little disturbed in their spirits. In her mind Mercy kept saying, *Satan, you are liar; Satan, you are a liar; Satan, you are a liar.*